Making Solid Contact

A Novel by Jeffrey L. Sakas

Published by:
Maudlin Pond Press, LLC
PO Box 53, Tybee Island, Georgia 31328, USA

ISBN: 978-1-959563-15-0
eBook ISBN: 978-1-959563-16-7

Disclaimer: This book is a work of fiction and any incidental reference to any person living or dead is unintended. While the events depicted are similar to those of the author's family and his own experience, this book is a fictional account of a character who is completely fictional.

*I have written this novel
with the support and encouragement
of my son Nick and I lovingly dedicate
this book to him.*

Introduction

I come from a family that enjoys watching baseball games. We also enjoyed playing baseball from an early age. When I was about 10 or 11 years old, and my family lived in Hopkinsville KY, I put on my first baseball uniform and played for the local post office Little League team. It just so happened that the regular catcher that played on the team was out on a family vacation and I was called on to become the starting catcher. That team had a history of being the premier team in the Little League of Hopkinsville. I was not very good at being a catcher in those first days of playing organized baseball. However, the coach of the team who was also the postmaster of the city have confidence in my abilities and that started me on the road to developing a love for the game of baseball.

It was also while my family lived in Hopkinsville KY, that I heard the call of Jesus Christ on my life. I did not know everything that a commitment to a Christian life would require. Similarly, to baseball, my desire to become a committed Christian took time to develop. It was my belief that if I was going to follow Jesus Christ that I had to familiarize myself with Jesus from the standpoint of what he said and did during his life. From an early time in my life as a Christian I decided to familiarize myself with the gospel accounts of the life and teachings of Jesus. As with my love for baseball, my love for Jesus has continued and has become deeper and more complex as my years have progressed.

I continue to study the scriptures, and to pray that the Holy Spirit will give me guidance in my study of the Bible. I continue to watch baseball since my playing days have come to an end. In many ways my desire to become more familiar with Jesus and to seek the wis dom of God in fulfilling my desire to be his witness, I will not come to an end to my life as a Christian as my baseball playing days. I will continue onward even as I approach the latter stages of my life to seek a closer relationship with my Lord and Savior.

I have written this book to explain that in every human activity there is the necessity for a spiritual commitment to every portion of every man's calling.

The game of baseball like every other human endeavor has a spiritual essence if it is going to be played in such a way that it brings glory and honor to God. It is my hope that in reading these pages that my readers will gain an appreciation of the spiritual dimension that must be taken into consideration as we live our lives in accordance with the directions that God lovingly places before us.

Contents

MAKING SOLID CONTACT

A Novel by Jeffrey L. Sakas

CHAPTER 1
SOME BASEBALL FUNDAMENTALS

Some people say that hitting a round baseball with a round baseball bat is the hardest thing to do in sports. To fortify their argument baseball fans, point out that the best hitters during any current baseball seasons only achieve a batting average of around 33%, meaning that a hitter fails to reach base by hitting the ball 66 times out of 100 attempts, and those are the best of hitters. The failure rate for a major league hitter is very high. Pitchers on the other hand, do not need to strike out every batter they face in order to achieve great success. Pitchers merely must prevent the opposing team from scoring an average of more than three runs per nine innings to be considered elite.

When a batter stands in the batter's box he stands alone. Of course, there is the opposing team's catcher, who is signaling the pitcher to throw a particular pitch that the catcher and pitcher agree will confuse the hitter. There is also in close proximity an umpire who judges whether the ball is thrown in the strike zone and whether the batter swung at and failed to make contact with the pitch. The batter cannot initiate the confrontation with the pitcher. The batter stands by himself and waits for the ball to be thrown towards him by someone who is sixty-six feet and six inches away and intends that the batter will either not make contact with the ball or if the batter does make contact with the ball, it will not result in solid contact so that the fielders who support the pitcher will field the ball in such a way that the hitter fails to reach base and is ruled out. Making contact with a baseball thrown by a pitcher who intends that no or weak contact occurs with a round bat is in fact a difficult task.

Geometry and physics play important physical roles in the game of baseball and in assessing whether a batter can reach base by getting a hit. Also, it is undeniably true that the eye hand co-ordination that allows a good hitter to get his bat squarely on a ball that is traveling at more than 90 miles an hour and is moving in many times unpredictable arches, is much more acute than normal or even average players, and it is essential to making solid contact with a baseball. Additionally, the intellectual aspect of hitting a thrown pitch was identified by one of the all-time great hitters as being 90% half mental. Then of course there is the question that I wish to examine in this story, is there a spiritual aspect to the game of baseball that transcends the physical and mental aspects of the game?

The story begins as all real stories should. I was born into a family that played and enjoyed the game of baseball. I was born the year that Jackie Robinson broke into the major leagues and broke out of the ban on race. I was born one year before Babe Ruth died. It was a time in baseball history just after the great war had ended and some of the best hitters were returning to the big leagues after serving in the military.

My uncle Lou made it to the majors for a short stint but had a great career as a minor league pitcher. Uncle Lou played for the Boston Braves, who later moved to Milwaukee, and then to Atlanta in 1966. I did not know Uncle Lou when he played baseball and only met him after his playing days were over and he owned a convenience store in McKeesport, Pa., my father's hometown.

My mother would secretly listen to the Braves when my father was around because he grew up in the suburbs of Pittsburg and was a lifelong fan of the Pirates. Mother, who was from North Carolina, played softball and my father said that she was a good player. Mother helped me play little league baseball and reported my progress in regular letters to my father when he was at sea.

My father joined the Navy after high school. He and his first ship, The Ogallala, were at Pearl Harbor when it was attacked on December 7, 1941. My father's ship was sunk, and he got some shrapnel in his elbow. At the time of the battle of Guadalcanal, dad was stationed on a hospital ship carrying the dead and wounded from the battle to New Zealand. He did not realize that his older brother, my uncle Andy, was fighting in that bitterly fought battle while he was not far away.

Evidently the Navy liked my father and during the remainder of the war he was sent to Officers Candidate School at Duke University. While at Duke he was watching a baseball practice and remarked, "If I couldn't do better than that I would hang'em up." He just so happened to be sitting close to the baseball coach when he said that, and the coach told him to prove it, and he did.

I recall seeing my father pitch for a team made up of sailors. I was probably 3 or 4 and my mother took me to see my father play. He was still in the Navy, and it was my first recollection of seeing baseball played. This was the era before television was in wide use. We lived across the river from Philadelphia where my dad was stationed at that time. It was the time when people listened to big league games on the radio, if there was a big-league team that was broadcast in your locality. It was my first time experiencing the sights, sounds, smells and atmosphere of baseball. I would like to say that from that very moment I was a baseball lover, but that would not be true. The love of baseball, like all true loves, takes time to develop. It requires a deeper appreciation of all the nuances that such a complex set of rules, shapes, and probabilities may and do produce. Love for baseball takes seeing it played well by highly skilled players and it takes seeing it played poorly by those not so gifted with the ability to hit, throw, catch, run, slide, tag, anticipate, argue, spit and scratch.

Baseball is played by a very wide variety of people. Those who possess the skills necessary to be a good player are a mixture of many different and cooperative abilities. The ability to accurately throw a baseball so that a teammate can catch the ball without excessively moving from the spot where the receiver is stationed is an essential ability. A poor player, on the other hand, will throw the baseball in such a way that the one to whom the baseball is thrown will need to lung or leap or move dramatically to catch the ball. A good player has the ability to field a batted ball by tracking the ball into his/her glove and then accurately throwing the ball to a teammate to achieve an out. A bad player cannot consistently catch and throw the ball to his/her team-mate. A good player can hit the ball with a bat at least most of the time that the ball is thrown in or near enough to the place that the batter can reach it with his bat. The poor player does not have sufficient eye-hand coordination to put the bat in the right position to make contact with the baseball. The good player can run fast enough to make it to a base in time to avoid being tagged out by the position player. The poor player just does not run fast enough to avoid being tagged out.

To distinguish between a good and a bad player is often a matter of degree. There are players that can field the baseball so well that their deficiency as a hitter is overlooked. Such a player is a rarity. There are players who possess the ability to hit the ball so well that their deficiencies in running and fielding are overlooked because they get on base and score at a higher rate than others that possess other skills. In order to accommodate such players, they are often relegated to positions on defense where they are less likely to be required to field the baseball and expose his/her other deficiencies or now days they become designated hitters and do not play in the field at all. Some players, most noticeably pitchers, only possess the ability to throw the baseball with such velocity and with such spin rates that even good hitters swing and miss the baseball on a regular basis. There are few players that possess all the skills that the game of baseball requires of a player to make that player exceptional. In major league baseball one such player that possesses all baseball skills to throw, run, field and hit is Shohei Ohtani of the Los Angeles Angels. Another player that had all the tools was George Herman Ruth, better known as Babe Ruth. As you can see such players are few and far between.

There is also a group of official arbiters referred to as umpires that continually evaluate whether the baseball thrown by the pitcher meets the criterion established by the official rules of baseball to be considered a ball (outside the strike zone) or a strike (inside the strike zone). The umpires, usually dressed in blue uniforms, also determine whether the batter has swung at the pitched ball or sufficiently held his bat back and did not commit to swinging at the pitch if the ball is thrown outside the strike zone. While the umpires also make decisions regarding whether a hitter/baserunner has successfully reached base or was not successful and thus declared to be out, the umpire behind home plate decides whether the pitch was a ball or strike or whether the batter swung on nearly every pitch.

In many ways there is a symbiotic relationship between the umpire and the catcher. The catcher position on the baseball team requires that the right-handed player receive the pitched ball from the pitcher in such a manner that the umpire can make his/her call of whether the pitch met the criteria in the official rules of baseball to be determined to be a strike. The catcher has a vested interest in having the pitch be declared a strike as the catcher works in tandem with the pitcher to have the batter to be declared out. This also requires the input of the umpire. In order to assist the umpire in determining whether the pitch is within the strike zone the catcher will frame the location of the ball as it crosses or nearly crosses the strike zone. Sometimes the catcher engages in sleight of hand maneuvers to give the umpire the catcher's prospective as to the location of the pitch when it is received by the catcher. The ability to frame the pitch by the catcher is a learned skill that often takes many years to perfect.

Being a fan of baseball must of necessity engender a spiritual awakening. Football fans crave the brutality that the game requires. Basketball fans do not need the same level of spiritual awareness as the baseball fan because the game moves at such a fast pace that it is difficult to ponder how all the parts fit during a series of fastbreaks and dunks. Soccer fans and hockey fans are satisfied with the beauty of the motion on the pitch or on the ice. Individual sports like tennis and boxing have their moments but it is the ultimate confrontation between pitcher and batter that produces a sweet satisfaction or the bitter dejection that occurs for 27 outs during a nine-inning game.

Twenty-seven outs for each team gives sufficient time to internalize the meaning of such aspects of the game regarding the ability to score, give up runs, rally, make spectacular plays in the field, steal bases, strike out, run the bases, avoid tags, and hit home runs. Even more amazingly, if the contest is tied after both teams have recorded 27 outs they play on until one team scores more runs than the other after providing equal opportunity to both sides to score the winning run. As a great baseball philosopher once said, "It ain't over till it's over." All other sports (I'm not sure about Cricket) have time limits. Baseball has no such confinement.

Fundamental equal opportunity is a basic principle of the game of baseball. In football the team that has the biggest and fastest players most usually prevails in the contest. Some would take exception to that observation, and say it is the desire to prevail that determines the victor. I will stick with the biggest and fastest as the most likely to win. On the other hand, baseball players come in all shapes and sizes. Even smaller players can accomplish extraordinary feats on the diamond. Take for example the size and shapes of two players that are considered elite. On the one hand is Aaron Judge who currently plays for the New York Yankees. He is 6'7' and has a well-developed and muscular body and is definitely an elite talent. On the other hand, Jose Altuve is currently playing for the Huston Astros. Altuve is at best 5'5" but his size is no impediment to his elite status on the baseball field.

Basketball is a big person's sport. Even in women's basketball it takes very tall people to play the game most effectively. In baseball the skill level of the player is not dependent on his/her size and that makes baseball a more egalitarian sport. The skill level of a major league baseball player cannot always be measured by size or even strength. While sometimes size and strength may make a difference in the ability to hit home runs, size and strength are not a factor in putting the bat on the ball. As Yogi was apt to say, "Hitting is 90% half mental." The mental aspect of hitting is thus pronounced. The defensive abilities of a baseball player have nothing to do with size. The ability to accurately throw a baseball also is not dependent on size or even muscle mass, and even the velocity and/ or spin rate of a thrown ball is not always determined by the size of the muscle in the arm of the man throwing it.

It has been said that it is impossible to teach someone how to run fast. Either you are built for speed or not. Being able to run fast is a blessing and should not be overlooked as a natural phenomenon. But even the ability to run like a deer is not a requirement to achieve success as a baseball player. It was often said of some of the best hitters that they were deceptively slow.

Even being left-handed is not a detriment to most positions on the baseball diamond. Some of the greatest hitters were left-handed. Babe Ruth was left-handed, as was Berry Bonds, Ted Williams, Willie Stargell, Stan Musial and many others. In fact, in major league baseball, it is often wise for a team to employ both lefties and righties in the batting order so that the pitcher cannot settle in a comfort zone as he maneuvers through the lineup, he is called on to face during his time on the mound. Further, the major league manager is in a better circumstance if he can deploy a variety of both southpaws and righties as the games progress.

The mental aspect of baseball is seen in the ability to anticipate a pitcher's next pitch, or whether a base runner will be stealing second-base on the next pitch. Also, the prudent manager must know at what time to insert a relief pitcher and to anticipate the other managers deployment of pinch hitters by keeping track of who might be available on the opposing team's bench at all times. That anticipation and mental awareness makes that aspect of baseball an intellectual pursuit.

I am getting a little far afield, however. It is the spiritual part of baseball in which I am most interested. As I spin this story, I will try not to get bogged down, too unnecessarily, in either the physical or mental aspects of baseball. Baseball is a beautiful game played by athletes with varying skill levels. A major league player has undoubtedly committed a large portion of his life in pursuit of his dream to play under the bright lights and before adoring fans. In order to reach that goal, a baseball player must make a spiritual commitment that will drive him on his journey beyond the physical and mental abilities with which he is blessed.

Chapter 2
Spiritual Awareness

In the book of Revelations, in the Bible, the seven churches to whom Jesus speaks, are admonished to hear with spiritual ears the words of the Lord. In the confrontation between Jesus and the Pharisees concerning a man that was born blind (John 9) and who received his sight, Jesus warns the Pharisees by saying, "If you (Pharisees) were blind, you would not be guilty of sin; but now that you claim you can see, your guilt remains." Jesus was telling the Pharisees that as opposed to the physical blindness of the man to whom he had just given sight; they were spiritually blind and did not even know of their inability to comprehend the requirement of mercy and forgiveness that is necessary in order to be shown mercy and forgiveness from God.

In the explanation to his disciples of the parable of the Sower (Luke 8; 1-15), Jesus says he speaks in parables because most of the people listening to him do not have a spiritual understanding. Jesus is telling his disciples they must hear with spiritual ears and see with spiritual eyes if they are to understand the true meaning of his words and actions.

In the first chapter of the New Testament book of James, the scripture says, "If any man lacks wisdom, let him ask God, who gives to all men liberally and without reproach, and it will be given him. But let him ask in faith, with no doubting, for he who doubts is like a wave of the sea that is driven and tossed by the wind. For that person must not suppose that a double-minded man, unable in all his ways will receive anything from the Lord."

Asking for spiritual wisdom and seeking spiritual

eyes and ears are closely aligned. One cannot see spiritually or hear spiritually without obtaining the wisdom that only God can give to those who call on His name. But as the writer of James chapter1 says, do not ask if you are unsure of your belief that God exist and that He will positively answer your prayer.

Remember how God answered Solomon's prayer when he asked God for wisdom so that he could effectively judge his people. Solomon was given the privilege of asking for whatever he desired. Solomon asked for discernment. That is the ability to listen clearly and see without distortion; so that he can govern fairly. God honored Solomon's request because it was also God's will that his chosen people be taken care of in a righteous manner. Solomon asked for the ability to judge his people as God would have them judged. We should ask for the same wisdom.

Everybody has a spiritual side. We are all spiritual beings whether we recognize it or not. We cannot actually see the good in someone's heart, but we can see the results of that person's good deeds and thus have evidence that good is prevalent in that person's spirit. We cannot see the evil that encompasses a person, but the results of evil are evident in the mass shootings and killing that are currently going on in the United States. We can measure evil by the outcome or result of an evil person's actions. Good and evil are not the only aspects of a spiritual existence. Desires, the ability to appreciate beauty, a feeling of closeness with another person, love, hate, kindness, joy, sadness and many other expressions of feelings have spiritual components.

That is not to say that there are no physical and mental components to the list of emotions that I have just stated, but for each of the listed emotions a spiritual aspect is usually evident. Science and especially research of brain functions show us that chemical components flooding through the brain and body of a person can and do cause mood swings. However, the presence of a particular chemical in your brain cannot fully explain the perception of beauty or the desire to do hard work. There are too many variables, imperceptions, and desires to find a degree of certainty in how the chemical components of the brain react to any given individual. For example, if the exact amount of dopamine, and serotonin were injected into a series of functioning brains it is uncertain how or if each brain would experience the same emotion or have the exact perception of beauty or engender the desire necessary to accomplish the work required to develop certain skills.

Humans connect on a spiritual level all the time. Our spirits interact with other spirits that belong to others human beings. There is a spiritual connection that allows humans to reach out to God and to know that God is a reality and that He interacts with us. Prayer is a deliberate act of spiritual connectiveness with the Almighty. Prayer can and should be a two-way street. We open ourselves to ultimately receive an answer from God to the burdens of our hearts. When we are thankful for God's blessings God becomes closer to us and we (person and God) are connected.

Many of us are not attuned to our spiritual beingness. Some deny the existence of God. Some believe that the ability to perceive beauty is a chemical reaction of the uptake inhibiters in the brain. How absurd. However, any human's perception cannot be argued against because the spiritual side of any human cannot be quantified in terms of any measurable amount of chemicals, brain function, intellectual capacity, or any other measurable standard that science can provide. A person's spirituality can only be manifested by the life of that person. Some would rightfully point out that there is the ability to reach out to God only because God has elected to reach out to any particular person.

For example, consider the life of Jimmy Piersall who

played center field in the major leagues for 17 seasons from 1950 to 1967. He was the subject of the book and subsequent movie, Fear Strikes Out, that chronicled Piersall's struggle with bipolar depression and his fight to overcome that disorder. In later life Piersall was heard to say that the best thing that ever happened to him was going nuts because who would have ever heard of him otherwise. Piersall underwent electroshock therapy and was prescribed lithium to treat his disorder.

The exact cause of bipolar disorder is unknown, but a combination of genetics, environment, and altered brain structure may come into play. Bipolar disorder can be treated but it cannot be cured. It can last for a specific amount of time or for the entire life of the person so afflicted. Is there a spiritual aspect to mental disorders? It would seem that people can be delivered from mental illness only by the intervention of the Holy Spirit.

Consider those afflicted by alcoholism that include many well-known baseball players. There is a spiritual basis for the treatment of alcoholism in the meetings and programs of Alcoholics Anonymous. Those that find their way to AA are encouraged to admit that they are addicted and need to confess that he/she is powerless to overcome his/her alcoholism. The addicted person is then encouraged to admit the need for the intervention of a higher power to deal with his/her addiction. Twelve-step programs offer help for addictions to drugs, sex, gambling, pornography and many other forms of addiction. Each of those programs has a spiritual basis to bring at least a temporary relief to those suffering from the evil of addiction. The spiritual basis urges those suffering addiction to put their faith in a higher power (AA does not call the higher power God in deference to all spiritual beliefs) to intervene in the life of the addict to relieve that person of his/her addiction.

Spiritual awareness is critical to developing a love for

the game of baseball. Spiritual awareness is also necessary for the development of the skills needed to become a baseball player. It takes dedication to the sport of baseball to become a good player. A player who develops the skills to become a good baseball player requires an awareness that a person's spirit must be accessed in such a way that there is a level of commitment to the development of that player's skills. As mentioned above, one of the spiritual components of a person's being is that of desire. Couple desire with dedication and an ability to commit to the hard work necessary to become a good baseball player; that my friend is a spiritual quest and is what we shall explore in these pages.

The spiritual nature of baseball is at least two-fold. The love of the game from a fan perspective is developed over years of seeing the game played well and seeing the game played poorly. From the player's perspective a desire and devotion to put in the work to develop the skills needed to be a good player is a spiritual quest that must be aided by a power above and beyond the player.

Chapter 3
The Story Begins

October is a glorious month. The stifling summer heat has subsided. There are cool evenings and warm days. The leaves on the maple trees, oaks, sourwoods, sweetgums, dogwoods, tupelos, cherry trees and persimmon trees are in their red stage. Hickories, ash, yellow popular, aspen, birch, cottonwood, sassafras and alder trees are yellow and gold when the chlorophyll in the leaves departs as the weather turns cooler and the true color of the leaf appears. October is also the month of the year in which the Major League Baseball teams start their annual playoffs. By the end of October, a new World Series champion will be crowned.

Many important people were born in the month of October. United States presidents were born during the month of October as were notable titans of business and world leaders. Of course, that could be said of other months during the year besides October but for the start of our story we must consider October as a unique month for it is the month in which the person about whom this story was written was born.

The Navel Medical Center, Portsmouth formerly the Portsmouth Naval Hospital sits in a spot that is unique in American history. The Naval Hospital was founded in 1827 and the first hospital building was built in 1832. It is the most continuously serving medical facility associated with the United States Navy. The hospital is located near Chesapeake Bay and at the mouth of the James River. That location is where the Civil War Battle between the two iron clad vessels, the Merrimac and the Monitor took place.

The Merrimac renamed the Virginia, was a Confederate vessel that was used effectively by the Confederates to sink wooden hulled Union ships moored close to Portsmouth and Hampton Roads, Virginia. The Monitor was built and deployed to counteract the Merrimac and the two vessels slugged it out on March 8 and 9, 1862. It is said that that battle changed navel tactics for navies all over the world.

Not far from the location of the hospital is the Revolutionary War Battlefield of Yorktown. The battle of Yorktown was fought from September 28 through October 19, 1781. In that battle, the American army led by George Washington with the help of the French Fleet defeated the British under the command of General Cornwallis. The American victory brought about the 1783 Treaty of Paris that sealed the independence of the United States from Britian.

Close to the Naval Hospital but further back in history was the founding of Jamestown, the location of which is only a few miles away as is Williamsburg, the seat of the colonial government of Virginia. The historic value to the United States of these locations is without dispute.

On an October day, when the leaves were in full color and the autumn skies were bright blue, a male child was born to the parents of an enlisted man serving on the USS Missouri and his young wife, a woman from rural North Carolina that often wondered what had brought her to this place at this season to give birth to a child whose father she hardly knew.

The child, a little hairy boy was the first child of the couple, and he looked more like a Simeon than a human because of the amount of hair that covered the child when he was born. It was said that the hair on his head met his eyebrows and that he had hair on his arms, legs and even on his newborn back. It was a wonder that the parents did not name him Harry. Instead, they named him Christopher after his mother's father. They decided to call him Chris.

The baby boy was not overly big at his birth, weighing in at 8 pounds 6 ounces. Nor was he particularly small. He was born with all his parts and no deformities except for the excessive amount of hair. What was unknown to anyone but the baby himself was that he had a well-developed brain that allowed him to see and perceive things that were going on around him from the earliest days after his birth. Even as a baby Chris was alert with bright eyes and an energetic way of moving his arms and legs.

As he was a first born and his mother was alone much of the time because the child's father was at sea a lot of the time a close bond developed between mother and child. All mothers love their first child but because of the circumstances of Chris' birth there was an extraordinary closeness between Chris and his mother. As soon as Chris could travel, he was taken to meet his maternal grandparents in rural North Carolina.

There was a strange feeling between Chris' mother and her father when Chris was presented for family inspection. Chris even at six weeks old recognized that there was tension in the relationship. Out in rural North Carolina where Chris' mother came from, bootleg whisky was an ongoing enterprise. Chris' grandfather drank moonshine whisky and drank a lot of it. When he got drunk, which was very often, he became belligerent and would curse and throw things at his oldest daughter who happened to be Chris' mother. Also, it was well known within the confines of the family but not publicized to anyone else that the grandfather sexually assaulted Chris' mother. That explained why a very beautiful and intelligent girl left the farm as soon as she could get out on her own and married a sailor from Pennsylvania who she hardly knew. Her given name was Lula. She hated that name and insisted on being called by her middle name, Kathrin. She accepted being referred to as Kay.

Kay's mother was aware of the abuse that her oldest daughter was enduring. In rural North Carolina in the mid 1940's there was no child and family services department. If anything was going to be done to protect her oldest child from the abuse of her drunken husband, it was up to her to help her child escape by getting enough money for bus fare and as much cash as she could to send her child to a safer place. Kay got on the bus in Lillington, North Carolina and arrived in Norfolk, Virginia in the summer of 1943. She found a job at a munition factory because World War II was still in full swing, and workers were needed to promote the war effort.

Chris' father a son of Hungarian immigrants, grew up in a suburb of Pittsburg. McKeesport, Pennsylvania was the home of an important US Steel mill that turned out large quantities of high-quality steel that was also needed in the war effort. Chris' father's father was a man among men. He had been a professional wrestler in the old country. He had huge, strong hands and was able to pick up a telephone pole and carry it for several blocks. Chris' father was the youngest child of the marriage between a good looking and very strong wrestler and a petit woman who had royalty in her blood. Chris' grandmother on his father's side was the equivalent to a duchess and her family had estates in Hungary. The youngest child born to the union between the wrestler and the duchess they named Joseph. Everybody called him Joe.

Joe had a wandering spirit that drove him to join the Navy soon after he graduated from high school. The great depression was still in its final stages, but there was work to be found if you wanted to work in the steel mills. Joe needed his father's permission to join the Navy and his father reluctantly gave in to Joe's request.

Joe's mother had died when Joe was 12 and Joe's father was stricken with almost unbearable grief at his wife's passing. When Joe joined the Navy, he believed it would be a great adventure and he got exactly what he dreamed of.

Joe was sent to basic training in Chicago. He was then sent to train on an old sailing ship in Boston. The Navy sent him to school in San Diego and he was assigned to the mine sweeper Ogalala that was docked in Pearl Harbor, Hawaii in the fall of 1941.Joe was asked to play softball with a group of sailors from his ship on December 7, 1941. As the group was getting ready to play, they saw the Japanese fighter/ bombers flying over and heard the explosions from the harbor where the Ogalala was tied next to the Battleship Utah.

While trying to make it back to his ship, Joe and the group of sailors he was with ran across a field near a pineapple plantation and were strafed by Japanese war planes. Joe was hit by shrapnel in his elbow. The ship he had been assigned to was sunk as were many others on that December 7, 1941. Many sailors were killed and injured. Joe eventually recovered from his injuries though the wound got infected, and the doctors threatened to amputate Joe's arm before it started to heal.

Joe was then assigned to a hospital ship. By that time, he was an electrician's mate and was required to change out light bulbs in the morgue where dead marines and soldiers' bodies were stored. The hospital ship eventually was assigned to station itself near the location of the battle of Guadalcanal (August 7, 1942-February 9, 1943). Enemy activity threatened that even hospital ships could be subject to attack so Joe would wrap himself in a life preserver and sleep on deck for fear of being trapped below deck if the ship was torpedoed.

Joe did not know that his oldest brother, Andy, had

been drafted into the army and was among the combatants at the Battle of Guadalcanal. Joe did not get that bit of news until the war was over for many years and the subject happened to come up at a family gathering.

Joe took all the required tests that the Navy specified, and Joe evidently did well enough for the Navy to send him to Officers Candidate School at Duke University, about 50 miles from the very rural farm where Kay lived. By chance Joe and Kay met in Norfolk, Virginia in the summer of 1944 while Joe was on leave from his duties at Duke OCS. They were with other friends and were out playing miniature golf when Joe spotted Kay and told his friend that he was immediately smitten and would marry that woman if she would ever let him get her attention. Joe finally got her attention and within a month they were living together in an undercover relationship because Joe had failed to get permission from the Navy to get himself into a marital relationship.

Joe and Kay could not legally marry. They would not separate or terminate their love affair. The Navy found out and Joe was kicked out of the OCS at Duke and returned to the ranks as an enlisted man. That act by the Navy allowed the parents of baby Chris to get married before Chris' arrival.

Chris was a happy child. His parents, Joe and Kay were loving and caring people who intended to raise Chris in a manner that was better than what either Joe or Kay had experienced in their formative years in the suburbs of Pittsburg or in the sandhills section of North Carolina. Joe intended to remain in the Navy because he kept being promoted at a relatively rapid rate. Kay was content to remain at home with her children. Children, plural, because within a short period of time another child was born to the union of Joe and Kay.

The new child was also born at the Portsmouth Naval Hospital in February 1949, and she was named

Swamp Goddess because her parents also had an unusual sense of humor. Her parents decided to call her Ali, short for alligator because as a Swamp Goddess she would naturality reign over all the alligators in the swamp. Ali was also a happy child, born with all her parts in perfect condition. The only unusual aspect of Ali's life was that she could not get over the fact that her parents named her Swamp Goddess and when the roll was called at the beginning of every school year, her name, Swamp Goddess would be called out loud and the other children in her class would snicker.

Because Joe remained in the Navy the family was relocated often as Joe was assigned to different ships at the whim of the Navy. The family never stayed in a location for more than two years. They were always picking up their furniture and household goods and moving. Any acquaintances they made at one location were quickly forgotten and new acquaintances were made at a completely new location.

The family moved from Portsmouth to Norfolk, from Norfolk to Philadelphia, from Philadelphia back to Norfolk, from Norfolk to Jacksonville Florida, From Jacksonville to Quonset Point, Rhode Island, from Quonset Point to Hopkinsville, Kentucky, from Hopkinsville to Clarksville, Tennessee, from Clarksville to Nashville, Tennessee, from Nashville to Murfreesboro, Tennessee and there they stopped moving for a while.

All along the way and from place to place the family would make new acquaintances and leave old acquaintances behind, usually never hearing from the old acquaintances again. After Joe had spent 23 years in the Navy he retired. By then he had achieved the rank of Chief Warrant Officer, W4 and was entitled to a pension from the Navy as well as benefits under the GI bill authorized by the US Congress and signed by the President that gave men and women who had honorably served in the armed forces during WWII housing and education allowances. The education benefits prompted Joe to return to college. After Joe was forced out of Duke, where he was studying electrical engineering, Joe had been sent to Los Alamos, New Mexico to learn how to construct nuclear weapons while he was stationed at Clarksville Base, Tennessee.

Joe had learned many things while he was in the Navy and felt as if he would like to try his hand at being a high school math teacher. When his time in the Navy came to an end his family of Kay, Chris, and Swamp Goddess moved to Clarksville and Joe continued his education. Within two years Joe had completed his bachelor's degree and had gotten a master's degree for good measure, and he still had unused benefits due him under the GI bill. So, the family moved again. This time the family moved to Nashville and Joe pursued a Doctorate from Vanderbilt University.

All the time the family was on the move the children experienced varying degrees of exasperation with the continuous movement from place to place as if the family were gypsies or better yet nomads. Swamp Goddess who always told her friends that the name Swamp Goddess was a joke that her brother had played on her and that her real name was Alison and that she should be called Ali was a particularly intelligent young lady.

By the time the family moved to Nashville, Ali could sing, collect bugs, write stories, and keep everyone entertained with her adventurous spirit. Chris, despite all the changes in scenery, had begun to develop some skills as a baseball player. Chris was still acutely aware of what was going on around him and even seemed to understand even complex situations in which others found themselves and needed help in resolving.

Chapter 4
The Development of Baseball Skills

Chris started playing little league baseball in Hopkinsville, Kentucky when he was selected to play on the best team in that age group. Chris was thrown into games quickly because the manager of the team recognized that Chris had a strong and accurate throwing skill. Besides, the kid who was selected to play catcher unexpectedly failed to show up for a scheduled game and Chris was put in the game as the starting catcher despite his complete lack of experience at that position.

Chris had developed his throwing skill when the family lived in Virginia in the early 1950's. Kay found an apartment in Norfolk while Joe was on an extended cruise in the Mediterranean when the Suez Cannel crisis began to unravel. Joe was assigned to a troop transport ship that carried a battalion of marines and their equipment around in the Mediterranean for about 18 months just in case they were needed to protect United States interest in that region of the world.

The apartment complex was only partially completed and there was still much construction going on when Kay and the children moved in. Chris was only 5 but at that time it was not a negligent act on the part of a parent to allow even a 5-year-old child to spend the day entertaining himself by playing outside in an unsupervised environment. Besides there were all sorts of other children playing outside, it was the middle of the baby boom. Thus, the term Boomers was coined to explain what was going on before the eyes of Kay and all the other young mothers who had children of the approximate age of Chris.

There were mounds of dirt and construction debris

throughout the apartment complex just waiting for boys and girls close in age to engage in dirt clod wars. One group of children throwing dirt clods at another group of children, what possibly could go wrong?

Chris found out that he could break up dirt clods into small enough chunks to allow him to throw the clods at the other children who were throwing clods at him. Unfortunately for the other kids, Chris could throw the clods further and more accurately than those throwing at him. When Chris determined his ability to throw was superior to other boys his age or even older, he set about to hone his throwing skill even more by throwing anything he could find in the construction debris at any target that presented itself. There was also loose gravel. Gravel had a higher density than dirt clods and rocks were particularly better than dirt clods at throwing and hitting someone. Hitting another kid with a piece of gravel usually ended the war. Chris became good at throwing at and hitting other kids with rocks.

Eventually, Joe made it back to Norfolk when things settled down in the Middle East. Joe, because he liked baseball when he was growing up in McKeesport, because his brother Lou had played professionally, and because Joe had played for Duke before he was unceremoniously kicked out of the OCS program, wanted to nurture Chris into becoming a baseball player. Joe had been around his brother Lou when he played professional baseball. Joe had hawked peanuts at the ballpark. Joe had seen the great Josh Gibson play baseball in Pittsburg and heard the distinctive crack of the bat on ball when Gibson made contact. Joe said it was like no other sound he had ever heard, and the ball traveled further than he ever thought it could when Gibson hit the ball so hard that it would leave a dent in the ball. People who had seen both Gibson and Babe Ruth play remarked that even the Babe himself could not hit a baseball as hard as Josh Gibson. But Gibson was a black man and during the thirties and before and all the way until 1947 black men were not permitted to put on the uniforms of the major league teams and compete with white men.

Joe had played baseball at Duke University until the Navy found out about his relationship with Kay. Joe even pitched on teams composed of sailors on a regular basis but because he was the youngest of his siblings, he had no experience in helping Chris understand the complexities of the game of baseball, or for that matter how to parent a child. Joe's mother died when he was 12. It was the height of the great depression, there were 8 mouths to feed and work and food was scarce. The family decided to send Joe and the youngest sister of the family out to Springfield, Illinois to live with an aunt who had a farm. Joe and his sister remained in Springfield with their Nania (Hungarian for Aunt) for two long years. For Joe they were very formative years. His mother had died of cancer. His father was overwhelmed with grief and experienced a severe depression at the loss of his beloved and Joe felt guilty that his mother had died, and his father was so sad.

In another sense Joe had been away from the family because of his duties aboard ship. In order to rekindle a relationship with his children it would take some dedication to becoming aware of the needs and even the different personalities of not only the children but also of his wife. Luckily for Joe, Kay was not about to create problems with her relationship with Joe because she had no place else to go or return to if things went south with her marriage.

Since the time that Joe and Kay had met Joe was gone a large portion of the time. He evidently was in port just long enough to father the two children of the marriage. Joe had no comprehension of the abilities of Chris to throw dirt clods or rocks at the other children that happened to live near the family. To his credit, Joe took responsibility for doing what he could to keep the family together and encourage his wife and children as best as he could.

Slowly Joe started to take an interest in Chris's personality and ability. By the time Joe returned from his duties in the Mediterranean, Chris was starting second grade and Chris had never swung a bat or had any idea of how baseball was to be played. On one of the first occasions on which Joe took Chris out to field to see if Chris had enough eye-hand coordination to hit a thrown ball, Chris hit the ball but had no knowledge of which way to run the bases. Chris hit the thrown ball. Joe said run to first base. Chris started running towards third. Joe should have been aware that Chris had the required eye-hand coordination to cause a round bat to make square contact with a round ball thrown in Chris's direction. Instead, the excitement centered around Chris's running the wrong way. Later that day, Joe decided to see if Chris could field a ground ball. Joe fungoid a ground ball in Chris's direction. The field was nothing but a grassy meadow full of rocks and construction debris. The grounder took a bad bounce and went straight for Chris's nose. A bloody nose ended baseball practice for the day and Joe had to explain to Kay how her darling little boy came home with blood on his shirt and a broken nose.

Things did not get any worse. I fact things started to improve form that moment on. Joe started to bond with Swamp Goddess now referred to as Ali, and Joe became a personality with the other children in the neighborhood. When Joe was not at sea, he would often pitch a rubber ball to Chis in the backyard of the house that Joe and Kay purchased in a lower-class area of Norfolk. When Joe would engage in pitching batting practice it was as if the Pied Piper had summoned all the neighborhood children to come and participate as well. Not only that, but Chris also showed an aptitude for hitting.

It was not unusual for Chris to make contact and drive the ball out of the yard, across the street and into a neighbor's yard several houses further down the street. None of the other children were able to match that ability to make contact and drive the ball as well as Chris.

CHAPTER 5
CHRIS'S PROGRESS AND THE REALITY OF DESIRE

At some point in time everyone starts to develop a desire to become something or give up on life and only take what is thrown at them without trying to make solid contact. Taking what is thrown either ends up being a called strike or a ball by the umpire. Taking pitches requires either a desire to not commit to anything or a fondness to just take whatever is thrown up in life and live with the consequences.

A good batter will have the depth perception necessary to distinguish between whether the pitch is out of the strike zone or even if it is in the strike zone whether the hitter can make solid contact. Even as that decision is made the pitch can be deceptive and the batter may only foul the pitch and not make solid contact. Life can be that way also. Swinging at a baseball requires a desire to play the game. Commitment to the development of the skills necessary to make solid contact and a determination to not let the pitcher best your efforts more than necessary.

When a hitter decides to swing at the ball it is necessary to follow the ball until that critical moment when the batter commits him or herself to the act of making contact with the pitched baseball. That critical moment can occur at different times depending on the velocity of the pitch, whether the pitch is a curve, slider, change-up, knuckleball, or any other of an almost inexhaustible assortments of pitches that pitchers develop in order to cause a swing and miss or soft contact. The desire to develop the skills necessary to become a good hitter requires a spiritual commitment, a good eye and excellent eye-hand coordination.

Chris had good eyes and could judge the location of pitches thrown at which he could swing and make solid contact. Chris's eye-hand coordination was sufficient to make solid contact on a regular basis. Chris needed a spiritual commitment to form the desire necessary to develop the skills that God gave him at birth. The spiritual desire that Chris needed was not that easy to come by and moving from place to place during his formative years did not help at all. It seemed that every time Chris got into a situation in which he could get instruction on the development of the techniques necessary to improve his skills, the family moved to the next location that the Navy picked for Joe.

Even with all the moving around and the lack of coaching that would have helped Chris to develop his hitting skills there came the summer of 1959. The family was living in Quonset Point, Rhode Island. Swamp Goddess was having a wonderful summer exploring the finger of the Narraganset Bay that was nearly in the backyard of the Navy housing project in which the family lived. They had moved from Florida in the summer of 1958. Swamp Goddess developed pneumonia when the family was in Jacksonville and there was apprehension about what so drastic a climate change would do to Swamp Goddess's health. She developed Scarlet Fever over the winter months and Kay was always concerned that Swamp Goddess would become chronically ill as she grew into adolescence. Then summer arrived in New England, and it was a glorious summer.

Chris was drafted to play for the little league team of the Junior Police. The team was coached by a man who lived in Wickford, Rhode Island, who was called Corky Cockren. The Junior Police were the class of the league and Chris was the class of the team. The Junior Police won nearly every game they played and by the end of the season Chris had a cool .512 batting average and was also pitching for the team as it won game after game all season long.

Joe was away most of the summer as his ship the WWII ventage aircraft carrier, Lake Champlain, was on duty off the east coast of the US hunting for soviet submarines. The Lake Champlain had been retrofitted to accommodate sophisticated electronic surveillance and detection equipment to locate the presence of soviet nuclear-powered submarines. Joe was responsible for maintaining the electronics on board the ship. When he was on duty, Joe would be at sea for six weeks and return to port for three weeks then back to sea. It just so happened that the Lake Champlain was at sea for most of the little league season, so it was up to Kay to keep Joe informed and to make sure that Chris got to his games and practices on time and fully equipped.

At the end of the regular season of little league baseball, all-stars are selected, and the all-stars were going to play other all-stars from other little league towns in the region. Chris was selected as an all-star and the North Kingston team played another team from a nearby town to see who would advance in the little league playoffs. Corky Corkern was not selected as the coach for the North Kingston team and Chris found himself in the unenviable position of being relegated to playing an unfamiliar position and batting near the end of the batting order. Little league games are only six innings long so by batting Chris at the end of the batting order Chris only got to do his thing twice. Each time he got a hit, but it was too little too late for North Kingston.

Chris overheard the manager of the team speaking to Corky Corkern. Corky asked why the locally appointed manager did not bat Chris higher in the order and Corky was told that Chris was an outsider and the local boys needed to have a greater role in the fortunes of the North Kingston team. Politics on the very local level was going to be a prominent factor in the development of

Chris's baseball skills. Chris was always going to be an outsider even if he possessed great God given abilities. Not only did Chris have to be a good player he had to overcome the prejudice of being an outsider in a world that often looked for excuses to overlook anyone that was different or did not fit the mold of the person making the decisions even if it meant that a better player was available.

One cannot overestimate the psychological trauma that always being an outsider plays on a young person's psyche. Some people may thrive in the knowledge that they will never have a close relationship with anyone while they are growing up. That would be the exceptional case. Humans are social creatures. When humans came out of the trees, they probably formed groups for mutual defense from animals and other humans who did not want the other group infringing on their sources of food and area of control. If an outsider attempted to insert himself (I say himself to the exclusion of herself because a male was trouble and could replace an established male member of the group while a female was considered as another worker/child barer that would enhance the power of the alpha male of the group) a war was eminent. The outsider was chased away of killed. So, it has been throughout the history of mankind.

The baseball season of 1960 started with Chris playing on the North Kingston Junior High School baseball team and he was doing very well until the baseball coach determined that Chris was not serious about baseball and benched Chris for the last few innings of the last game of the short season. Chris aged out of little league and was recruited to play for the Tigers of the Connie Mack league. In his last at bat for the Tigers, Chris hit a ground rule double. Before the season was finished the family again packed their belongings and moved. Chris found himself and his family in Clarksville, Tennessee.

Chapter 6

An Outsider Again in Clarksville, Tennessee

Joe re-entered college after a 20-year hiatus from his days at Duke. The family lived in married student housing right across the street from the college baseball field. It was late in the local baseball season, but some games were still being played at night on the college field. The games were played mainly by semi-pro teams composed of older men who just loved the game and could not get playing the game on a team composed of their peers out of their systems. There was a smattering of players on those semi-pro teams that had played professional baseball and even a very few who had reached the big leagues. Such is the draw of the game of baseball that once baseball is in your system it is very difficult to wean it out of your conscience and to my thoughts out of your spirit.

Kay busied herself with homemaking and becoming involved with the First Baptist Church of Clarksville. The church served as Kay's social outlet and provided her with likeminded people with whom she could talk and become acquainted; as Kay and the family had done throughout the many years that the family spent following Joe from assignment to new assignment in the Navy. Joe spent much of his time at the college library trying to get himself back into his studies. Joe's professors were impressed that a man his age would re-enter college. Joe had no trouble impressing his classmates and professors with his knowledge and his ability to score high grades.

Swamp Goddess required everyone in the family to refer to her as Ali. She quickly made friends with some of the other children that lived around the married student housing on the campus of Austin Peay State College. There were parks, classroom buildings, dormitories and recreation facilities to explore and hide in if you were being chased by anyone.

Chris became acquainted with a kid who was about his own age, and they hung out together until the start of the school year. The same age kid's name was Tim and Tim had absolutely no interest in baseball. All Tim was interested in was getting himself and Chris into trouble. Tim's family consisted of Tim's father who had been recently hired to be the Chairman of the English Department at Austin Peay. Tim's father was also a member of the Church of Christ and had extremely conservative beliefs and acted them out. Tim's mother, Elizabeth, also a conservative member of the Church of Christ was the mother of five children and absolutely adored her husband. As soon as Jim, her husband, walked through the door after work, Jim and Elizabeth would passionately kiss and embrace in front of anyone who was in their presence. After the passionate kissing, the couple would retire to their bedroom for an extended time and refuse to be disturbed by their children. Tim had an older brother, two younger brothers and a sister who was the same age as Swamp Goddess.

One day before the end of the summer break from school, Tim thought it would be great fun to hide in the bushed in front of Tim's house and throw rocks at cars as they passed that location. Tim enlisted Chris to engage in that criminal activity and Chris, who had lots of experience in throwing rocks at moving targets joined in.

Chris was accurate and hit several cars with small pieces of gravel that was readily available. Most of the drivers did not know that their car was being hit by gravel thrown at their car until they got home and inspected their car and found that the car had a dent and some of the paint had been scraped off their shiny automobile. Lack of knowledge was not the entire case, however. As the rock throwing event went on the size of the rocks thrown by Tim and Chris got larger. Eventually, Chris threw a rock the size of a baseball at a passing pickup truck and the driver of the truck took immediate exception to the game of hit the vehicle that was being played at his expense.

The truck stopped. The driver got out and saw the size of the dent in the side of his pickup truck. The truck driver then saw Tim and Chris hiding in the bushes in front of Tim's house. The truck driver's face was bright red with anger. He shouted, "You boys are going to jail, and your father is going to pay for the damage to my truck."

Without further discussion Tim and Chris ran in the opposite direction from the street on which the now dented red pickup truck was parked. Tim took a left and went into his house. Chris took a right and ran into a classroom building on the Austin Peay campus. The truck driver followed Chris. Chris ran into a classroom and hid under a table. He could hear the running steps of the truck driver and realized that if the truck driver ever got his hands on Chris, that going before a judge would not occur because the truck driver was so mad that he would have committed murder as soon as he got his hands around Chris's scrawny neck.

Time passed. It seemed as if a whole day must have been spent under a table in a classroom building on the campus of Austin Peay State College by a boy whose heart was not pounding because he had accurately thrown a rock the size of a baseball at a moving target and hit it squarely at the exact spot at which he was aiming. His heart was pounding because he knew he had done something very wrong. It was stupidity to throw rocks at passing cars and especially at pickup trucks driven by men that could have caught Chris and called the police or even worse.

Soon summer school break was over, and the memory of the rock throwing incident faded. Chris went to Greenwood Junior High and as usual he was an outsider facing a new group of classmates who had been with each other from the start of first grade. Coming from a school in Rhode Island to a school in Clarksville, Tennessee was not very challenging to Chris as most of the subjects covered at his new school had been covered the year before in Rhode Island. It was almost like repeating a grade. Chris was able to entertain himself because the college students had shown up and the freshmen class was full of students from very rural Tennessee, and it was fun to see all the young men from places like Dickson, Hohenwald, Paris, Franklin, Portland, Lebanon and the various towns, villages and unincorporated areas in and around north central Tennessee.

The new students from "small town" Tennessee were long on excitement and short on experience. For the most part they were away from home for the first time in their lives. It was only 1961 and America had not become as homogenized as it later became when national TV gave the American public stereotypes for fashion and behavior that became standardized by watching Father Knows Best, Leave it to Beaver, and the Brady Bunch.

California standard had not reached north central Tennessee, there was no awareness of the English invasion that occurred just a few years later. John F. Kennedy was president, but Tennesseans supported Nixon by a 53% to 48% vote in the Presidential election of 1960. Country music was still king, and Roy Acuff the famous country music performer was owner of Dunbar Cave, a resort (later Dunbar Cave was purchased by the State of Tennessee because it had significant historical value) near Clarksville. Roy Acuff would often appear at Dunbar Cave and perform his most famous country classics The Great Speckled Bird and The Wabash

Cannonball before audiences made up of the freshmen students from Austin Peay.

The largest men's dormitory was just across the street from the married student housing where Chris and his family lived. Next to the large men's dorm there was the dorm that housed male student athletes. That dorm was much nicer, had a better student lounge, more vending machines and a better television than the larger men's dorm. On Saturday mornings Chris and Swamp Goddess would walk across the street and arrange themselves in the athletic dorm lobby and watch cartoons on the athletic dorm's TV. They would generally have enough change to buy sodas and vending machine cookies and enjoy being out of the control of their parents. Chris and Swamp Goddess would watch Fireball XL 5 and mimic the mechanical voice as it said, "firing retro rockets". They also enjoyed watching Underdog, The Flintstones and George of the Jungle.

Sometimes Chris would be required to walk across the street to shower at the athletic dorm because Swamp Goddess would take up residence in the bathroom at the married student apartment that he shared with the family.

Soon, however, school started, and Chris was showering at the Jr. High facilities because the coaches recognized that Chris was a good athlete and they wanted him to play football, basketball and compete on the track team. The Jr. High did not have a baseball team and that was a drawback to Chris in the development of his baseball skill level.

The football coach told Chris that he should "come out" for football. Chris had made friends with a fellow student named Pat. Pat was tall and lanky and convinced Chris that he should try to become an end so that he could catch passes if the quarterback threw the football. The coach had other ideas. Chris found himself playing quarterback and learning to run plays. Chris was athletic enough to handle the football and hand it off to the star of the team, a running back who was faster than any other 13-year-old in middle Tennessee. Jimmy Heaton could do one thing and he did that one thing really well. When the football was handed to Jimmy Heaton more often than not, he would burst through the line and out run anyone on the field all the way to the endzone.

Spring football practice replaced spring baseball. Chris was expected to concentrate on learning the playbook and preparing himself to take up the responsibility of being the quarterback in training not only for the Jr. High team but also for the Clarksville Central high school team after he matriculated. Such was the love of high school football in Clarksville, middle Tennessee, and the entire south in the 1960's. That love of football for men of the south, also has political ramifications of which most 13-year-olds are only tangentially aware. Whose child should be allowed to be quarterback on a high school football team is a matter of political intrigue.

Chris's status as an outsider worked against him in that setting. The quarterback position had to be entrusted to someone whose family had roots in the community. An outsider like Chris had to be a super athlete to even be considered as a potential for the position. It was something that was unknown to Chris. Joe was not in a position to help the situation because, like Chris, he was also an outsider with no ability to understand that politics were involved even in Jr. High football.

Besides Joe was busy studying and trying to move on with his life while supporting his family and dealing with his professors and fellow college students. The fall quarter at Austin Peay had all sorts of excitement. The college football team practiced on the baseball field next to the married student apartments. The high school football team played their games at the stadium adjacent to the campus and the segregated black high school also played their games at the same stadium. The black high school was Burt High, and their games and fans were much more entertaining than anything else going on in and around Clarksville in the autumn of 1961.

Burt High's distinguished alumni included Wilma Rudolph, the Olympic gold medalist in all the women's sprint events at the Rome summer games of 1960. Burt High's band was much more entertaining than its white counterpart at Clarksville central. Burt High had a running back named Lester Barker who would electrify fans with his ability to reverse field and escape the grasp of defenders who often had nothing to show for their efforts of trying to catch Lester than a hand full of turf.

It was not hard for Chris to get in to watch all the football games at the stadium next to the college campus. He merely had to walk about 500 yards and jump up to the ledge of the 8-foot wall surrounding the stadium, pull himself up to the top of the wall and jump down into the stadium. As easy as pumpkin pie.

After getting into the stadium the fun really began, especially when Burt High was playing. More often than not a fight would erupt in the stands. Pint whisky bottles were thrown at the field by opposing team fans. A drunk fan would shout, "they hurting my brother, I gonna kill them boys what is hurting Willie." On more than one occasion Chris was confronted by a black man who was curious to see some white teenagers wandering around the Clarksville football stadium at a Burt high school football game.

The black man asked with somewhat slurred speech, "What you doin in here?'

"I came here to watch the football game." Chris replied without giving much thought to the fact that he was the only white person in a crowd of black people in

the early stages of the Civil Rights movement at a segregated high school football game on a Saturday night
in the deep south. Schools were integrated in Rhode
Island and in the Naval housing project black and white
families lived in close contact with each other. Chris's
friend, a black child named Henry even would spend
the night with Chris from time to time. Not so in Clarksville.

The black man continued, "You want a drink of whisky?" as he pulled a pint bottle from his back pocket.
Another less drunk man standing close by grabbed the
whisky bottle and took it from the first man's hand.

"You need to leave this kid alone, you going to get
us all thrown outta here." The second black man said
as he pushed Chris away from the first black man and
towards the stands were most of the fans were seated
and paying attention to the game. "You need to get up in
them stands and sit down before any of these guys see
you and want your ass." The second man said to Chris.

Chris quickly did as his protector said and found a
seat on the home team side of the stands. Chris stood
out among the fans as he was the only white face in the
stands and soon people sitting around him were asking
why Chris was there. The game was eventful. Burt High
was playing Pearl High School from the inner city of
Nashville. Burt and Pearl played on a regular basis and
were both completely segregated schools where only
black students attended. As mentioned, Burt High's star
running back was a shifty ball carrier whose name was
Lester Barker. On multiple plays, Lester would carry
the ball and be met by a solid tackle at the line of scrimmage. Lester would appear to be mortally wounded by
the tackle and remain on the turf while his teammates
gathered around him. Someone would grab Lester's belt
and pull him up and down until life flowed back into the
running backs fragile body. This course of action would
continue for several plays. Then all of a sudden, the

football would be pitched to Lester and off he would go around the end and no one, I mean no one was about to catch Lester Barker in the open field. It was a certain touchdown as soon as Lester Barker got loose.

Not only was Chris enjoying the action on the field, but he was also taking in the Burt High cheerleaders. Those young ladies were an unknown commodity to Chris. Chris, who had had black female classmates in Rhode Island, had never seen cheerleaders with such pretty legs as those cheerleaders. Their black legs seemed almost polished as they danced around while leading the crowd in cheers. Perhaps it was the lights or the cool evening air that caused Chris to react as he did on seeing the Burt High cheerleaders, but everything considered, it made a lasting impression on a 13-year-old white boy sitting in the stands of the Clarksville Municipal Stadium while watching a crowd of black people as they were cheering on Burt High and Lester Barker.

It was not long until Chris also had the opportunity to play football under the lights of the Clarksville Municipal Stadium. Greenwood Junior High's football season started, and Chris was named the starting quarterback much to the consternation of the local fans of football in Clarksville and Montgomery County. The local fans wanted one of their own to be the quarterback even at the junior high school level politics would be a factor in who was selected to play and who would be relegated to a backup role. Greenwood's first game, the first football game of Chris's playing experience, was against Murfreesboro's junior high team.

Before the game the Greenwood coach told Chris that the first three plays that would be called would be first a hand off to the running back over left tackle. The second play would be a hand off to the other running back over right tackle. On both of those plays Chris was to fake a pitch out to the other running back after handing the football off. On the third play Chris would fake the dive play, pitch the ball to the right running back for a sweep around the left end. The right running back would in turn hand the ball to the left running back in what is known as a double reverse. When the game started, Chris took his position at quarterback and performed the plays as directed by the coach. On the third play Jimmy Heaton, a very fast and shifty running back wound up with the ball and ran 60 yards for a touchdown. Unfortunately, there was a penalty on the play and the touchdown was called back. The next thing that Chris knew was that a replacement quarterback was sent onto the field and Chris was relegated to a backup role until the other quarterback got hurt several games later.

Greenwood lost its first game that first night of the season. A rematch with Murfreesboro was scheduled for the last game of the season. Greenwood won every game it played except the first game loss to Murfreesboro. The rematch would allow Greenwood to get revenge.

Before the last game, the coach told the players that as an incentive for the team to do their best the school would allow the players to keep their home game jersey if the team got its revenge and beat Murfreesboro in the final game of the season. The team was excited. Chris was somewhat indifferent because the other quarterback was to start the game. However, things can change quickly. After the first few possessions neither team scored a touchdown. The teams went into half time with the score still tied without any team having been able to get into the endzone.

When the teams came back on the field Murfreesboro moved the ball quickly down the field and was poised to score when its best running back was hit solidly and coughed up the ball and a Greenwood defender pounced on the football and prevented Murfreesboro from scoring. Greenwood took over at its own 20-yard line.

Within a play or two the Greenwood quarterback was hit hard, and it affected his ability to fully concentrate on the called plays. The coach motioned for Chris to come to the sidelines and to get ready to go into the game. The play calling would be simple. Chris directed the line to increase their splits, meaning that the offensive linemen would line up at a greater distance from each other than they had normally been accustomed to. Chris was given the opportunity to run the offense, but the coach told Chris not to get too fancy and to keep giving the ball to Jimmy Heaton for as long as he was gaining yardage.

When Chris entered the game, it was already the fourth quarter and time was beginning to run out. Chris smoothly handed the ball to Heaton, and he gained 7 quick yards. Chris quickly called another play and handed the ball to Jimmy Watson the other running back and that confused the defense because they expected that Heaton would continue to get the ball on every play. Watson got 10 yards. As soon as the team was back in the huddle Chris again called a play and the team was back at the line of scrimmage before Murfreesboro's defense could get set. Greenwood marched the ball quickly down the field. From the 20 Heaton got loose and scored. The ball was given to Watson to score the extra point and the game came to an end.

The Greenwood students rushed onto the field. The cheerleaders hugged the players that stayed on the field all except Chris. No one seemed to notice that Chris took over as quarterback and directed the team to victory. The cheerleaders and the other students only recognized the other quarterback because he was local and they all thought that the outsider, Chris, was just that, an outsider not worthy of their acceptance.

Chris realized that he would always be an outsider whether it was in Rhode Island or Clarksville, Tennessee. It did not matter if he was a good player or not, there were going to be other factors always revolving around him that could ultimately dictate how he would be received or even perceived as a player and as a human being.

Chapter 7
On to Nashville

Chris was selected to play on another Connie Mack baseball team in Clarksville the summer following the end of his 9th grade school year. The high school baseball coach regularly came to the games at the field on which Chris's team played. The high school coach approached Chris about his interest in baseball and offered some instruction on stance and hitting to Chris. When Chris had played little league baseball in Florida, he was instructed to hold his bat at an angle more parallel to the ground than in a 90° angle as most hitters do. Chris used that stance and was extremely successful in making solid contact for the next several years. In Florida he hit double after double and had a very high batting average. When he played in Rhode Island he hit for high average, and he had power to go with average. By the time Chris got to Clarksville the high school baseball coach thought that Chris's stance and bat angle was odd and stepped in to make a significant change.

The high school coach, the only hitting instructor that ever actually instructed Chris on the fine points of hitting a baseball up to that point, told Chris to hold the bat in an upright position and think of the bat as a hammer with which to drive nails. Joe was at the game that night and heard what the coach told Chris and did not object. It turned out that neither man actually had any idea about how to teach the art of hitting a round baseball with a round baseball bat to anyone.

Physics tells us that the speed at which a bat makes contact with a baseball is an all-important factor in determining the distance the ball will travel. Additionally, the launch angle of the ball as it leaves its contact with the bat is an important factor in the measure of the distance the ball will travel. A good hitter will recognize that there is also the issue of hitting the ball on the "sweet spot" of the bat.

The sweet spot on a baseball bat is that location on the bat so that when the batter makes contact with the baseball the impact of ball on bat does not sting the batter's hands. If contact between bat and ball occurs, especially on cold days, at a spot on the bat other than the sweet spot a batter will feel stinging on his/her hands caused by the excess vibration in the bat as the inertia of bat and ball goes from 0 to high velocity. If the ball makes contact at a location towards the end of the bat (above the sweet spot), the hitter's top hand on the bat will feel the sting. If contact is made at a spot below the sweet spot, (a location on the bat closer to the batter's hands) the hitter's bottom hand will feel the greater stinging. However, if the hitter makes solid contact with the baseball at the sweet spot on the bat the hitter will feel no vibration or sting in his/her hands. (As an aside, once while playing baseball in college, on a cold March Day in Tennessee, I hit a ball at a spot on the bat that sent so much vibration into my hands that it cracked my thumb nail in half.) The sweet spot is roughly two thirds of the length of the bat as measured from the hitter's hands.

After the baseball season was finished the family moved to Nashville. Prior to the whole family moving Joe took Chris to Nashville to get him enrolled in high school. The high school closest to the Vanderbilt campus was West End High. The family decided that they would live near Vanderbilt because they only had one car and if Kay needed to drive during the day, Joe could walk to his classes or more importantly to the college library. As Chris was enrolling at West, Chris and Joe were greeted by the football coach at the school as he was preparing for fall football practice.

Coach Kennedy introduced himself and gave an inspection of Chris's body. Chris felt as if he was being given a physical exam right there in the lobby of the high school even before Chris decided whether or not he wanted to continue playing football on the high school level. On the other hand, neither Joe nor Chris knew anybody from the high school and Coach Kennedy seemed to take an almost fatherly interest in Chris and assured both Chris and Joe that he would look out after Chris, and all would be well if Chris would commit to playing football at West high. When asked about his preferred sport Chris told Coach Kennedy and anybody else who would listen that he wanted to play baseball more than anything else. Coach Kennedy told Joe and Chris that that would not be a problem because all that playing football would entail was keeping Chris in shape so that when spring came around Chris would be ready to play.

What happened could not be further from the assurances that Coach Kennedy gave to Chris and Joe. Football practice for an outsider was hell. Chris was physically abused at every turn. The other team members were friends for life. They all grew up together. They all liked each other. Chris again was an outsider, and he had no advocates either on the team or on the coaching staff.

The other team members decided that Chris could and should be the target of their aggression before the season started. Football requires aggression. Football thrives on aggression. Chris just happened to be the odd man out and the natural recipient of the pent-up aggression that the naturally aggressive members of the West high football team had and needed to express. Either the coaching staff were unaware that Chris was getting beat up at almost every practice or turned a blind eye to what was going on.

The West high football team boarded a bus and traveled to a remote location in middle Tennessee to engage with two other high school football teams in an extended football camp. Practices were to include early morning workouts and afternoon workouts. The team stayed in rooms that housed six or seven players. The rooms had no bathrooms or anything more than bunkbeds, screen windows and a place to put the football gear that each boy was assigned before they set off to football camp. After practice the boys would go to their room strip off their equipment put on a pair of shorts and walk down to the shower facility in order to wash off the grime and sweat that had covered their bodies during practice.

On more than one occasion Chris would walk down to the shower facility and hear the other boys talking about him in very threating ways. The other boys were not aware that Chris heard their discussion of how they would bully and hurt Chris for no other reason than he was not one of them even though they all were supposedly on the same team. Such is the fate of being an outsider even in today's world in which primitive instincts take over the heart and mind of a group when someone that has not been a part of the group shows up even if he/she is invited. Perhaps the us versus them mentality is not even a conscience choice. Perhaps the instinct to fight and drive an outsider away from the group is so instinctive that it manifests itself in all situations where an outsider poses a threat to the position of any member of a group that has an established hierarchy. In the situation in which Chris found himself, the hierarchy of the members of the West High School football had been established before Chris arrived in Nashville and he again would suffer as a result of his position as a newcomer even at high school football practice.

After a week of torture at the hands of his team mates the football team ended football camp and returned to Nashville and to civilized society. Joe had secured the rental of a duplex house on Blair Boulevard in fairly close proximity to West High and the Vanderbilt campus. Chris could walk to school as long as the weather was decent, and Joe could walk to the library where he spent long hours. Swamp Goddess was enrolled at Calvert Junior High which was also within walking distance from the family's residence. Kay within a few days after arrival in Nashville visited the First Baptist Church of Nashville and shortly thereafter the family as a group joined the church.

As it turned out the church was infinitely more welcoming to Chris than anywhere else, he had tried to gain acceptance from his peers. Even though Chris always appeared to be bruised and beaten when he showed up at church, he was allowed to participate with other young men of his age group, and they did not seem to notice that his face was cut, and his hands were always swollen and deeply bruised. As it turned out there were other boys who also appeared in the same situation from other schools who also played football and who were also considered outsiders on their team. The group of outsiders that also included Chris formed an alliance and at least for a few hours on Sunday mornings Chris was a part of the group.

There were also girls about the same age as Chris who wanted to get to know Chris and find out all about his troubles. One particular girl, Marsha, from Buffalo, New York, also an outsider, wanted to take Chris under her wing, so to speak, and engage in conversation and even some hand holding. Before long, Chris was asked to join the youth choir and to help lead the music of the church at its early service. As opposed to what was going on at high school, church at least provided a place where Chris could be with people of his own age without the fear of being subject to injury and insult.

Not only was football physically demanding, but it also caused Chris to fall behind in his studies. Football practice started on Sunday afternoons. The team would gather for a film viewing of the team that they were to play on the following Friday night. Additionally, the players had to watch film of the game they had just played, and the coach would point out mistakes that each player had made during the game. The film sessions were boring and long. On weekdays, the team practiced from 3:00 until dark. By the time Chris got home from school he was so tired that he could not eat and all he wanted to do was to lie down and rest. After resting for a few hours, he would have a desire to eat. By that time Joe and Kay were already in bed and Chris was on his own to forage for whatever was in the refrigerator that he could stuff into his mouth.

On Friday afternoon Chris would come home right after school and prepare himself for the football game that was scheduled. If it was a home game Joe would take Chris to the barber shop to get a haircut, Chris would eat a descent home cooked meal and then he would go back to the school to be taped and outfitted for the game that night. When the team played away games Chris had to gobble down whatever he could stuff into his mouth and hurry back to the school and get taped, put on his uniform and ride on the bus with the team to the opposing team's field to play in the game. After the game Chris would go home and go right to bed because he was physically beat up, mentally exhausted and spiritually weakened by the threats and insults that he had endured for the whole week.

On Saturday Chris would rest. He did not want to get up from his bed. Chris did not want to go outside or go for a ride in the car. Chris had almost no friends except for the guys at church for as long as football season went on when Chris was in 10th grade. It was a miserable experience. To make matters worse Chris was falling behind in his studies. Chris failed algebra and he failed Latin. He did alright in English and in biology. Chris did very well in American history. Joe became very angry with Chris about his grades in algebra and Latin and threatened Chris with more insults and punishment when all that really needed to happen was that Chris was not allowed to continue playing football. Mercifully, the football season ended at the end of October 1963. By then Chris had been beaten up almost every day since football practice had begun in August, had to endure threats, humiliation, and physical violence in what seemed to be a never-ending hell.

When the football season ended Chris's life got better. Then on Friday November 22, 1963, President Kennedy was assassinated. Kay and Swamp Goddess were at an overnight girl's camp sleep over. Chris and Joe were at home. By then Chris was playing basketball but not on the varsity team. A heavy rain fell that night and a cold front form the west moved across middle Tennessee. All day Saturday there was nothing on television but the events surrounding the assignation of President Kennedy. Kay and Swamp Goddess got home in the early afternoon and the family watched the television in unbelief concerning what had happened in Dallas, Texas on the day before.

Stores were closed, football games were called off. The country went into a standstill. When the death of President Kennedy was announced over the loudspeaker at West High, Chris was in Ms. Demsky's Latin class. The school's Principal Mr. Oliver broke in and put the radio broadcast of the events in Dallas throughout the school. In the class in which Chris was sitting some of the students expressed joy that Kennedy had been shot and proclaimed that, "He had it coming to him for what he had done."

Chris had no idea that other 10th grade students could have developed such hatred of the duly elected President of the United States. Ms. Demsky, a small single lady who had immigrated to the USA from Poland expressed her sadness and told of her feelings when she learned of the death of Franklin Roosevelt. Ms. Demsky had never married. She dyed her hair bright red and smoked Home Run cigarettes in the teacher's lounge. How Chris learned that Ms. Demsky smoked Home Run cigarettes is a mystery but a fact, nonetheless.

After school Chris and another basketball player walked across to the Jewish Community Center on West End Boulevard to kill time while the varsity squad used the basketball court that was on the third floor of the school building. After the varsity finished the B-team had its turn. Chris was not the only outsider on the b-team and a kid named Phil took most of the abuse from the insider team members. Phil was often referred to as the "scholastic spastic." Phil's father was Jewish, and his mother was Christian. Phil's mother had lost both of her arms as a result of an electrical accident, she had hooks and prosthetic arms that allowed her to drive. She always seemed to enjoy the company of Phil's classmates when Phil brought them to his house that was close in proximity to West High.

The student population of West High was about 50% Jewish. The school mascot was a Blue Jay, but other schools referred to West as the Blue Jews. Phil did not fit into the Jewish group or the other group. Phil was an outsider to a higher degree than Chris and was thus treated in a harsher manner than Chris. A natural affinity developed between Chris and Phil. They were not close friends, but they shared similar experiences and thus looked at life in a way that they both understood.

On Sunday November 24, 1963, the family went to church at the First Baptist Church of Nashville. It was a somber service. The pastor, Franklin Pascal, preached a sermon that expressed sadness at the killing of the president and cautioned the congregation to not get caught up in right-wing rhetoric that had been expressed by some who considered the death of Kennedy as a good omen for the country. Joe did not adhere to far-right beliefs, but he was not a liberal either. Joe and Kay had voted for Nixon and were not happy that Kennedy had become president. Joe would often make jokes about Kennedy. Once, while he was still in the Navy, he brought home a quarter with George Washington's head colored with nail polish so that it looked like old George was wearing a cap something like the Pope would wear. Joe pronounced that the new president of the United States was the Pope because Kennedy, a Catholic, took his politics and orders from the Pope.

After church the family went home for lunch that usually consisted of roast beef that Kay had prepared in an electric pot that cooked the roast while the family was at church. When Chris got home the whole living space of their house smelled of roast. They all ate and were happy that they did not have to wait for their meal to finish cooking. The TV was on, and it was still only dealing with the events surrounding the Kennedy assignation. The cameras and the news reporter were on the scene in Dallas when deputies were moving Lee Harvey Oswald from the city jail to the county jail that was 10 blocks away. The NBC news reporter, Tom Pettit, was no more than a few feet away from Oswald when Jack Ruby emerged from the crowd and shot Oswald in the stomach. All of that action was on live TV for the entire nation to view. Oswald died from his gunshot wounds and Jack Ruby died from cancer on January 3, 1967.

Kennedy's assassination, the arrest and murder of Lee Harvey Oswald, the swearing in of Lyndon Johnson as the new president, the reporting of Jacqueline Kenney's bravery in light of her husband's death, the Kennedy funeral procession, the Jack Ruby trial, and all the other news that surrounded those events filled the news in the entire country for an extended amount of time. While all the country was focused on the news, Chris was focused on why he was in the particular situation that he found himself. He had no close friends. The only people that he really knew were Joe, Kay and Swamp Goddess. Joe was busy with his studies; Kay was busy with her homemaking chores and Swamp Goddess was busy fitting in with the other students at Calvert Junior High.

Swamp Goddess had a much easier time of making friends and fitting in than Chris had. Young girls are usually more accepted than young boys. Boys were seen as threats in ancient history. Girls were accepted because they could help with work and could bear children as they advanced in age. Boys were prone to rebellion and posed a risk for the leaders of the tribe. In Indian cultures, when the tribe went on raiding parties the conquering tribe would take hostages and make slaves of the hostages. Boys that were above the age of puberty were slaughtered. Young boys were put to work tending livestock and especially horses among the Plains Indians like the Comanches. Girl slaves were made to work and depending on the needs of the tribe were used for sex by the dominant men. That mentality must have been hardwired into the brains of people because that is what was happening to Chris and to other outsiders, male outsiders were not physically killed, but their lives were made so difficult that it was often hard to explain the trauma inflicted on the group in which Chris found himself.

Chapter 8
High School Baseball

The remainder of Chris's sophomore year in high school was punctuated by a continued acceptance at church, hostility from the players on the football team, making an effort to bring his algebra and Latin grades up and then Spring happened, and it was time to play baseball. The baseball coach was also the varsity basketball coach, and his heart was clearly more in tune with basketball than baseball. Chris was good enough to play baseball without much coaching but the lack of instruction or even encouragement from the coach assigned to help his players improve their skills was a negligent way of coaching. There was a group of players that could have improved if the school and the coach had taken their job seriously. The team had a few potentially good players. Chris, if properly instructed, was potentially a great player.

West won a few games but lost more than they won. Chris played in the outfield and was as usual a very good hitter. There was no encouragement to work on his hitting skills. There was no program in which any of the players were to participate during the summer. It was a haphazard set of circumstances that found Chris playing on three different teams during the summer after his 10th grade year in high school came to an end.

Chris played on the church team in the church league for young guys. The games were played on Saturday mornings at the Centennial Park baseball field. Chris played the outfield, and on occasions shortstop, pitcher and catcher usually depending on who showed up to play on any given Saturday morning. Chris also played on a team of high school players that was only slightly more organized than the church league. The games in that league were played generally at midday on Saturdays so they did not usually interfere with the morning games in the church league. The third team was the most organized of the three leagues. While there was no formal program of development for Chris or any of his teammates to follow there was plenty of playing time and at bats to at least keep Chris and his good friend Buddy playing together in the summer of 1964.

Chris and Buddy played together at West high school. Buddy's father had been a major leaguer and played for a few years in the St. Louis Cardinals organization. Buddy and his family moved to Nashville around the same time as Chris and family moved to Nashville. Buddy was the oldest of three brothers. Buddy's father wrote a column on baseball for the Tennessean, the local Nashville newspaper and also covered pro wrestling for the paper. Pro wrestling is not usually covered in the sports section of most newspapers because it is not considered to be an actual competitive sport. The definition of a pro wrestler is that the wrestler is a "struggling actor." That is not to say that the men and women who put on skintight wrestling costumes are not good athletes, however the actual pro wrestling matches are staged events designed to promote a soap opera like storyline that will entice simple minded men and women to follow the pro wrestling circus on TV and in the arenas. Chris often watched pro wrestling on TV because it was funny, and he got a good laugh when the Scufflin Hillbillies took on the Bavarian Boys. The Hillbillies would use a cowbell as a hidden weapon and the Bavarian Boys would get a submission from the other wrestler if he got him in the pretzel hold.

Chris played a lot of baseball that summer. On Saturdays he would get up and have a quick breakfast. He would put on the church league uniform, catch a ride to the baseball field, play one or two 7-inning games. Chris would then go home, change uniforms, and gobble down some lunch. He would then get a ride to the next game, play another 7-inning game, go home change uniforms again, drink as much water as he could hold, ride to the next game and play another 7-innings. On any given Saturday from May until the end of July Chris could play as many as 28 innings. While the experience of playing that much baseball allowed Chris to keep active in the actual playing of the game in which he wanted to become the best, there was no help in the development of the skills needed to become the best. There was also the stigma of being an outsider and not having the support of the in crowd.

At church, the youth choir was preparing to go on a choir tour from Nashville to Fort Worth, Texas. The youth choir under the direction of Robert Sneed boarded a chartered bus on a Friday morning with about 40 choir members and adult chaperones and headed to Birmingham, Alabama. The choir performed a concert at a local church and were housed by church members from that church in their homes. The next morning the individual choir members were fed breakfast at the local church members' home and then taken back to the church to again board the bus. On Saturday night the choir performed again this time they were in Meridian, Mississippi. Again, the individual choir members were housed by the local church members but this time there was something different. At the house where Chris stayed there was a teenage guy that wanted to take some of the choir members in his car to a drive-in restaurant. On the way they passed by a place where there was a confrontation between a group of black people and a group of whites.

It was the summer of 1964. The civil rights movement was in progress. Martin Luther King Jr. had rallied those interested in racial equality to take to the streets and protest the segregated society that predominated the country and especially the south. Meridian, Mississippi was in the center of the white backlash against any change in the place to which blacks had been relegated since the days of slavery.

It was a Saturday night. Many people were on the streets of Meridian, Mississippi. Cars full of whites drove past blacks walking in groups on the street. Shouts of "nigger" and worse were hurled at the black people. At one street corner a fight broke out and blood was spilled. Chris had been around black folks from his days in Rhode Island and to some extent while he lived in Clarksville, but he had never experienced the hatred that spewed forth from and was expressed that evening by a group of white people intent on causing injury to black people merely because they were black.

After seeing first-hand the tension between a group that would not accept change in the social order and those who sought to bring about change and racial equality, Chris became convinced that the old south was dying and that something dramatic was about to happen in the United States.

The young man that was driving the car from which Chris got a first-hand view of the hatred that white people could and did express to the people who were exercising their rights to peacefully walk the streets of the town in which they lived, took Chris and the others back to the house where they were staying that evening. The young man who was a church member expressed his hatred of the blacks and left no doubt as to where his sympathies laid. He did not like black people, and he felt the world would be better off if they were never seen again.

The next morning the local news in the Meridian newspaper told the story of the arrest of several black protesters who had broken the law by not having a permit to gather on the streets of the town where they lived.

The church folks that had housed Chris that night said that the black folks who they also called "niggers" deserved to be jailed and worse. Chris took all that he had seen and heard and thought deeply of what it all actually meant and what place he would have in a society filled with hatred.

The bus full of choir members and chaperones pulled out of Meridian and Chris hoped that he would never have the pleasure of coming back. The bus rolled on to Louisiana and another stop with the same procedure of staying with church member families after a concert. The next day the bus moved on to Texas. Chris had never been to Texas before, but he had often heard that Texas was the state where real cowboys worked on ranches, rode horses and carried guns on their hips. What he mostly saw was everybody driving a pickup truck and driving fast.

The bus headed for Fort Worth and the Southwestern Baptist Theological Seminary where the choir members and chaperones would be staying for two nights. The youth minister informed Chris that they would be sharing a bed together that evening. Chris thought it was somewhat odd that the youth minister would not have his own room, but it was not so unusual that Chris expressed any concern to any other person in authority. As it turned out Chris should have expressed his concerns.

The youth minister said, "Chris don't be concerned if my hands wander during the night. I'm used to sleeping with my wife and I may reach out for you during the night."

"That was an odd thing to say," Chris thought to himself, but by that time Chris was tired and ready to get some sleep.

During the night as Chris was sleeping, he felt the youth minister's hand reaching for his groin. Chris rolled over on his side so that his back was to the direction of the youth minister's wandering hand, and yet the youth minister persisted in moving his hand in order to grab Chris's penis. Chris further positioned himself out of the reach of the youth minister's hand and after a struggle that lasted for several minutes the youth minister got up from the bed in which they were sleeping and went to some other room.

Chris thought about the confrontation between the youth minister's hand and his penis and had the fear that the man was some sort of pervert. Perhaps Chris should have said something about what had happened, but Chris was still an outsider and Chris was also embarrassed about the whole affair and he did not want to make waves on a church youth choir tour while he was in Texas and so far away from family. Besides, Chris had met Phyllis and they were becoming friends. The choir was to go to Six Flags over Texas that day and Chris and Phyllis were going to hang together, and ride rides together and hold hands and make out when no one was looking.

The bus was loaded with the choir and off they went. The Six Flags franchise had only a few locations in 1964 but the location in Arlington, Texas was a great attraction for a group of teenagers from Nashville. While Nashville had the Grand Ole Opry, it lagged behind in attractions for children and even young adults. That all changed a few years later when Opryland was built, and the Grand Ole Opry changed locations from the downtown Reymond Auditorium to the new Opryland location near Old Hickory Blvd. Chris and Phyllis sat next to each other near the back of the bus and got as close to each other as their young bodies would permit.

Phyllis was one of five children. She had an older sister, two younger sisters and a younger brother. Phyllis's family lived across town from where Chris lived and her family had moved to Nashville from the area around

Buffalo, New York. Phyllis's father was a member of the United Brotherhood of Industrial and Ornamental Ironworkers. Phyllis's mother had grown up in Derby, New York and her grandfather had been a railroad engineer. Phyllis's maternal grandparents were originally from Hattiesburg, Mississippi but the railroad relocated them to Buffalo during the great depression of 1932. Phyllis's mother was a devout Christian and met and married Phyllis's father who also came from a strict Christian background.

All of the girls from Phyllis's family were well accepted in their high school and each one of them became a cheerleader. Phyllis's family would relocate every summer from Nashville back to the home of Phyllis's mother's parents. The father whose name was Blake, would get more steady work around Buffalo in the summer than in Nashville. They would return to Nashville for the children to go back to school in the late summer and Blake would find work in and around middle Tennessee in the winter and not have to worry about the ice and snow of Buffalo.

Chris and Phyllis got on the tunnel of love ride at Six Flags, and they kissed the whole time the cart in which they were seated was in the cover of darkness. They got off and rode the same ride again and again until the chaperone saw them a demanded that they ride some other ride and not grope each other because it was embarrassing, and all the other choir members knew what was going on and were laughing. That did not stop Chris and Phyllis from holding hands and kissing when no one was looking. Chris was 16 and his hormones were running wild. He walked around with an erection all day long.

From Chris's standpoint the day at Six Flags and even the choir tour was over too quickly. After all, kissing and hugging with a willing recipient was a new experience and he wanted to continue doing that for as long as Phyllis was willing to do just that. After the choir tour was over Phyllis and her family returned to Buffalo and Chris was alone except for his family and the love of baseball.

A few weeks after the baseball season ended, fall football practice started again and new trouble was right around the corner. A new family moved to Nashville from Oklahoma and the oldest child of that family was a guy named Ronnie and he was a big-time football player who loved to inflict pain and suffering on opposing players and on his own teammates when he could not find anyone else to punish.

At first Chris and Ronnie hit it off well. They were both outsiders and they came from similar circumstances. Ronnies father was also enrolled at Vanderbilt and was a candidate for a PhD in guidance and counseling. Joe had met Ronnies father at Vanderbilt and they had exchanged information about their son's football aspirations. Chris met Ronnie and told him about West High and the football program. Chris drove Ronnie to practice and life was well until an unfortunate event occurred that made Chris and Ronnie bitter enemies.

One afternoon after football practice Chris drove Ronnie to his house. Ronnie was a line man and was physically bigger than Chris. Ronnie also had a mean streak that predominated his personality. Chris was a quarterback/ running back and considered himself to be more of a finesse player relying on speed and movement to make plays rather than on brute strength as was the preferred method of play used by Ronnie.

Ronnie and family had a small dog that they named Princes. It was a family dog that was loved by all. When Chris took Ronnie home the dog ran out to greet Ronnie. Ronnie did not see the dog. Princes ran under Chris's car and Chris ran over the dog. Chris did not see Princes and just started to pull away from where he was parked. Chris heard a crunch under the tires of the car. Chris got out of the car and to his complete horror Princes lay dead in the street. Chris picked Princes up and carried the little dog up to the house were Ronnie and family lived. Ronnie came to the door. Nothing was said, Chris just handed the dog's body over to Ronnie.

From that day on Ronnie wanted nothing better than to hurt Chris. At football practice Ronnie would line up so that he could smash his fist or elbow into Chris face. If Chris ran the ball Ronnie was sure to pile on any time Chris was tackled. Ronnie had such a temper that later in the year he would always get into a fight with anybody that he lined up against. Later in life Ronnie was given a scholarship to play football at Middle Tennessee State but it only lasted one semester. He got into a fight with one of the coaches and was thrown out of school.

None of this was of any help to Chris. He was injured in the second game of the season and had a blood clot in his left leg that caused his whole leg to turn purple. His leg was so stiff that he could not bend his left leg and had to have sonic shock treatment in order to break up the blood clot. Chris could not practice and that probably saved him from several beatings at the hands of Ronnie. When Chris was finally able to return to football it was so late in the season that no one much cared about physical violence so Chris was spared the rath of Ronnie.

The situation with Phyllis also turned sour. Phyllis decided that she did not want the relationship with Chris to continue. Phyllis became distant and Chris could not figure out what he had done wrong that would cause Phyllis to back away from Chris so abruptly. Chris pushed too hard and that made matters even that much worse. Chris would call Phyllis and Phyllis would be too busy to talk. Chris would see Phyllis at church, and she would turn her back and walk away.

It was just puppy love but to an outsider rejection was almost impossible to imagine. Chris was beside himself dodging Ronnie and feeling the hurt of breaking up with Phyllis and being injured and not able to bend his leg. His life was miserable. But then when all else seemed lost baseball season started. Chris had to be cautious because Ronnie was on the baseball team and Chris knew better than to get too close or to even talk to Ronnie. To Ronnies credit, he was a powerful hitter and Chris, and Ronnie complemented each other from a batting order standpoint. Chris would get a hit and would be on base when Ronnie would drive him in. Unfortunately, that was all that West had from an offensive point of view. West scored but also gave up more runs than they could ever hope to score.

Chris and Buddy were teammates and Buddy was also a good hitter. Buddy did not get along with Ronnie either because of a confrontation at football practice. Ronnie wanted to fight almost everybody with whom he came in contact. Chris and Buddy were good friends. Buddy's father was interested in teaching Buddy to make solid contact and was interested in teaching Buddy to be a better player. What Buddy's father was not interested in was allowing Buddy to get mauled by Ronnie.

One afternoon West played Hillcrest High in baseball. Ronnie was up to his usual antics. Ronnie had several hits and drove both Chris and Buddy in producing several runs. On the other team was a player whose name was Manley. Manley was a good player and was a very good football player. Manley and Ronnie had had a confrontation when West played Hillcrest during the football season. When the baseball game came to a conclusion Ronnie got in Manley's face and as usual wanted to pick a fight. Manley did not back down as he also had a reputation to uphold.

Ronnie began, "Manley you are a queer."

Manley replied, "you are a loser, and we just beat you to prove that you are loser."

Ronnie picking up a baseball bat and approaching Manley said, "I just called you a queer and you must be one cause you are too scared to do anything about it."

"Ronnie, you are a turd and not worth shit." Manley said also picking up a bat with which to defend himself. Ronnie became more enraged and went after Manley with the bat and would have beaten Manley to death if Ronnie's father had not been at the game and intervened. Ronnie was still cursing and was so overcome with hate that he almost took a swing at his own father.

Buddy's father saw all that had transpired and told Buddy that he could no longer play baseball on his high school team as long as Ronnie was allowed to participate. That was a real blow to the team because Buddy was a good player. Ronnie was a good player. He was very strong and could hit the ball a mile when he made solid contact. Ronnies problem was between his ears. Ronnie took immediate action to respond to any adverse call, pitch, errant throw or any other real or imagined slight that he perceived that was unfavorable to him and would fight anybody at any time. Fortunately, the season ended, and Ronnie graduated, and Chris never saw him again.

Towards the end of the school year, Chris was visited one evening by the coach of an American Legion baseball team who was also the coach of a high school team from across town. The coach had followed the box scores from the games that Chris had played in that spring and wanted to invite Chris to play on the American Legion team that he was putting together. The team would be mostly made up of players that the coach knew from the high school at which he coached baseball. Chris by then had a reputation of being a good hitter who made solid contact and the coach wanted him to play with the guys that he already knew. The other players were mostly graduating seniors but there were also a few players like Chris who were still juniors in high school. Even though Chris knew that he would undoubtedly be considered an outsider, in his mind playing with a traveling team would be of benefit to his skills and a learning experience.

Chris accepted the invitation to play on the American Legion team and started playing on the team shortly after the high school season ended. Chris continued to play on the church league team and he and Buddy would get together and play catch and hang out together when there was nothing else to do.

Chris got a call from Buddy's father one afternoon and was told that Buddy had been injured the night before while playing at a baseball field in North Nashville. Buddy was playing center field when a ball was hit into the gap in right center field. Buddy went after the ball and would have caught it but for the light pole that he ran into. The force of the impact was enough to cause the light pole to sway, but more importantly the impact also crushed the ocular bone in Buddy's face and Buddy was taken to the hospital. The crash into the light pole ended Buddy's season and prevented him from playing football when the season started in the fall.

In the meantime, Chris continued to play for the American Legion team and that team was doing very well. There were several very good players. There was a third baseman who had an exceptionally strong arm and was a reliable hitter. There was one guy that was very fast. If the opposing pitcher ever walked that guy, he would not just trot down to first base, he would race all the way to second before the surprised catcher could get the ball out of his mitt.

The American Legion team was invited to play in the annual American Legion tournament in August. The tournament was held in Jackson, Tennessee, a small town located closer to Memphis than to Nashville. Despite the fact that Chris played the whole summer with the guys on the American Legion team he was definitely an outsider and never was engaged with the other players from a social or personal point of view.

The team arrived in Jackson and were housed in a downtown hotel. The hotel was one of those old hotels that traveling salesmen would stay in when they had to make service calls in that area of Tennessee. Jackson was more of a sleepy deep southern town that supported the agriculture business of the surrounding countryside. During the Civil War, General Grant had his headquarters in Jackson while he directed the movement of the Federal troops in the siege of Vicksburg.

The team checked into the hotel and were treated to an old fashion all you can eat banquet by the sponsors of the tournament. All the teams and all the players were given all they could eat and most of the teenaged players ate plenty. Chris stuffed himself with steak, fried chicken, potato salad, coleslaw, fried fish and even turkey. The next day the tournament began and the team that Chris played on quickly won the first two games they played.

The games were played in the early evening and extended into the night. During the day and when the team from Nashville was not playing there was not much to do in Jackson. Next to the hotel was a pool hall and half a block down the street was a movie theater. The pool hall was always crowded with players playing 8-ball and betting whatever money they could come up with. The movie theater happened to be showing Bikini Beach with Annette Funicello and Frankie Avalon. The movie was all that was available that week in Jackson. This was in an era before there were cable television or movie channels on TV. There was nothing to do in Jackson.

Chris played a few games of pool but did not have any money with which to gamble. He went to the movies, but you can only watch a movie so many times without being bored out of your mind. That was especially true when it came to the 1964 addition of the love affairs of Frankie Avalon and Annette Funicello. Don't get me wrong Chris admired the looks of Annette and would have liked to have met her but the acting and repetitiveness of watching the same movie over and over again was just too much. Chris, by the time he had watched the movie twice, could recite the entire script of all the parts played by Annette, Frankie, and all the other actors.

The team that Chris played on was eliminated in the semifinals by a very good team from Memphis. The Memphis pitcher was unhittable. Chris struck out and only managed to hit a few foul balls off the Memphis pitcher. No one from the Nashville team did more than hit a loud foul.

After being eliminated all hell broke loose at the hotel at which the team was staying. One of the players produced a bottle of whiskey. The players morphed from conscientious ball players into wild animals uncaged and willing to destroy the entire floor on which they stayed. Nothing was spared. Rooms were trashed. Fire extinguishers were emptied, toilets were destroyed, the guys ran naked in the halls and eventually the police were called. To his credit Chris avoided the mayhem and cloistered himself in his room and kept quiet when confronted by the police as to who had caused all the destruction.

The Nashville team left Jackson as soon as the sun came up the next morning and before all the damage to the hotel could be accessed. Chris was home by midafternoon and happy to see his parents and even Swamp Goddess.

Football practice had begun at West while Chris was in Jackson. Chris would have been a senior and would have been the starting quarterback, but he could not decide if he wanted to go through another season of getting his butt kicked by his teammates and then beaten down by opposing teams. West as mentioned was in the Jewish section of Nashville and the Jewish students did not play football, West's football team had a relatively small number of students from which to recruit players. The fewer the number of players the more each player would have to play. With the number of football players available it was certain that many of the players would have to be two-way players, playing both offence and defense, and thus greater the likelihood of injury.

Chris's friend Phil had decided to try out to be the punter on the football team and Chris knew that Phil would take the brunt of the beatings from the insiders that had played together from elementary school days. Chris also knew that he would be subject to scorn from the football coaches for not returning to play football in his senior year of high school. To the coaches it was a form of rejection even if Chris was an outsider. The year before Chris had suffered a separated shoulder and blood clots in his left leg from playing football. Chris chooses to not subject his body to playing football and concentrate on baseball.

Phil made the team as punter. Actually, there was no one else that wanted the job. Phil was not good at punting and in the first game he was called on to punt, he missed the ball with his foot and was not asked to punt in a game again. Phil endured all kinds of ridicule not only from his teammates but also from the student population in general.

Chapter 9
Senior Year Baseball and the Beginning of Professional Baseball

Chris's senior year in high school was important to the family. Joe was working on his dissertation in International Comparative Education and was engaged with his major professor who was from Australia. The major professor had a keen interest in Chinese foreign policy and Chris and the family would be invited to the home of the major professor on occasions and Chris would listen to the latest news from China and the economic outlook for trade between China and the United States. In those days China was a mystery to the average American. It was not until President Nixon engaged in diplomacy with China in 1973 that there was much interest in China.

Joe would take Chris along to international conferences hosted at Vanderbilt. On one occasion Chris was introduced to Adlai Stevenson the U.S. ambassador to the United Nations. Chris was able to say that he knew Ambassador's cousin, Miss Anne Stevenson because she had been Chris's third grade teacher when the family lived in Hopkinsville, Kentucky. Meeting Ambassador Stevenson was very interesting because not long before the meeting at Vanderbilt Stevenson had a prominent role in the showdown between the United States and the Soviet Union over the supply of ballistic missiles by the Soviet Union to Cuba. The Cuban missile crisis had the country on the edge of nuclear war in October of 1963 and had been reported extensively on television. President Kennedy had addressed the nation regarding the foreign policy that the United States was following, and a speech delivered by Ambassador Stevenson was a key development in the strategy to stop the delivery missiles to Cuba.

Chris also attended gatherings of international students at Vanderbilt. Many of those meetings involved covered dish meals prepared by the students and the cuisine of different countries was an adventure in food for Chris. Joe, as a graduate student, was often given the responsibility of acting as the chaperone for the gatherings of the international students and he had to remain at the site of the party until the last student left the building. After eating and mingling with the students Joe and Chris would retire to the professor's office and Joe would quickly fall asleep. Chris could not sleep sitting up in a chair, so he sat idly by until the party ended, and Joe made sure the place was clean and securely locked.

Chris also assisted Joe as he was writing his dissertation. On Saturdays and sometimes on Sundays after church Chris would accompany Joe to the college library and pull books off of the shelves for Joe to review and add as references to his dissertation. The book that Joe was writing was a comparison of the educational systems of several different countries and an analysis of the strengths and weaknesses of the American form of public schools. Joe worked on his dissertation for what seemed like an eternity, but it was necessary to be finished so that Joe could apply for and receive a professorship when he graduated and received his doctorate.

Chris was happy enough to help his father in any way that he could because he realized that he was also ensuring that Joe and Kay would be able to achieve some stability in their lives. The family had been vagabonds for way too long and needed a permanent home. At the same time Chris realized that he would be graduating from high school, and he was interested in playing college baseball or getting drafted by a professional team.

One day Chris received a letter from the Pittsburg

Pirates saying that they had been watching Chris's progress in his baseball career and that they would be watching him during the next season in high school. When the high school baseball season started, Chris went on a hitting spree that was a sight to behold.

In the first game he went four for four and had two doubles and a homerun. In the second game Chris went three for four and again had two extra base hits. He kept on hitting and was scoring runs at an exceptional pace. Chris kept noticing men with stop watches showing up at his high school games and realized that these men were there to watch Chris and to send reports back to their home offices about what they were seeing.

These were the years before the major league draft of high school and college players was widely anticipated. There were no televised productions of the selection of players and the major league teams kept information about baseball players to themselves. Teams made direct contact with a player and initiated contract discussions in a secrete manner without any other teams being aware of the interest that any particular team had in any particular player. There was interest in Chris from the Pirates and in another team that did not want their interest to be known.

The Pirates drafted Chris in the 4th round of the 1966 amateur baseball draft and signed him to a small bonus of $15,000. Pittsburg assigned Chris to their rookie league affiliate in the Florida Complex League at Pirate City, Bradenton, Florida.

The Pirates have a long and varied history. They are currently in what could be considered a rebuilding phase of their operation. Some would argue that they have been in a rebuilding phase for way too long for that assessment to be the team's correct situation. The Pirates are perennial losers. The Pirates have had a losing season for the last 20 years, but it was not the case in the 1960s and 1970s when the Pirates had such stars as Roberto Clemente, Willie Stargell, Berry Bonds and Bobby Bonilla. The Pirates won the World Series in 1960 by beating the Yankees who were led by Micky Mantle, Yogi Berra, Whitey Ford and Bob Turley. The Pirates were outscored by a lot of runs but won the series on a walk off homerun in the 7th game of the series. The homer hit by Bill Mazeroski is the only walk off homer in a game 7 of the world series in baseball history.

Joe, a big fan of the Pirates, was very happy with the outcome of the World Series that year. The Pirates had three players, Bob Friend, Roy Face and Vern Law that Joe renamed Friendless, Faceless and Lawless as a claim of greatness for his hometown heroes. It did not matter that Bob Friend still has the record for the most losses by a Pirate pitcher, nor did it matter that the Pirates were outscored by a very large margin. All that mattered was that when it counted Pittsburg would win by a single run. All that mattered was that the Pirates had won the Word Series for the first time since 1925 and Joe was happy all winter.

The Pirates won the World Series again in 1971 with the great Roberto Clemente and the pitcher Steve Blass who pitched a complete game for the game 7 victory. They also won the World Series again in 1979 singing the song "We are Family" and being led by a group of black and Latino players. Willie Stargell was the team leader. Stargell had a buggy whip batting style and could hit a round baseball with a round bat for great distances. The 1979 Pirates were given the nickname of "The Lumber Company." That name was given to them because the whole team could hit for average and power.

I have digressed from my story. Chris was drafted by the Pirates and sent to Bradenton, Florida to become acclimated to playing professional baseball and to compete with other skilled players in order to advance in the Pirate organization and ultimately play in the major leagues. There were no high expectations for players drafted in the 4th round of the draft of high school baseball players because only a very few of the players selected to play professionally ever made it all the way to the major leagues. The chances of progressing through the organization were stacked against someone like Chris.

Yet, Chris traveled to Bradenton dreaming just like every player who puts on a baseball uniform that one day he would play at the highest level of professional baseball. He dreamed of making solid contact with such regularity that he could not help being noticed by the coaches and other players and more importantly being noticed by the amorphous organization.

The organization is the business end of baseball. The organization is made up of bean counters who place value on every piece of property that the organization possesses and that includes the players that play for the organization. To the organization a player is a property owned and possessed by the organization and can be quantified in money or in money's worth. Either the player has a positive value or creates a cost that detracts from the bottom line of the business interest of the owners/ investors of the organization.

On arrival in Bradenton, Chris was assigned to a room with a roommate. Chris was given a schedule of daily activities that he would be expected to participate in without variation. The regimentation of schedule and events was more closely watched and overseen by the organization than being in bootcamp in the army. In 1966 the Pirates drafted in the first round Ritchie Hebner a shortstop from the suburbs of Boston. In the second round the Pirates took a pitcher, James Minshall, and in the third round another pitcher, Richard Grimaldi. In those days there was a never-ending supply of Latino players because the draft only included players from high schools or colleges in the United States.

Baseball organizations were free to scout and sign foreign players, mainly from the Dominican Republic and Puerto Rico without subjecting those players to the draft. Previously, organizations had signed players from Cuba, but when Cuba was taken over by Fidel Castro in 1960 major league organizations stopped trying to sign Cubans even if they could. Players such as Roberto Clemente were not drafted to play as the players in the United States. Clemente was signed while he played on a Puerto Rican team by the Brooklyn Dodgers and was assigned to their Montreal Royals farm team in 1954. Clemente was then drafted in the first round of the Rule 5 supplemental draft by the Pirates in 1954 and made his major league debut in 1955.

Again, I have digressed. Chris came from a family that attended church and as I have mentioned, Chris while in high school had found solace at church from the torment of being attacked on the football practice field and in school because he was always considered to be an outsider. Chris had become a Christian when the family lived in Hopkinsville, Kentucky and his profession of faith was preceded by a distinct call on his life by Jesus Christ. Chris did not understand the precise essence of a spiritual encounter with Jesus, but he did know that Jesus had called him to believe, and his belief was very real.

Chris did not understand the presence of the Holy Spirit. In fact, it was not until a few years after he made a profession of faith that the presence of the Holy Spirit in Chris's life began to manifest itself. Suddenly and out of nowhere Chris was competing in a game of basketball in junior high school and he was overcome with a feeling of power to change the course of the game by a sheer will to cause his team to win. He did not know where the power came from, but he recognized that the power of a will to win came over him and permeated its expression as a force that was unstoppable and pushed Chris to the inevitable outcome of the game.

Chris did not equate the will to win as a spiritual power nor did Chris apprehend that there was a power that emanated from God with in him that could control his ability to play a game or be a factor in his own life. You could say that there was just an inkling or an awareness that there was a power within Chris that motivated him beyond his natural talents to control his and his team's ability to perform. Where the power came from at that point in Chris's life was a complete mystery. Chris did not even think about using that power in most instances and merely relied on his God given talent to make solid contact with a round baseball with a round baseball bat.

It was not many days into the rookie baseball camp in Bradenton that Chris was challenged by the coaches assigned by the organization to teach and monitor the progress of the newly acquired assets of the organization and to evaluate the value that these assets might have. The coaches were hardened older men who had been in baseball all their adult lives and who acted more like drill sergeants than baseball coaches. The coaches in fact acted as drill sergeants in putting the players through their paces. These coaches woke the players up at dawn. Hustled the player through breakfast, drilled them in calisthenics, had them throw to each other at the distance of 90 feet for an hour, conducted infield drills, hit fungo flies to the outfielders, pitched batting practice and divided the players into teams to compete against each other. All this was accomplished before lunch. After lunch scrimmage games were played on a daily basis. The games would last until it was too dark to see, and the day would abruptly end with the new recuits being too tired to do anything else but to take a shower and go to bed.

Rookie league lasted for 8 weeks. After 8 weeks

the players were given a week's pass to return to their homes. The players would then be required to return for another session of rookie league. While there was a break in the Pirates rookie league activities, Chris returned to Tennessee.

Joe had been hired as a college professor at Middle Tennessee State University in the education department and he, Kay, and Swamp Goddess found a house in a new subdivision near the campus and settled in. Swamp Goddess found new friends quickly and enrolled at Murfreesboro Central High School. Kay found a new church and joined the ladies of the church in doing good works among the people of Murfreesboro.

Chris was very happy to be with his family. He found comfort in the familiarity of being at home and eating the special food that Kay prepared for him. She made stuffed cabbage, chicken paprika, and fried chicken. Joe had a gas grill installed on the patio of the house and they grilled steaks and chicken when neighbors came over to inspect the rookie league baseball player that was in their neighborhood. Mainly the neighbors were interested in Chris because they had never been around a professional baseball player and wanted to see if he looked or acted any different from the other young men of his age that lived near there.

Joe tried to persuade Chris that he needed to enroll at MTSU during the winter semester and begin his college education during the baseball off season. Rookie league would take a break from the end of October through the end of February and that did not leave time for Chris to go to college. At best all Chris could do was to sit in a few classes without registering and get a feel for what a college freshman would be like if he gave up his hopes of being a major league player and went to college.

From Chris's perspective the weeklong break from

rookie league was both too short and too long. Chris was a loner having been an outsider all of his life and the only stability that he had was his family. On the other hand, his desire to be a great baseball player required that he continue his baseball education in Florida. Chris desired to learn how to make solid contact with every pitch thrown his way no matter the velocity, break, or location of the pitch. He had a spiritual will to succeed that he recognized as the gift of God. Chris intended to go as far as the Holy Spirit would take him.

Joe and Kay took Chris to the airport in Nashville with the promise that their prayers would be always for Chris success and safe return. Swamp Goddess did not share her parent's belief in the power of prayer, but she wished her brother well as he departed for the second session of rookie league.

Chapter 10
What Could Go Wrong Goes Wrong

At some point in our lives, we are all tested. Men of distinction are tested. Strong men are tested, and weak men are severely tested. Women are not exempt from testing, but women have different mechanisms to cope with the paths of adversity that are thrown in their way. The ability of women to deal with adversity is a mystery to men. A man's testing takes many forms, and a man is not always successful in coping with adversity. A man, even a strong man, can be overcome by his testing. Testing can drive a man down a path from which there is no return. Bars are full of men and women that can only find relief from their troubles with alcohol. Young people make their own adversity by using drugs.

Chris was not exempt from testing. He was tested when he played football. He was tested because he was an outsider all of his life and he was about to be tested again. It would be the spiritual essence of baseball that was to be the only saving grace that would see him through to the next phase of his life and career as a baseball player.

When Chris returned to the Pirates' rookie league training facility in Bradenton, Florida he was put in a room with a Spanish speaking player from the Dominican Republic. Manny Alverez was from Punta Cana a resort city on the southern end of the Dominican Republic and was a catcher that could hit. Manny spoke only a few words of English and Chris spoke only a few words of Spanish. They got along with each other very well because they both knew how to stay out of each other's way. If they communicated, it was in rudimentary sign language in which a gesture of putting your hand to your mouth as if you were putting something in your mouth and then chewing motion meant' "Let's eat."

They would also use these types of signs to provide help in batting stances and bat angles. Manny because of his position as a catcher had to spend longer hours learning the art of catching on the professional level. Manny had to communicate with the pitchers in a meaningful way in order to not only know what pitch to signal to be thrown from the pitcher but also to understand that each pitcher threw each pitch in the pitcher's arsenal differently from each other pitcher who Manny was assigned to catch during each pitching session. At first there was a Spanish interpreter that assisted in the language barrier between Manny and the English-speaking pitchers. Manny was also given English lessons to help with the communication. Before long Manny could speak enough English to let the pitchers know what was on Manny's mind when he had to go to the mound to let the pitcher know what was on Manny' s mind. The pitchers also started to pick up some rudimentary Spanish as well and communication happened.

As an outfielder the learning curve for Chris, while important, was nowhere near as complicated as that for Manny. They each, however, savored the chance to make solid contact and improve their skills as professional hitters. For the first time in his life Chris was getting constant and detailed instructions on hitting a baseball. His instructor was a former major league player who was assigned to be a hitting instructor at the rookie/ instructional facility in Bradenton.

Forrest Harrill "Smoky" Bartlett became the Pirates hitting instructor after a long career as a player for the Reds, Phillies, Pirates and White Sox. Bartlett held the record for the most pinch hits as a major league player. After playing his last game for the White Sox, Bartlett was hired to be a hitting instructor and his path crossed with the path that Chris was on at the rookie/ instructional league facility of the Pirates.

Smoky Bartlett was from a small town in North Carolina and spoke with the distinct accent of anyone who had grown up in that part of the country. That is to say that he drew out certain vowels in words that were distinctive from other accents, even other southern accents of which Chris was aware as he had lived in the south. Even though Chris had no particular accent of his own, he had been around his mother's family in North Carolina on many occasions and immediately recognized Coach Bartlett's accent as being familiar and pleasing to his ear.

"Chris, how you going to drive the ball standing with an over exaggerated closed stance." Smoky Bartlett growled at Chris when he looked at the batting stance that Chris was employing at the time Bartlett first made a visual inspection of the Rookie outfielder.

"Move your front foot back so that you have a more balanced stance." Bartlett continued.

It was a time before video tape came into wide use and way before computer generated pictures were employed to analyze every move that a player made on every play and even every swing of the bat. Bartlett employed the method of evaluation that had been employed on a baseball field since baseball was invented by Abner Doubleday (that supposition is open to question) in Cooperstown, New York in 1836. Bartlett looked Chris over and applied his own hitting style to instruct Chris on the technique that Chris should adopt to make Chris as good of a hitter as Bartlett had been when Bartlett hit .363 for the Phillies in 1954.

None of the instructions that Bartlett gave Chris took into consideration the makeup of Chris's unique body or the coordination that was obviously evident when Chris made solid contact with the round baseball with the round baseball bat. It just happened that luck was on Chris's side because the adoption of Bartlett's style of hitting was agreeable with the kinesiology of Chris's body and manner of making solid contact.

While Bartlett had been a major league catcher, he was not expected to give instruction to the catchers at the Pirates training facility. Bartlett had refused to take that assignment because he was still a southerner, and his racial prejudices were not so easily overcome when he was put in a position of instructing a foreigner like Manny and he was most adamant that he would not instruct black players beyond watching and shouting instructions from outside of the batting cage.

Old prejudices for an older man from a heritage of hate could not be overcome easily. On the other side of the equation, Chris had no thought of prejudice either with his roommate or the black players he came in contact with while starting his professional baseball career. One of the best players on Pittsburg's roster was Roberto Clemente who was both black and Latino. Clemente had to overcome racial prejudice from the standpoint of a black man from Puerto Rico who spoke very little English when he was taken in the Rule 5 draft by the Pirates in 1954.

At the time of the instruction given him by Smoky Bartlett, Chris had seen the effects of racial hatred on the streets of Meridian, Mississippi, during the summer before his junior year in high school while on the church choir tour. Chris was aware of the hate that could fill a man's heart and cause damage to a man's soul. Kay's sisters' husband, Uncle Roy was a member of the KKK. Uncle Roy spewed hatred of black people whenever Chris would be required to have dinner at Aunt Buela and Uncle Roy's house when the family visited relatives in the Sandhill region of North Carolina.

Aunt Buela and Uncle Roy died tragically. Roy suffered from a back injury that did not allow him to straighten his back and he had to walk doubled over after he was around 50 years old. Aunt Buela died in a traffic accident as she was coming home from work and Roy died in a house fire because he was unable to move quickly enough to get to safety. Tragic endings to lives filled with hatred are not only sad but wasted. What would have been their lot had they been more caring and less hateful? We can only speculate but it did have a profound impact on Chris because he believed that he should be tolerant of all men.

Chris started to live up to the promise of his recruitment and would make solid contact and drive the baseball into the gaps of the instructional league ballpark on a regular basis. The pitchers that pitched batting practice could not get the baseball by Chris without Chris making solid contact. It did not matter if the pitcher was a flame throwing right hander. Chris, a right-handed hitter, was able to get the bat on the ball even if the velocity at which the ball was thrown was faster than Chris had seen in high school. It did not matter if the pitcher was a left-handed junker (a pitcher who threw nothing but off-speed pitches designed to keep the hitter off balance) Chris was still able to make solid contact and drive the ball into the gaps (the area of the field between the outfielders in right and left center fields).

In the afternoon games played by the new recruits Chris excelled in hitting, fielding, throwing and running the bases. Before too much time had passed in the second session of the rookie/ instructional league Chris was being noticed as was Ritchie Hebner. Ritchie, like Chris was making a great impression on the organization. Ritchie Hebner was taken in the first round of the armature baseball draft of 1966. He was from Middleboro, Massachusetts and played shortstop.

Hebner had a great eye for hitting. When the expression "great eye for hitting" is used, it generally connotes that a hitter is able to see a pitched ball all the way to the bat and actually see the ball leave the bat after contact. It was said of the great Ted Williams that he had such a vision that he could read the label on a vinal record playing at 78. (In olden days vinal records, played on record players, spun at different speeds. Some at 45 rpm and some at 78 rpm. The higher the rpm value the faster the vinal record would spin on the record player.) In other words, Ted Williams' eyesight and brain function allowed him to be able to follow the flight of a baseball from the pitcher's hand all the way to the bat and to adjust his hands and swing to make solid contact with any pitch that was thrown. Ted Williams was the last major leaguer to hit over .400 for an entire season. Williams accomplished that feat in 1941, the same season that Joe DiMaggio had a 56-game hitting streak. The accomplishments of Williams and Di Maggio have not been matched since the year that the United States was attacked by Japan and entered WW II.

Chris also had a great eye for hitting. Chris could see the spin on the ball as it left the pitcher's hand. He could not do that on every pitch, but he could generally see the spin on the baseball and make unconscious adjustments to his swing as the ball traveled the 66'6" from the pitcher's mound to home plate. There are times when a hitter can see the ball better than at other times. What causes the fluctuation in being able to see a pitch and make contact is a great mystery. A player like Chris would go through streaks when it was almost impossible to miss making solid contact. The baseball would appear to be as big as a beachball and adjusting his swing was so easy that the pitcher had no chance of getting Chris out. On other hand, but on less often occasions, either atmospheric conditions or brain function caused the ball to seem as if it was the size of a BB and hitting it was more problematic.

Remember the difference between a great hitter and

an average hitter is a matter of degree. It is generally accepted that a great hitter will reach base as a result of hitting the ball no more than 33% of the time. That is not to say that the hitter did not make solid contact on a majority of times he/she faces a pitcher. Even if solid contact is made there are 8 other players behind the pitcher assisting the pitcher in getting the batter out. A hitter can drive the ball into the gap but if the outfielder is positioned toward the gap there is a chance that the fielder will catch the ball on the fly and despite having made solid contact the hitter will make an out. An average hitter gets on base by hitting a pitched ball anywhere between 24% and 27% of the time he/she faces a pitcher. There is also an element of luck in being considered a great hitter and an average hitter may be just unlucky. Hitting below 24% is a sign that the player is having a streak of bad luck or is such a good fielder that a low batting average is tolerated.

Baseball organization scout, draft and sign only players that they believe possess a great eye for hitting, unless of course the player is a pitcher. It is said of Latin players that the only way that they could get off the island of their birth is to be able to make solid contact no matter where the ball is thrown. Latin players are notoriously bad ball hitters. That means that Latin players from the Dominican Republic or Puerto Rico realized that they had to impress the major league scouts by hitting the baseball even if it was bounced up to the plate by the pitcher. It was either hit or stay at home.

While there are many examples of bad ball hitters, none is more noteworthy than Yogi Berra. Berra was not a Latin-American player. He came up in the Italian section of St. Louis known as the Hill. The Hill is a community of Italian descendants that have many local restaurants, serving some of the best Italian cuisine you could imagine. Berra's parents were immigrants from what Yogi called the old country.

Berra grew up on a street in the Hill that was across from Joe Garagiola's home. Garagiola, another catcher from the Hill was selected by the St. Louis Cardinals before Yogi Berra was selected by the Yankees. Berra was a renowned clutch hitter because he could and did hit pitches that were out of the strike zone. Berra was able to hit those pitches because he had the ability to control his bat angel to hit low pitches by swinging the bat like a golf swing, and also hit high pitches by chopping down on the ball to hit line drives. Opposing managers feared Yogi Berra as a run producing hitter in the late innings of games because he consistently made solid contact. In 1954 Yogi only struck out 12 times in over 500 at bats. The ability to cover the entire plate and adjust the bat angle to a pitch as it is being thrown is a gift that made Yogi Berra a most productive hitter.

Chris also had the ability to adjust his swing to the speed and location of any pitch that might be thrown his way. That ability does not come to many hitters. Many hitters choose to not swing at pitches outside the strike zone and prefer to make the pitcher throw strikes. In modern baseball strategy forcing the pitcher to throw more pitches and thus driving up the number of pitches the pitcher must throw to record an out requires the opposing team to carry more pitchers on its roster. A strategy referred to as getting into the opposing team's bull pen (the location where relief pitchers await the call from the pitching coach to get ready to relieve the preceding pitcher). The strategy of getting into the bull pen has caused the adoption of a counter strategy on the part of many major league teams of getting more skilled relievers so that when an in-game pitching change is made the reliever may be as or more unhittable as his predecessor.

Chris's ability to adjust his swing so that he could hit a pitch in any quadrant of the strike zone is also referred to as being able to hit the ball where it is pitched.

Generally, a right-handed hitter like Chris could hit for more power (drive the ball deeper into the outfield or out of the park) if the pitch was thrown on the inside part of the plate. When the ball is thrown on the inside part of the plate Chris, or any right-handed hitter would bring his hands closer to his body. The motion of bringing his hands closer to his body caused an increase in the speed at which the bat traveled through the strike zone. An increase in the speed of the bat from a physics perspective increased the energy transfer so that the ball would travel farther when it left the bat. If you notice on games played on television today, when a homerun is hit a graphic shown on the screen gives a value for the speed at which the ball leaves the bat. Also referred to as the EV (exit velocity). Just the other night in a game played between the Braves on the Pirates (August 24, 2022) a ball was hit by rookie shortstop O'Neil Cruz for the Pirates that left his bat at a speed of 122.4 miles per hour, the fastest speed recorded for a hit ball that year. The ball was hit so hard that it ricocheted off the right field wall that it bounced back to the right fielder on the fly and Cruz was held to a single even though the ball was crushed (an expression by play-by- play announcers indicating that the ball was hit really hard).

On the other hand, if the pitched ball was thrown in the outside lower quadrant of the strike zone, Chris would have to extend his arms and thus slow down the speed of the bat. That usually meant that the bat angle would also lower and cause the bat to make contact with the pitch at a flatter angle. The result was that the ball would be driven in a more or less flat trajectory towards the right field foul line. The result was referred to as a liner to right. That was not a bad result. If there was a base runner on second base, a liner to right that finds grass in most instances produced a run.

Hitting breaking balls is also a difficult task. Think about the cliche, "he threw him a curveball." Generally, that means that in any given setting a difficult task is said to be a big curveball. The meaning of course is that the person who is setting the task has unexpectedly made the task more difficult than was originally intended. The same is true for a hitter that is trying to make solid contact with the baseball. If the ball is thrown so that the spin placed on the ball by the pitcher is such that the ball is moving in an arc away from the batter, then the batter must adjust to the arc of the pitch by making an adjustment in his swing that brings the barrel of the bat into the path of the ball as it moves along in ark away from the batter. Additionally, the velocity at which the pitch is thrown is generally slower than the normal velocity that is expected, thus causing an unexpected variation as to when the ball will be in the zone at which the batter can make solid contact.

Pitchers also very the rate of the spin so that the curveball can either spin at a relatively slow rate and rotate on the axis in what is referred to as a slow curve or if the pitcher induces a spin rate on a hard thrown ball, generally referred to as a slider, then the arc of the ball as it moves away from the batter is much sharper and the movement can be even more deceptive. Some pictures are so skilled at throwing a slider and the break of the ball is so sharp that it is almost impossible to hit. For a time, former Braves pitcher John Smoltz had a devastating slider that rendered it almost unhittable, and he had great success not only as a starting pitcher but also as a relief pitcher. It also did not help the situation for the batter that Smoltz could throw the ball in the mid 90's so that not only was the ball traveling fast it was also sharply breaking away from a right-handed hitter.

Sorry, I have again digressed. I apologize. Chris was doing well at the rookie league training camp in Bradenton. He was getting along with his roommate Manny from the Dominican Republic and was well liked by the coaches and more importantly by the amorphous and unknown faces of the organization. All seemed to be going very well. There was the usual anxiety caused by being away from his family. Chris even missed Swamp Goddess. There were regular long-distance telephone calls from the training facility to Murfreesboro and the calls seemed to lessen Chris's anxiety about being away from the only people with which he had a long-term relationship while he was alive.

Joe, who was not one to speak for extended periods on the telephone, would ask how Chris was doing from the standpoint of his playing and nothing more. Kay was much more concerned with Chris's well-being from a health and psychological standpoint. Kay was also concerned with whether Chris was going to church, whether he had met any Christians, and whether he was saying his prayers. Kay always told Chris that she loved Chris and prayed for him daily. Swamp Goddess would just get on the phone and say hello and then be back at her studies and social contacts.

Chris's side of the conversation was always filled with enthusiasm. He was having a good time playing baseball and getting the instruction he wanted on how to anticipate the potential pitch that any pitcher might throw in any given situation. He told Joe that there was a lot of pressure on the rookie players and that they were judged every day on how they performed during the games that they played on a daily basis.

After all it was baseball and records were kept on every pitch and every swing of the bat. Chris was evaluated and re-evaluated because he was an investment that the organization wanted to place a monetary value on so that its investment in Chris would produce the proper return.

The organization's evaluations were based on the reports that the coaches at the instructional league made to the bean counters at the operations offices in Pittsburg. The coaches were also evaluated by the general manager of the baseball operations branch of the business. Evaluation on evaluation up and down the line produced pressure on each part of the organization to produce a player that made a positive contribution to the business. To be certain, professional baseball was nothing more and nothing less than a business that expected to be a profitable business even if it did not produce a winning team on the baseball field.

Ultimately, the organization put pressure on the coaches and instructors and they in turn put pressure on the rookie players to perform up to their highest level. Chris was no exception to the pressure exerted on him by the instructors and coaches. Chris began to feel the pressure to make solid contact at every at bat that he took. Sometimes pressure can be a good thing because it forces the batter to concentrate on every pitch. On the other hand, too much pressure can be distracting and put the hitter into a slump.

A slump is a curious thing. Slumps happen and they happen to even the best of hitters. There is not a hitter alive that has not gone through a slump.

A slump is a prolonged period of time when the hitter fails to make solid contact. There are many reasons for a slump. A slump can be brought on by a psychological condition that causes the hitter to lose faith in his ability to make solid contact. A slump can be brought on by an injury to the hitter's hand, wrist or back. Sometimes the injury can be minor and yet it causes a big impact on the hitter's comfort at the plate or in his swing. Maybe, a slump can be caused by an evil spirit, or more likely an evil pitcher.

At the very least opportune moment Chris hurt his hand while playing in one of the afternoon games at the training facility and went into a slump. At first Chris thought that the injury to his left hand was of no consequence. He hurt his hand while fielding a ground ball in the outfield. A ball was hit in his direction and Chris charged the ball. As he bent down to follow the ball into his glove the ball suddenly took a hop in an unexpected direction and that caused Chris to lunge for the ball. When he lunged his feet went out from under him and he fell on his hand at an awkward angle, and he landed with his whole weight on his glove – hand. Chris felt the bones in his left hand give under his weight and felt a slight pain in his hand and wrist when he finally got back to his feet. One of the coaches came running out to where Chris had fallen.

"That was quite a spill you took there Chris, are you all right fellow?" the coach asked.

"I'm ok. The ball just bounced funny, that's all." Chris replied.

"Yeah, they will do that sometimes. Are you sure everything is ok with you? It looked like you took a hard fall on your glove hand." Coach Tanner asked as he was examining Chris's left hand.

"No, I'll be all right just give me a minute to settle myself down, I'll be fine in a minute." Chris assured Coach Tanner.

Chris was not all right. He had sprained the ligaments in his left hand, meaning that he had stretched the ligaments in his hand to an extent that there were tears in the connective tissue in his hand and that would cause pain in his hand when he attempted to swing a bat. Chris had never experienced an injury to his hand and thought that it was no big deal at first. As time went on however, it became more problematic. Chris's left hand was swollen. He could not grip his bat in the way he normally did and when he did make contact with a pitched ball it felt as if someone had stabbed his left hand with a knife. Chris went into a prolonged slump.

What happened while Chris was in a slump is difficult to explain. He lost confidence in his swing. Chris had to alter his stance in the batter's box. Chris felt responsible for causing his own injury and for falling behind in the progress that was expected of the rookies in the Pirates training facility. Chris was told that the other players were passing him by and that he could do better. Strangely, it seemed to Chris that no one equated Chris lack of performance to the injury to his left hand.

Through it all Chris continued to play and train as if he had not hurt his hand. He was afraid to say anything to the coaches. Chris was afraid to tell Manny that his hand was hurt and that he could not swing his bat properly. Chris did not say anything for fear that he would be sent home and fear that his dream of playing at the highest levels of baseball would go up in smoke.

Finally, when Chris was about to give in to his injury and tell everyone that he was going home, Chris was sleeping, and he had a dream that would change the course of his professional baseball career. At first Chris did not know if he was sleeping or if he was awake and thinking of how much his hand hurt and what he should do. Chris, since the time that he had heard the call of Jesus on his life as a 10-year-old boy in Hopkinsville, Kentucky had prayed on a regular basis. That night, as was his habit, Chris prayed.

When a person becomes a follower of Christ, The Holy Spirit enters that person, and The Holy Spirit takes up residence in the person who has become a committed follower of Christ. (The Holy Spirit does not have a particular gender but is often referred to as He. The Holy Spirit could just as well be referred to as She but for the sake of my readers I will address The Holy Spirit by using the proper name Holy Spirit in every instance.) The mission of The Holy Spirit is sometimes mysterious. Jesus in various passages in the New Testament referrers to The Holy Spirit as the Comforter and as an advocate or in some cases as the helper. In each instance Jesus assures his/ her followers that after Jesus was raised from the dead that he would send the Holy Spirit to dwell within those that Christ calls to believe in him.

That night the Holy Spirit spoke to Chris. Chris was assured that he was called by Christ. Chris was assured that his hand would heal and that he would be able to return to playing baseball in the manner that he had been playing before his injury. Chris was assured that he did not need to fear telling the coaches about the severity of the injury to his hand and that he would receive treatment from the training staff for the hand and any other ailment that he had while playing. Chris was given confidence that God was aware of Chris's situation and that God had given Chris the talent he needed to be a good if not great baseball player. Chris had only to play as if he were playing for God and the rest would take care of itself.

With those assurances Chris got up the next morning and reported his injury to the coaches and the training staff. To his surprise Coach Tanner asked Chris why he had not reported his hand injury before now. Everyone knew that he had hurt himself and that he was having difficulty gripping his bat. The coach told Chris that it was up to the players to report their status and not for the staff to guess what was going on with the players.

Chris then said, "I received a message in a dream that I had last night that I was to report my injury to you this morning."

Coach Tanner asked, "What kind of a dream was that?'

Chris summoning up courage from a source that he did not know that he had in him said," Coach Tanner, I am a Christian. I believe in Jesus Christ. I believe that I was contacted by the Holy Spirit in my dreams last night and I was assured that I could trust you to see me through this slump in my hitting."

Tanner looked intently at Chris and replied, "Chris, not many players or even coaches know that there is a spiritual nature to baseball and to life. Most people are unaware that God actively wants to be involved in the lives of his chosen followers. God has given you a gift as a player that you must develop and use for God's purposes. What purpose God has for you is something that you must find for yourself with the leadership of the Holy Spirit. The Holy Spirit will direct you to the path that you must follow, so be alert, keep your mind focused on the movement of the Holy Spirit in your life and you will be a blessing to all that you encounter."

When Chris heard Coach Tanner's words he was filled with emotion and could not immediately respond. After a few minutes finally the words formed in Chris's brain and he said, "Coach as a part of my dream I was told that you would have understanding of my situation and that you would see me through this time that I am going through. I was afraid to tell anyone about my injury, but I now have enough courage to let you know that I will be alright and that I will regain my swing. Thank God for the Holy Spirit's help when all seems lost."

With that being said, Chris went into the training room and let the trainer take a look at his left hand.

CHAPTER 11
CLASS A

As reported earlier, Chris had sprained the ligaments in his left hand. He had fallen on his glove hand while tracking down a ball hit to right field during an afternoon game played at the Pirates rookie league facility in Bradenton, Florida. This had occurred in the summer after he was drafted in the fourth round of the 1966 amateur baseball draft. The injury to his left hand had caused Chris to go into a batting slump and it had weighed heavily on his mind. That is until Chris was visited by the Holy Spirit and given direction as to the path that Chris should take.

The trainer looked Chris's hand over carefully and told Chris, "I have seen this injury a hundred times. It is a common condition for players to sprain their wrists, hands, ankles, backs, necks and all other connective tissue and joints in their bodies. When you fell on your hand and wrist you were lucky that you didn't break something. You will be fine in a day or two. I'm giving you a two-day exemption from baseball activities, also I want you to soak your hand in Epson salt water every two hours and avoid using your left hand for lifting anything over 2 pounds."

Chris was very relieved that the trainer did not offer any other advice concerning his hand and took the meeting with the trainer as confirmation of what he had been told in his dream the night before. Chris realized that playing baseball could cause injury because it was a physical activity that required the player to exert his body and put his body into extreme positions. It was therefore necessary to properly stretch and condition his body.

In fact, the trainers insisted that all the players engage in exercises designed to keep their bodies as strong and as supple as possible. One aspect of the trainer's recommendations was that the players engage in weight training. Also known as weightlifting, and body building, weight training consisted of visiting the weight room that had a variety of devices that a player could use to develop his muscles. It was a combination of lifting weights to build especially the upper body of a player along with stretching exercises that Chris had to commit himself to that caused Chris to renew his faith that his efforts would be rewarded.

The determined players could be found in the weight room and using the weight machines whenever the baseball activities of the day ended. Ritchie Hebner was always pumping iron. Manny was not in the weight room as much as Chris because he had extensive meetings to go to in order to develop his catching skills. When the day finally ended and Chris and Manny were ready to fall asleep, Chris would tell Manny of his faith that all would go well for the both of them as far as their commitment to baseball went. Chris would say, "Manny, we will make it to the show. You are a great catcher, and you have a good eye as a hitter. We are becoming good friends and we can depend on each other to watch each other's backs. There are forces all around us that will try to interfere with our progress, but we will make it. We just have to keep the faith, work hard and avoid stupid stuff."

By the time Chris had finished making his speech Manny was snoring and Chris realized that he was really only talking to himself. Chris understood that he had an obligation to do whatever he could to fulfill the promise he had made to God to be the very best person and best baseball player that his body and mind would allow him to be. He had to follow the trainer's advice concerning his physical conditioning, he had to study the game of baseball from a mental point of view so he could anticipate the pitch that was about to be thrown and he had to allow the Holy Spirit to keep him on the right path to the goal set before him.

Chris's hand healed within a few days, and he was able to return to the baseball activities in which he was expected to participate. Coach Bartlett, the main hitting instructor, began to see a very real potential in the batting approach that Chris brought to the plate. Chris constantly made solid contact and started driving the ball to the gaps on a regular basis. Bartlett made his report to the general manager every Thursday.

Bartlett's report evaluated each of the players with which he interacted from a hitting standpoint. The reports were on standard 5 by 3 index cards with prescribed categories of evaluation for such issues such as plate coverage, contact frequency, power ranking, swing and miss rate, and other significant aspects of the batting coach's evaluation of each player's progress. This was the era of baseball before the invention of computers and none of the information on the index card reports was digitized. The other coaches often meet to compare notes regarding players. The coach in charge of the rookie league, Coach Tanner, was required to make sure that the reports were sent to the home office so the organization was well informed about the players in his charge.

When the player evaluations were received at the home office a chart was made of player progress and the General Manager of baseball operations would hold weekly meetings to discuss player progress with his assistants and scouts. On a monthly basis the various managers of the farm teams were brought into the team's headquarters in Pittsburg for an organizational meeting to go over the baseball operations of each minor league team. At that time there were no women involved in the organizational meetings. The farm team managers, the general manager, the GM's assistants and the scouts met in a large conference room at Forbes Field in downtown Pittsburg.

The Pirate's General Manager was Joe L. Brown and he reported to the owners of the team. John W. Galbreath was a wealthy general contractor who had his fingers in many business enterprises including horse breeding and racing. Galbreath became interested in horse breeding through his second wife, and they owned Dandy Dan Farms in Ohio. Galbreath held the majority stake in the Pirates. Bing Crosby the singer/entertainer and Thomas Johnson, a prominent Pittsburg attorney, held the minority interest in the organization. Bing Crosby met Joe L. Brown, through his father who was the comedian/ entertainer Joe E. Brown. Crosby and the senior Brown had a distinct love of baseball and Crosby bought a minority interest in the Pirates. The Pirate organization had a strong farm system that culminated in World Series Championships in 1960, 1971, and 1979 under Joe L. Brown's leadership.

The Pirates were also cost conscience. The market share for the Pirates as a member of the National League was small. The Pirates were considered to be a small market team. They had to compete with New York, Philadelphia, Chicago and Cincinnati for television coverage and fans. Also, the Pittsburg Steelers posed as competition for fans dollars in the local economy.

The baseball season lasts from mid-February when the pitchers and catchers report to spring training until the first of October when the last regular season games were scheduled to be played. Before 1969, after playing 162 games the team with the best record in the National League would play the team with the most wins in the American League for the World Series title. In 1969 baseball following the other major sports leagues (the National Football League and the National Basketball Association) initiated a playoff system in which both

American and National Leagues were divided into two divisions, the NL East and the NL West, the Al East and the AL West. The champions of each division would play a 7-game series to determine which teams would play in the World Series. Baseball traditionalists, of which there were many, regarded the initiation of a playoff tournament as sacrilege.

Baseball purest decry any change in the way baseball is played and any rule changes that are made to the game. In 1973 the American League adopted the designated hitter rule. Major League Baseball Rule 5.11 allows a designated hitter to hit in place of another player (usually the pitcher) during a game. The rule was adopted by the National League in 2022. From 1973 until 2022 the respective leagues played by a different rule when it came to designated hitters. There was much debate and fervor about the use of the designated hitter. Baseball purest hated the rule. Why should the pitcher not be allowed to hit, they would protest. After all Babe Ruth was a great pitcher and he could also hit.

On the other side of the isle, those who favored the designated hitter rule pointed out that fans came to the games to see teams score runs. The use of the designated hitter caused teams to have more exciting games because more runs were definitely scored. When the American League employed the designated hitter rule, they began to win more All-Star games and the World Series was won by more American League teams when only the American League had a designated hitter.

Sorry, digression must run in my family. Back to my story. Chris had been in a slump because he had injured his left hand. The left hand for a right-handed hitter is the top hand on the bat as the hitter stands in the batter's box facing the pitcher. The top hand guides the bat to the proper location of the bat to make contact with the ball while the right hand, and more particularly right arm produces the power to move the bat into the ball. In actuality, the whole body of the hitter must move in a coordinated effort to make solid contact with a ball moving at a high velocity as it moves in different arcs and locations while the ball travels the distance from pitcher's hand to a place where the bat can make contact. However, the left hand is an integral part of the process of hitting a baseball for a right-handed hitter.

When Chris hurt his left hand, he did not think that the injury was serious. He did not report to the trainers and did not tell anyone that he was experiencing pain in gripping his bat. If you cannot properly grip your bat, you cannot make solid contact no matter how good of an eye you might have. It is after all eye-hand coordination that we are talking about here. The eye engages the brain to bring the bat into the right location and the hand corresponds with the brain to accomplish the task.

Chris's eyes and brain were willing but his left-hand was not and the effect was predictable. No solid contact. No solid contact as long as the left hand could not do what the eyes and the brain was telling it to do. Gradually, slowly, Chris's left hand began to respond to the treatment that was prescribed by the trainers. Eventually Chris's left hand regained its ability to properly grip the bat and do what the other parts of Cheris's body wanted to do all the time. After being in a slump for what seemed like an eternity to Chris, one afternoon on the instructional league field of the Pirates in Bradenton, Florida a fastball was thrown as Chris was batting.

The pitcher who threw the ball expected Chris to make no contact or at best weak contact as he had been doing for the last couple of days and weeks. Instead, Chris moved the bat effectively. His whole body moved in unified coordination. The muscles in Chris's legs responded exactly as his mind directed. Chris's hips rotated precisely. His left leg lifted, and his right knee bent. The left leg came down and the right leg acted as a brace. Chris's left hand guided the bat to the right location and angle to intercept the flight of the ball. Chris's right hand and arm pulled the bat at a rapid speed through the zone in which the ball was traveling. A round wooden bat made solid contact with round leather covered ball and an explosion occurred. The speed of the bat intersected with the speed of the ball. The force was transferred from bat to the force of the ball and a thing of beauty happened. The ball hitting the bat made a sound that is dear to the ears of those who love the game of baseball. A "thwack" that those who know and understand can only mean one thing. The ball changed direction by more or less 180°. The catcher reached for the ball, but it was not there, it had been translated, it had been rotated, it was moving away at a pace that was not measured in those days but is measurable now. The ball took flight. It soared. The ball was shot like a rocket from Chris's bat and the men in the field could only behold the glory. The ball followed a path that caused the outfielders to only have time to turn their heads and watch as the ball flew past their positions and over the fence in dead away center field. The ball did not stop its flight until it was out of sight.

When Chris swung the bat, he knew that he had made solid contact. The vibration that usually occurs when bat meets ball can be felt in the hands of the batter. On cold days the vibration stings the hands and especially the bottom hand on the bat. Sometimes the vibration is so severe that fingernails are split, but when solid contact is made there is no sting. When perfect contact is made the batter only feels slight pressure on his hands and the ball seems to jump off the bat as if it had a mind of its own. When Chris made contact on that day there was no sting. There was no perceptible vibration. The bat responded to the brain, body and hands. Solid contact is the kind of contact that every hitter dreams of having and does have on some occasions. Solid contact does happen and when it happens it takes the batter's breath away if only for a second. Chris felt it. Chris knew that that ball had been dispatched to a location far away, and he knew that he wanted that feeling over and over again.

Coach Tanner took notice. Hitting instructor Bartlett saw what had happened and said, "He got all of that one." Tanner and Bartlett took notes. They had seen homeruns hit by some of the great ones. Bartlett was there when the Yankees hit a bunch of them against the Pirates in the 1960 World Series and had seen Bill Mazeroski' s walk off homer to win the series. Both men had seen Babe Ruth hit long homeruns and had heard the distinctive thwack of the bat on ball produced by the Babe's swing. Tanner had even heard the loud thunderous sound when Josh Gibson hit one a country mile in Pittsburg. Both men knew that the sound that they had just hear was in the same category as Babe and Josh. Both men knew that they had to see that happen again before they would report what had just happened to the organization. On the other hand, they were both impressed enough to look at each other and acknowledge that they had seen something that they were not used to seeing.

Chris was just 18 years old. He had not fully grown into his body. Chris was 6'1" and weighed 170. He was muscular and could run very well for his size. From a personality standpoint, Chris had a winsome personality and would easily laugh at seemingly odd times. When asked about why he had just laughed he would often say he had remembered something funny he had seen or heard. Chris was a good student of the game of baseball and also of the history of baseball.

When talking about the game of baseball Chris would always remind those listening to him that it was the best game in the world. "Baseball involves both a team game and an individual contest between the hitter and the pitcher. The hitter faces the pitcher alone in the batter's box. None of the hitter's teammates can help him. He's alone as he tries to make contact with a pitch. The pitcher is just as intent on getting the hitter out as the hitter is in hitting. There is nothing like it, no nothing at all." Chris would say when asked about his feeling regarding playing.

Chris's left hand continued to allow him to hit the ball with increasing consistency. He was hitting the ball where it was pitched and spraying hits to all fields, and he was hitting with power. After the homerun that Chris hit that impressed both Coach Tanner and hitting instructor Bartlett, he hit another long homerun that had the same thwack sound as the one before. Then a few days later he hit two prodigious homeruns in a single rookie league game that brought the coaches and players to stand in aww as the ball sailed over the fence and out of sight on consecutive at bats.

Tanner and Bartlett discussed the developments concerning Chris and reported their opinions to the home office in Pittsburg. Tanner recommended that Chris be promoted to the Pirate's Class A affiliate in Gastonia, North Carolina of the Western Carolinas League. The manager of the Gastonia Pirates was Bob Clear who looked after his players with affection and saw to it that they did not go too far astray.

Gastonia, North Carolina, is 21 miles west of Charlotte and is the county seat of Gaston County. In 1966 Gastonia was the center for the production of spun yarn and the home of Parkdale Mills, the world leader in spun yarn and also the largest employer in the county. Gastonia was a baseball city, and the Gastonia Pirates were the biggest source of entertainment in town. Gastonia was the hometown of Earnest Angley, the televangelist, and Crash Davis a professional baseball player who was the inspiration for the main character in the book and movie Bull Durham.

There were 8 teams in the Western Carolinas League in 1966. Spartanburg was a Phillies affiliate, the Greenville Mets, the Thomasville Hi-Toms were a Twins affiliate, the Rock-Hill Cardinals, the Salisbury Astros, the Statesville Tigers, and the Lexington Giants along with Gastonia composed the teams in the league. The season consisted of 124 games played from late April until the end of August.

By the time Chris arrived in Gastonia the season was more than half over. Chris was called up on Monday, June 27, 1966, and he was the youngest player on the squad. Chris walked into the club house and was greeted by an older man who was there alone because the team had played a three-game set in Lexington and the Sunday game had gone into extra innings. The team bus had arrived back in Gastonia late. The players were given the day off to recuperate from their travels.

Chris was unaccustomed to life in the minor leagues but understood that this was a new place for him, and he was again an outsider. The older man was the club house attendant and had seen hundreds of players just like Chris pass through the Pirates Gastonia affiliate. There had been some very good players and some troublemakers. For the most part the players who had come and gone through Gastonia ended their careers in the Western Carolinas League because their skill level was not great enough for them to advance beyond that level of play. They were good players and maybe even exceptionally good players in their hometowns and in their high schools. They had been given a chance at playing professional baseball and they did everything within their ability to advance, but they ended their professional careers in class A baseball. The largest number of players went home from the Western Carolinas League to be factory workers, firefighters, accountants, lawyers, real estate agents, insurance salesmen farmers, burglars, pimps, gamblers or whatever else they could do to survive as their dream of the big leagues vanished before their eyes as smoke dissipates from a bonfire. They could still smell the smoke and even feel the warmth of the fire but their dream of playing beyond Class A ended as it began with a bus ride home.

"You must be Chris. I was expecting you this morning. My name is Elijah Parks, and I am the club house attendant and assistant trainer for the Pirates." the older man stuck out his hand for Chris to shake.

Chris took Elijah Parks hand and felt the roughness that had come from years of hard work.

"Yes, Mr. Parks, I am Chris. How did you know that I would be here this morning?"

"Everyone calls me EP son and that's how I prefer to be addressed. Don't call me Mr. Parks or even Elijah. I'm just EP. I'm here because I am paid to be here to take care of boys like you who come here to find out if they are baseball players or not. You put your bag down over at the dressing stall in the corner and I will get you set up with your new uniform." EP spoke as he pointed to the corner dressing stall.

The club house smelled of old tobacco smoke and of the ancient toilets that sat behind a thin wooden door very close to the dressing stall that EP directed Chris to store his stuff. The floor of the dressing room was cracked concrete with small cheap shag throw rugs in front of each dressing stall. The walls were sticky with brown streaks the residue of tobacco smoke as players during that time period smoked cigarettes and cigars in the club house on a regular basis. There were also spittoons for the players who chewed tobacco to spit and many of the young men who played baseball at that time chewed tobacco or dipped snuff while they played. Chris had tried to chew tobacco but found that it made him dizzy and unable to focus on the ball.

Yellow paint pealed from the walls, and everything was just plain old. In the toilet room there were 5 toilets lined up for use by the players so that multiple players could relieve themselves at one time. Chris knew that there would be action aplenty on those toilets just before game time on any given game day during the season. Chris knew that men's bowels tended to want to empty when the game was getting ready to start. It had often happened to Chris that when he was getting ready to play any game, whether it was football or baseball, it was necessary to empty his body of whatever was in his intestines just before the game started.

EP looked Chris over to judge his size and said, "How does number 27 suit you young man. It really doesn't matter if you like that number or not, it's what's available today and that will be your number for at least the rest of the season. If you ever need to go down to AG's sporting goods and get a new pair of spikes or a new glove or new bats come to me first and I will go with you and pay for the equipment. The club has an account at AG's that we use for stuff like that."

Chris looked on with an expression of being lost and a little apprehensive at the prospects of being around a group of professional baseball players that were used to the daily grind of being on their own, working out on their own, eating on their own and meeting new people and especially girls on their own. While Chris was in rookie training camp everything was orchestrated. It was like being in the army. The players were told when to get up and when to go to bed. In class A ball it was more like going to college. There was plenty of time to get into trouble if a player was so inclined.

Chris was told that he could temporally stay at The Esquire Hotel in downtown Gastonia. There would be a room waiting there for him. All that he needed to do was give his name, everything had been arraigned.

Chris had never stayed in a hotel room by himself. He had never checked into a hotel and had no idea about how to get lunch or dinner. EP did not give a telephone number where he could be reached. Besides, cell phones had not been invented in 1966 and there was no internet.

Chris was alone in the middle of a place he had never been before. Chris found the Esquire hotel, which was not too far from Sims Legion Park, the field on which the Gastonia Pirates played their home games and to where he had been taken after his taxi ride from the Trailways bus station in Gastonia. The Esquire hotel was built in 1918 as a bank building, underwent years of neglect and had been transformed into an old-style hotel complete with ballrooms, a high-class dining room and a bar in the 1930's.

When Chris checked in the man behind the desk told Chris that the team had made all the arraignments and that he was free to eat in the dining room for as long as he was a hotel guest. All that Chris needed to do was to sign the bill and indicate that he was with the Pirates. Chris was happy to get that bit of information because he only had the $50 in his pocket that had been given to him by the team secretary in Bradenton.

Chris found his room on the third floor of the hotel and lay down on the bed because he had been on the bus from Bradenton all night and was weary from his travels. He was fast asleep when someone rang the phone next to his bed. Chris found the phone and answered.

The voice on the other end of the line started, "Chris this is Bob Clear. I'm the Pirates manager. Welcome to the West Carolinas League."

"Yes sir, thank you sir." was all that Chris could manage to get out of his lips.

Manager Clear continued, "Chris, I am in the hotel lobby. Why don't you come on down so that we can get to know each other."

"Yes sir, I'll be right down. Just give me a minute to wash my face." Chris replied.

"Then meet me in the dining room. I will tell the host to point me out when you say who you are." Bob Clear told Chris.

Chris quickly got himself ready and rode the elevator down to the lobby and found the dining room. Chris asked the host to help him find Bob Clear and the host directed Chris to a man sitting alone in the far corner of the dining room. It was around lunchtime and there were men dressed in business suits dining in the room. Many of the businessmen were having martinis or other drinks from the bar. In 1966 the United States was still in an era where business was conducted at lunch between company representatives and salesmen over drinks of alcohol.

Chris sat down at the table with the manager of the Gastonia Pirates and noticed the manager was drinking iced tea and not a martini. Bob Clear looked Chris over and said, "How was your trip? An all-night bus ride can be rather taxing if you are not used to it."

Chris said, "It was alright. I'm happy to be here and to meet you, Mr. Clear."

"Call me Bob or better call me Pop. All the players in the West Carolinas League either call their manager by his first name or just call him Pop." The team manager told Chris as if he were his own son. The manager now referred to as Pop when on, "I have read the report that Tanner and Bartlett sent to the home office about the way you abuse a baseball. I'll be anxious to see how you play once you settle in. I'm not going to start you in games right away because that would not be fair to the guy playing right field now. I'll gradually phase you into games as a little time goes by. The first thing you need to do is to get yourself acquainted with your teammates. For the most part they are a few years older than you and know their way around Gastonia and the Western Carolinas League."

Chris summoned up enough courage to speak and said, "Pop, I sorta feel funny calling you Pop. I don't even call my father Pop when I'm at home, but you make the rules, and I will do my best to follow everything you say and do my best."

"That's the right attitude to have. I'm here to help you to become the best player that you can become. Most of the kids that come to me, and this league, have been told that they are the best thing since sliced bread. They come here expecting to set the league on fire and move up to the next level overnight. That's not what this league is all about. I'm here to bring players like you to the game and life of baseball. The game is only a part of baseball. There is the life of baseball too."

Chris again spoke, "I have never heard the expression of "life of baseball". I always thought that baseball was played between the foul lines and once the game was played you were on your own to do anything that you needed to do to get along in this world."

"That is not exactly the way things are. On a baseball team playing 124 games during a season, you are on the road for half of the time, living with your teammates, eating on the bus, sleeping on the bus, in other words living with the team on the bus going from town to town. You get up in the morning, eat breakfast at the hotel, go to the stadium, take batting practice, eat a bite in the locker room, take infield practice, change into your game uniform, sit in a dugout, play the game that lasts 2 to 3 hours, shower, change clothes, go to the hotel or the bus and eat a late dinner, relax for an hour or two, and start the day all over again. It's really a gypsy's life during the season and a player has to adjust his life to that grind or find something else to do." Pop sitting across from Chris made his speech with such conviction and in such a way that Chris started to understand that the players' life was something that he would have to learn to get along with if he was going to fulfill his ambition to play in the major leagues.

The Pirates were due to play the Spartanburg Phillies at 7:00 PM and Chris was expected to arrive at the ballpark no later than 1:00. Pop told Chris that he should get dressed in the pre-game workout clothes furnished by the club and go to the outfield to shag flies until Larry the assistant manager called him in to take his cuts in the batting cage. Chris was excited to get to Sims Legion Park and get in the outfield, shag flies, and begin his journey as a minor league player.

After standing by himself for a few minutes one of his teammates, Charles Howard came close to Chris and said, "You must be the new guy. You get here this morning from Bradenton?"

"Yeah, I'm Chris and I was sent here to play with you guys." Chris replied in as casual a manner as he could because he did not exactly know what to say.

"Well don't get your hopes up too high, this is a pretty tough league when you first start out. Just keep out of everybody's way for now and you will get along." Chuck Howard warned.

Chris did not know how to respond but said, "I'm here to do my best. I'm not here to get under anybody's skin. When I get into the game, I will give it all that I have and let it fall where it falls. I hope we can get along with each other because you can show me the ropes. This is my first time playing professional baseball and I want to enjoy the experience."

"You just keep your head down rookie." was all that Chuck Howard had to say in return.

With that Chuck ran at a slow deliberate pace towards the batting cage and got in line to take his swings during batting practice.

Batting practice was pitched by one of the team's trainers who everyone called "Buckets." Buckets had played ball in a semipro league for a few years and earned a few extra dollars pitching batting practice when the Pirates were in town. After what seemed to be an interminable wait Chris was called to come to the cage and take his swings. Larry, the assistant manager, stood behind the batting cage that was on wheels so that it could be removed from the field after batting practice was finished, spoke to Chris when he was in the batter's box.

"Let's see what you got kid. Lay down a few then take 10 cuts and get out of there."

Chris was the last Pirate to take his swings and the Phillies players were already standing near the batting cage waiting their turn at batting practice. Among the Phillies players was a young shortstop, Larry Bowa, who already had a reputation as a feisty individual who liked to get under the skin of a rookie player like Chris.

"Your swing is like a rusty gate, rook!" Bowa shouted at Chris as he took his cuts.

Chris said nothing but realized that the Philly shouting at him was nothing to be concerned about, especially because Chris was driving the batting practice speed pitches into the deepest part of Sims Legion Park and causing those shagging flies to run back to the fences or more importantly watching the balls disappear over the left field fence.

Someone in the Pirates dugout shouted back, "Bowa you only wish you had this kid's swing."

There was good natured jawing back and forth during the next hour as the Philly players took batting practice with each team giving the other team a constant barrage of cat calls criticizing everything from the size of their shoes to the size of their waste and especially the length of hair that certain players wore. After all it was the late 1960's and hair styles had undergone a radical departure from the crew cuts those players often sported in the 1950's.

After spending an afternoon in the hot sun in Gastonia and after all the Pirates had taken infield practice, Chuck Howard yelled out to his teammates, "Take it to the house." Immediately everyone quickly headed to the club house in order to get ready to play the evening's game. Because Chris had never been in the club house of a professional team, he did not exactly know what to expect.

Chris went over to the dressing stall that had been assigned to him and found that his stall was next to that of Freddie Patek, the shortstop for the Pirates. Freddie was an engaging guy and held out his hand to Chris as introductions were made all around the club house.

The introductions of the veteran players followed a set ritual in which each player would say where he was from and the position that he played. When it was Chris's turn to speak, he followed suit until it came to the position that he played because Pablo Cruz had already through another Spanish speaking player announced that he was the left fielder in residence. Chris merely said, "I'm Chris from Murfreesboro, Tennessee and I'm happy to be here."

Everyone came over to the dressing stall where Chris was putting on his uniform and shook his hand and said they were happy to know him, whether they meant it or not. In any team sport there is always an undercurrent of caution and fear that someone will take the place of another player. A player's position is secure as long as he is better than any potential replacement that may be waiting on the bench or further down in the organization.

Chris played right field which is the position that the best hitters play. Henry Aaron, Roberto Clemente, Aaron Judge, Babe Ruth, Frank Robinson, Tony Gwynn, Mell Ott, Al Kaline, and Ichiro Suzuki were just a few of the great right fielders who made solid contact and drove the baseball to its limits. The current right fielder for Gastonia was Charles Howard and he led the league in homeruns two years in a row. All that was keeping Chuck Howard in class A baseball was the people in the organization who were ahead of him, starting with the great Roberto Clemente and down the line. For that reason, Chris refused to indicate a position and only said how happy he was to be in Gastonia and that he was ready to give his all to making the team successful.

As we learned earlier Chris was given number 27 as the number he wore on the back of his jersey. The uniforms for the Pirates were the old fashion wool uniforms that players had to ware before rayon nit fabric came into fashion in the early 1970's. The home uniforms were white with black block lettering and gold trim in keeping with the parent teams colors and styles. Players wore their black stirrup leggings at various lengths. Some players liked to show the white sanitary socks higher on the leg than others. Some players did not like to show any leg and wore their pants leg to the top of their spikes. The amount of stocking worn by a player was a matter of individual choice.

Chris sat at his dressing stall and pondered what was going to happen that evening if he got into the game and what the next few weeks would bring to someone like himself. He was away from family and had no friends that he could call on to even talk about his feelings and concerns. Telephone calls to home were increasingly more sporadic as Swamp Goddess monopolized the phone when she was at home and Joe was at work during the day. Kay filled her time with church activities and all of this left Chris without an outlet to express his feelings, his fears, his expectations and hopes to anyone other than God. Chris prayed. Chris had always prayed when he was a child. He prayed in a childlike manner. As he grew his prayers became more complicated. He prayed for others and neglected to come to grips with his own needs. Finally, out of desperation to be heard by anyone he cried out to God and said how sorry that he was for not coming before God and admitting his need to be comforted because he was along and was always an outsider. Chris prayed right there in front of his dressing stall. Chris needed an assurance that he was pursuing the right path for his life, and he needed to not feel as lonely as he was at that very moment.

A peace started to surface in Chris's mind. Peace about where he was. Peace about playing baseball in Gastonia. Peace about how he would get along with the other players on the team. Peace about his living condition and peace about his relationship with God. Chris prayed. God answered. God answered Chris's prayer in a manner that Chris knew that it was God speaking to him.

Chris finished putting on his new black and gold trimmed white home uniform tied on his spikes and made his way to the field. Players go through a series of stretching exercises before games. The pitchers who are pitching that night run sprints, engage in what is referred to as a long toss and stretch their arms before they get dressed. When pitchers are getting ready to pitch the game they are worked over by the trainers. The pitcher is massaged and rubbed down. After that the pitcher goes to the bull pen and warms up by throwing a given number of pitches including the full assortment of pitches that the pitcher has in his arsenal. The warm-up takes as long as the pitcher thinks he needs to get his arm ready for the game.

The position players do not need the attention and pampering that a pitcher needs. After dressing and stretching the outfielders will throw the ball back and forth to each other at a distance of about 150 feet to get their arms loose. The infielders will receive ground balls thrown by the first baseman to the other three fielders at their normal positions,

The managers meet at home plate with the umpires to go over any unusual ground rules that may have been unique to Sims Legion Park and the managers exchanged line up cards with each other. The line ups had been provided to the official scorer who was also entrusted with determining whether a ball put in play was a hit or whether an error had been committed by a fielder. Records were kept of every pitch, hit, error, and all other potential aspects of the game that was being played that evening and every evening and day that a professional game was played.

As Gastonia was the home team, they would take the field first and their pitcher would start the game. The players took their positions and the pitcher walked to the pitching mound. The catcher took his position behind home plate and received the 7 warm-up throws from the pitcher that were permitted by the official rules of baseball and by more than a hundred years of tradition. After the warm-up throws the catcher threw the ball to second base as if he were trying to throw out a base stealer. The ball was then thrown around the infield in what is referred to as being thrown around the horn.

When the ball is thrown by the catcher to second base just as the game is to begin, the shortstop fields the throw. The shortstop flips the ball to the second base man and he in turn throws the ball to the third base man. The third baseman either walks the ball over to the pitcher or softly tosses it to the pitcher. This ritual of throwing warm-up pitches, the catcher throwing the ball to second base and the ball being thrown around the horn is repeated in every ballpark across the United States and anywhere baseball is being played thousands of times by thousands of teams and tens of thousands of players every day that baseball is being played.

Tradition is an important part of baseball. While rule changes may be inevitable because of technological advances such as video replay, player's strength training, surgical advances in muscle and tendon repair, to name a few. It is the tradition of the game that makes baseball fans watch games, follow their team in the news, hope their team will get into the playoffs, and causes players to put on their uniforms in certain ways to allow them to be identified as a baseball player. Tradition causes baseball fans to discuss who was the greatest hitter, pitcher, base stealer, relief pitcher, catcher, or you name the subject category, and you will find baseball fans willing to debate their choice of the player that fits that category and bests the choice of the person with whom they are discussing the issue.

Tradition causes baseball players to become superstitious in their approach to the game. They dress to meet their superstitions. They perform pre-game rituals. Player's shave or don't shave on game days because of superstition. Some players will not step on the chalk line as they go to and from their position on the field because it would bring them bad luck when they come to bat. Some players stand in the batter's box and in front of a crowd of people will adjust their equipment (we are all grown-ups here and know that baseball players wear protective cups in their jockstraps to prevent injury to the family jewels and the shifting of the protective cup can be irritating and uncomfortable) in a certain way that you would not expect a civilized person to do in mixed company. Baseball players scratch and spit and some do that because it is a ritual founded in superstition.

Chris was no stranger to superstition. Chris wore his pant legs long but not to the tops of his spikes. Chris always pulled the colored outer stocking up just a little bit so that his sanitary socks could be seen but just barely. Chris carried a handkerchief in his back righthand pocket because if he had to slide, he felt that the handkerchief would absorb some of the impact of the ground as he slid on his right hip. Chris had learned these traditions as he played with other boys in little league and in high school.

On the other hand, the lengths that some of the players went through in order to appease their superstitions went too far for Chris and he backed off from believing that the way he played baseball was influenced by superstition. Chris ultimately believed that his abilities were God given and that he had to live up to the call and talents that God had bestowed on him. Chris saw baseball as an opportunity to serve God.

The game between Gastonia and Spartanburg began. The Pirates pitcher that evening was Bob Moose, a stocky 5'11" tall pitcher who showed great promise as a starting pitcher. Moose was opposed by John Penn a 6'2" 190-pound pitcher for the Phillies. Bob Moose finished his warm-up throws and Wilbert Hammond, who was catching that evening, threw the ball down to second base. Chris sat on the bench and watched everything as it unfolded. When Chris was in high school, he had played at the old minor league field in Nashville, Sulphur Dell, and was anxious to get started in playing for Gastonia. He knew that his time to play would begin shortly because he had faith that he was at the place that God wanted him to be at the precise time that God wanted him to be there.

Bob Moose was pitching a gem of a game for the Pirates. He was only 18 years old but was almost unhittable that night. Moose was from the Pittsburg area and had been an outstanding high school pitcher having thrown two no hitters, he was also a great athlete also playing football and basketball in high school. Moose was sticking out hitter after hitter and the Pirates were experiencing a rather easy time in getting ahead in the score. After five innings the Pirates were ahead by 6 runs and the Phillies were not making any solid contact with the pitches being thrown by Moose.

In the bottom 6th inning, Pop came down the bench and told Chris to get a bat because he was going to pinch hit for Chuck Howard even though Chuck had hit the ball out of the park and was 2 for 3 at the plate. Chris had mixed emotions. He was excited to get the chance to get in the game, but he was also nervous about taking the place of a power hitter like Chuck Howard.

Pablo Cruz led off the inning with a solid single to right, but Freddie Patek hit into a double play, and it was Chris's turn to come to the plate. In a situation like the one Chris was stepping into, the batter has the slight advantage because the pitcher has never seen that batter before and does not know what weakness the batter may have. On the other hand, Chris had watched the pitcher while he was standing in the on-deck circle (the location at which the batter stands or kneels in preparation to be the next batter, and where Chris would be expected to take warm-up swings and study the pitcher). Chris noticed that when the pitcher was going to throw his breaking ball, he gripped the ball more tightly than when he threw his fastball. To Chris that was a tip-off as to what to expect on the next pitch.

Chris stepped into the right-hand batter's box and carefully studied the pitchers grip on the baseball. Chris was aware of the catcher and the umpire standing behind the catcher. The pitcher went into his motion and Chris knew that the pitcher was going to challenge him with a four-seam fast ball. It seemed as if everything went into slow motion for Chris. Perhaps it was the adrenalin rushing into his bloodstream or just an unconscious reaction to his first professional at bat, but for Chris it was impossible for him not to make solid contact at that precise moment. The pitch came to the inside half of the plate, low in the strike zone. Chris's left leg lifted, his back leg braced, his hands moved the bat to the proper location and proper angle, his eyes were focused on the ball, his head did not move, his left hand guided the bat, and his right hand and forearms pulled the bat at a high velocity to the exact location of the ball.

Thwack!!!

The ball changed directions by 180 degrees and acted as if it had been shot out of a guided missile launcher. The flight of the ball was straight and traveled at a 45-degree angle to dead center field. There was a second thwack when the ball hit the aluminum score board. The Phillies outfielders only had time to turn their heads as the ball shot past them. The Phillies pitcher, after following through on the pitch and hearing the ball hit the scoreboard slowly turned and gazed at Chris as if he expected Chris to express an emotion. Instead, he saw Chris drop his bat and slowly and deliberately run to first and then around the bases until he got back to home plate where his now admiring teammates greeted him with a smile and pats on Chris's butt. Chuck Howard said, "You got all of that one rookie." and that was all that was said.

Back in the dugout, Pop congratulated Chris on his first hit and told him that he should always treat a baseball so rudely.

Chuck Howard came by the place where Chris was sitting, shook Chris's hand and said, "Don't think for one minute that you are going to take my place, but that was pretty sweet."

After the Pirates went back into the field Chris trotted out to right field and some of the few fans that were in attendance (the Gastonia Pirates averaged about 650 fans in seats during 1966) yelled their greetings to Chris and he acknowledged them with a tip of his cap. Chris did not have any chances to make plays in the field and that was good because Chris's mind was on hitting and not on fielding for the rest of the game. When they finished the Pirates won 7 to 4. As the teams were walking off the field, Larry Bowa came up to Chris and said, "Way to go rookie. Baseball can be a great experience on some days, but it is also a harsh mistress that can demand your soul if you let it."

Chris thought about what Bowa said and wondered what exactly he meant. It would have meaning in his life sooner rather than later.

Chapter 12
Winter Baseball

Chris continued to play in Gastonia for the rest of the 1966 season. Gastonia finished the season in fourth place with a record of 67 wins and 57 losses. Chris did fine in a limited playing time situation. His average was .286 and he had 7 homeruns and 12 doubles. In order to keep his eyes in shape the organization told Chris that he should consider playing winter baseball in Puerto Rico and Chris, despite knowing that he would miss his family, decided that he should take the offer to play winter ball.

La Liga de Béisbol Profesional de Puerto Rico (The league of Professional Baseball of Puerto Rico) begins its season around the first of November and plays through January. The winner of the Puerto Rico League then goes on to play in the Caribbean Champion Series. Chris was to play for the Gigantes de Carolina that was managed by Roberto Clemente and Clemente also played for the team. Manny, Chris roommate in the rookie instructional league also played for Gigantes.

Chris and Manny again became roommates and Manny was good about watching out for Chris as they traveled from game to game in the five-city league. Chris was very grateful that he had a friend to help him get around because Chris did not speak much Spanish and everything from finding something to eat to getting his laundry done required having the ability to speak and understand Spanish. While Chris was a quick learner speaking another language was not his strong suit.

Chris was also surprised by the poverty that he saw outside of San Juan and especially in the small towns of Southern Puerto Rico as the team traveled from city-to-city crisscrossing the island. The team played in San Juan the largest city and capitol of Puerto Rico, but the team also played in much smaller towns. Enthusiastic fans came to the games and supported their hometown heroes with louder cheering than Chris was used to hearing in the Western Carolinas League.

All the games were competitive and produced excitement not only in the stands but also in the dugouts and on the field. Each confrontation between pitcher and batter caused waves of chanting for both pitcher and batter. The fans beat drums and sang the team's songs with excitement and loud voices. The stadiums in which the games were played allowed the fans to be close to the players. The stadiums were colorfully decorated with banners and local advertisements extolling local products like beer and Coke-a-cola. Of course, everything was written in Spanish. Even though Chris did not speak much Spanish the enthusiasm was more than enough for Chris to know that the home team was held in esteem and the visiting team was not so much.

Chris reflected on the poverty from which the baseball fans came and the love that the baseball fans expressed to their home teams. Chris thought how a baseball team could cause a baseball fan to forget at least momentarily about the daily struggle of life and how was it possible that the poverty of their daily existence was put aside when baseball was being played?

Then Chris thought about how the players on the opposing teams from the hometown crowd could be so demonized by the home team's fans. Considering this, Chris also thought of the confidence of the away team's players. Chris thought that it was the game of baseball and the God given skills that each player possessed that allowed them to not give into the taunts of the opposing team's fans that kept them preforming at their best despite the adversity that they were experiencing while playing. Baseball itself and the ability to play the game gave each good player confidence that the game was sufficient to meet the challenges of playing before a hostile crowd.

Chris's thoughts turned to the sacrifice that baseball players make to play the game at its highest levels. Each player had to keep his body, mind, and spirit attuned to the rigors of playing a schedule of games during the season. The physical demands of playing a major league schedule of 162 games or even a class A schedule of 124 from April to August took a great toll on the body and mind. The spiritual part of baseball was not quite as apparent as the physical and mental parts of the prolonged season but was equally or even of greater importance to good players. A good player had to sacrifice body and mind to keep on playing when he was weary, hurt, and mentally exhausted. The spiritual component was expressed in a faith that body and mind would receive strength from an inner source that was more than sufficient and powerful to carry the body and mind past its perceived limits and to making solid contact despite sour hands, sour feet, sour back and legs and mental exhaustion. Only a few players had that spiritual component of their game. The spiritual component separated good players from all other players and made good players into champions and heroes.

Champions find a way to raise themselves above everything that is thrown in their path to win. Champions find a way to get on base. They find a way to make solid contact even against the nastiest of pitches. Champions score the last run, drive in the last run, hit the walk-off homerun and find a way to win when no one thought it was possible. Champions rise above the game and function on a different level. What makes them champions? Chris thought and believed that there was a connection between the spiritual component of a player's life, and a connection with the Holy Spirit that made the difference, but he was still unsure how a person's spiritual component worked.

Because of his Christianity, Chris prayed that God would give him wisdom and understanding regarding his life and especially as a baseball player keep himself physically fit, mentally focused and spiritually active to open a path to become a champion.

Chris played left field during the Puerto Rican winter league season and did not do too badly either. He was hitting a solid .270 with 10 home runs and 28 RBI over a 35-game schedule. Chris and Manny stayed together. As you will recall Manny was from the Dominican and he like Chris was away from his family. Manny did have a girlfriend in Punta Cana, and he was anxious to see her when he could get back home. Also, there were visa problems that Manny had to concern himself with when it was time to go back to the USA.

Manny invited Chris to visit him and his family in the Dominican and told Chris that Manny's girlfriend had a beautiful sister that Manny was sure that Chris would like if he got to visit Punta Cana. Manny showed Chris a picture of his girlfriend and her sister. Manny's girlfriend was Henrietta, and her sister was Polonia. The thought of meeting a beautiful Latin girl did perk Chris's manhood interest and he told Manny that he would take Manny up on his invitation after the winter league season was concluded. Chris did have second thoughts about traveling to the Dominican Republic, mainly because he missed his family in Tennessee, but the lure of meeting a beautiful Latin girl in a beach set-ting was enough to cause him to make up his mind to travel to Punta Cana when the winter season ended.

Winter baseball was a great experience for Chris. He was introduced to a different lifestyle by the peo-ple of Puerto Rico. The team played well enough to fin-ish in second place in the league and Chris played well enough to be invited back for the next season. Chris was able to play with major league players. The Puerto Rican league had many major league players who were either currently on the 40-man roster of a major league team or who had played in the majors at one time in their careers.

By playing with and observing the work ethic of the current and former big-leaguers, Chris began to realize that commitment to and focus on a baseball lifestyle was a total commitment to eating and breathing baseball. That meant that in order to play at the highest-level Chris had to discipline his body, condition his mind and offer his spirit to the game of baseball.

Up to that point in his baseball career Chris knew that he needed to refrain from any activity that would negatively impact his body. Chris realized that baseball required a mental focus not only on the pitched ball but also on every aspect of the game including how the pitcher approached each batter. The almost imperceptible nuances of the pitcher's rhythm in delivery, leg-lift, placement of the ball in his hand, and a thousand other observations that a hitter had to take into account before he stood in the batter's box. Chris also began to realize that the spiritual commitment to baseball left no room for much else.

However, Chris's observation of the big leaguers caused a re-evaluation of his understanding about what it would take to play at the highest level. He thought that merely refraining from activities that would negatively impact his body was not good enough. Big leaguers eat a diet that builds up the body and makes it much stronger.

Big leaguers work out with weights that increase their strength and flexibility. They think positively about how to nourish their bodies and build themselves into super athletes. They rest and hydrate in efficient manners and stay away from foods that are unproductive.

Major league players have a very high concentration level regarding all that goes into the position they play and the hitting stance and swing that they maintain. Big leaguers can remember the pitches thrown by the pitcher and the outcome of every at bat. They know the sequence of pitches thrown and the usual location of the pitch. Major leaguers maintain a notebook that provides information that will prepare the player for how to face a pitcher at any particular event that may occur during a game.

The spiritual aspect of baseball requires that a big leaguer player commit his life to playing baseball and the lifestyle that accompanies playing at home and on the road for an extended period of his life. A player on the highest level must leave family and friends behind for the sake of the game.

As Chris observed the attributes of truly professional players he wondered if he had such a commitment to the game of baseball that it would take to make him a big league player. He wondered if he was physically able to discipline his body, mind and spirit to baseball in such a way as to give up all other aspects of life. Chris wondered about this while he played winter baseball in Puerto Rico. When the winter season ended, he and Manny set sail for Punta Cana.

CHAPTER 13
CHRIS IS TEMPTED BUT SURVIVES

Temptation comes to all men. All men are tempted, and some cannot escape the pull of temptation and find themselves mired down so low that it seems there is no way out. There are temptations of the flesh. Temptation of the eye is a curse that can only be overcome by running away or by closing your eyes so tightly and for so long that the temptation dissipates. The temptation of pride in life is particularly prevalent in the self-righteous.

Temptations of the flesh were once the province of young men but in the modern era temptations of the flesh is not uncommon even among older men and for both sexes. A man sees a woman and he says to himself, "she is beautiful, and I need to be with her." He dreams that she will respond to his advances in a like manner. A man will think to himself, "I deserve to be with her because I am a good and attractive man, and she should be happy to give in to me." He lusts after her. He commits sinful acts in his mind and is apt to seek after her. She in return looks at him and thinks, "He's not so bad and he will spend his money on me if I lead him in the right direction. Let me play along to see what will happen."

They wind up in compromising situations. They are not satisfied with each other because it was just a temptation of the flesh that brought them together and nothing else. They go from temptation to burdened conscientiousness and finally despise each other. The consequence is a guilty conscience and a broken spirit.

The temptation of the eyes is found in the desire to possess something that is not yours and that you cannot afford. We all see things on television that we are told we must possess. Whether it is a new car, a better phone or even a new body, we are told that we will be better when we spend our money or go into debt to have what everybody else has. The last of the Ten Commandments tells us that we should not covet. "Thou shall not covet your neighbor's house. You shall not covet your neighbor's wife, nor his male or female servant, his ox or donkey, or anything that belongs to your neighbor." We have the temptation of the eyes when we want what we think others have.

The temptation of pride in life causes us to become self-righteous. A self-righteous man will justify himself and shall be condemned by his own mouth. If a man says, "I am perfect." it will prove that he is perverse because we have all sinned and gone astray. If we say we have no sin, we make God a liar and we place ourselves above God. The self-righteous man is a solipsistic person that only thinks that what goes on his own mind is reality. He is egocentric and will eventually fall into despair.

Temptation came to Chris. When Chris and Manny arrived at the airport in Santo Domingo, they were greeted by Manny's girlfriend Henrietta and her sister Polonia. Manny was immediately embraced by Henrietta and the embrace was long and emotionally and physically provocative. Chris and Manny had shared many long conversations about Manny's plans to continue their respective baseball careers, but Manny had said nothing about his plans concerning his life with Henrietta.

Because of their flight from San Juan to Santo Domingo Chris and Manny were dressed in slacks and button up shirts. The weather in Santo Domingo was warm because of the south Caribbean climate. The two young ladies were dressed in very provocative clothes. The hem length was short and the bustlines worn by both Henrietta and Polonia showed lots of cleavage. Both of the girls were very attractive. They had long legs and olive brown skin that was very attractive to Chris.

Polonia came close to Chris, and he greeted her in English, and she responded in Spanish. Immediately Chris realized that there was going to be a communication problem the moment he and Polonia were not around Manny. Chris took Polonia's hand and squeezed it with a friendly and reassuring grip that he thought would mean that he was happy to make her acquaintance. The next thing that Chris knew was that Polonia had put her arms around Chris and held on tightly. Chris was surprised but was tempted to hold her tightly as well but thought differently enough to pull back and wait for Manny to make a proper introduction.

After the PDA between Manny and Henrietta subsided, Chris spoke up and said, "Manny, please tell these beautiful ladies that I am happy to be visiting their country and that I hope we can all become friends."

Manny replied, "Don't worry about that, these girls are great baseball fans, and they will show us a very good time while we are here."

Chris had to think about that for a little while. Even though Chris was not unpopular in high school he was not very sophisticated when it came to knowing how to deal with girls. As you will recall he had had a relationship with Phyllis on the choir tour between his sophomore and junior years in Nashville, but he had no experience with being in a relationship in which he was expected to be with a girl for 24 hours a day. He had never slept with a girl and was not even sure how he should approach the situation.

Chris did what was the exact right thing to do, he prayed. Chris's expectation when he decided to accompany Manny to Punta Cana was that he would be staying with Manny's family and that he would meet Polonia and that they would get together and get to know each other. What he now faced was that he was expected to stay in a hotel room with a young girl with whom he could barely communicate and who he did not know for the duration of his visit to the Dominican Republic.

Polonia was an extremely beautiful girl. She was of medium height with large brown eyes. She had full lips and breasts, long legs and long black hair. Polonia had a sweet smile and was well dressed. After the meeting at the Santo Domingo airport the two couples drove to Punta Cana in a shuttle bus that made regular commutes from the resort hotels to the airport in Santo Domingo to transport resort guests to and from their air travel. It took about 90 minutes to make the trip from the airport to the hotel that the girls had chosen for their stay at the beach resort.

Chris had packed all that he possessed. What he possessed was only a few changes of clothes and a bathing suit. Matty and Henrietta departed to their own room and left Chris and Polonia alone to make their own accommodation. Polonia was able to talk to the hotel clerk and she was presented with a key to a room, and she motioned for Chris to follow her to a room that had a view of the beach and only one bed. Chris did not know what he was going to do. He did not speak but a little Spanish and certainly not enough to get himself out of the situation that he found himself in at that particular moment.

Then unexpectedly a peace that passed understanding came over Chris and he felt the presence of the Holy Spirit directing him to the door. Chris took his suitcase, turned to Polonia and said come with me and motioned towards the hotel lobby. Polonia had a disappointed look on her face as they approached the check-in desk. To Chris surprise the clerk behind the check in counter said to Chris in perfect English, "Is everything all right Mr. Remerez?"

Chris was somewhat surprised by the question and replied, "Sir, I am not Mr. Remerez, but I understand the confusion. I would like to have a separate room from this young lady. Can you accommodate me?"

After a moment of silence, the clerk was able to understand the problem and allowed Chris to register in his own name and have a separate room from Polonia. Much to Polonia's disappointment. Chris then took Polonia by the hand and led her, and they found the room where Manny and Henrietta were staying.

Chris knocked on the door and waited for several minutes before Manny appeared at the door. Chris said, "Manny, I need you to translate for me so that Polonia and I have a clear understanding of how my time in Punta Cana is going to happen. "

Manny looked at Chris and did not understand what Chris was talking about, and said, "Don't you and Polonia get along? Is she not giving you what you want?"

"I think there is a big misunderstanding about what I want. I did not come here with you to have sex. I came here because I am interested in meeting people and getting to know your family and finding out if Polonia is someone that I would like to be with and if she would like to be with me," was Chris's reply.

"Please tell Polonia that I cannot stay in the room with her. Tell her that I like her, but we need to get to know each other before anything serious happens between us." Chris went on speaking.

Manny looked at Chris and did not understand what all the fuss was about. Manny said, "I'm not sure what you are getting at, Bro. Polonia is a good girl, and she will treat you right. She has been with baseball players before and she knows what men want and will do all that you ask her to do."

"That is not what I'm talking about. You are going

too fast for me. I don't want to shack up with Polonia. I want to find out if there is any possibility that we will like each other first and then we can decide if the relationship is worth the effort of becoming friends and whether we can go to the next level of commitment." Chris said with an earnest look in his eyes so that Manny and even Polonia knew that he was being sincere.

Henrietta appeared at the door and told Manny and Chris to stop their conversation and for Manny to come back to bed with her. While Chris did not understand the words, he understood that he needed to move away and find someone who could help him convey his message to Polonia. Chris took Polonia by the hand, and they went to the dining room, found a table and sat down. Chris was still carrying his suitcase and it was awkward but manageable.

A waiter came to the table and spoke to Chris in English. Chris told the waiter that he could not speak Spanish and that Polonia could not speak English and that Chris needed someone to help them communicate with each other. The waiter told Chris that there was a priest on the property that the resort hired to help people with problems such as these and that the priest could be summonsed to speak to both Chris and Polonia because the priest was bilingual.

Chris took the waiters suggestion and found the office that the priest employed by the resort was located and Chris knocked on the door. An elderly man with a clerical collar appeared at the door and looked Chris and Polonia over and said, "Are you here to get married?"

Chris's response was quick and emphatic, "No sir we need someone to help us communicate with each other."

"Then come in and find a seat" the old priest replied.

"I think there has been a misunderstanding between me and this young lady from the time we met this morning, and it is because of the language barrier." Chris said as he looked at the priest and then looked at Polonia who was beginning to have tears fill her large brown eyes.

The priest then looked at Polonia and in Spanish asked her to say her name and what was she doing at the resort.

Polonia said her name but then went silent. The priest sighed and then again turned to Chris. "Young man tell me what you want me to tell this young lady."

"Sir" was all that Chris got out as he was interrupted by the priest.

"You may call me Father Emilio. That is how I prefer to be addressed. By the way what is your name and why are you here?" Father Emilio said as he again looked Chris over.

"Father Emilio, my name is Chris, and I am a professional baseball player. My teammate Manny invited me to come to the Dominican Republic after the winter league season ended. Manny told me that I would stay with his parents. When we arrived this morning, we were picked up at the airport by Manny's girlfriend Henrietta and Polonia and brought here. Manny and Henrietta went immediately to a room and left me and Polonia to get a room. Father Emilio, I have never been in a room by myself with a girl, I have never slept in the same bed with a girl and that is not what I want to do now. I think Polonia has the wrong impression of who I am and what I want." Chris blurted out in a rapid expression of thought and words.

Father Emilio thought for a moment and replied, "Chris this is a rather unusual situation. Young men like yourself do not usually turn down an opportunity to be with a young lady as pretty as Polonia, but I admire your resolve not to take advantage of Polonia. I will tell Polonia that you have decided that you cannot have a room with her and that she will need to go home to her family."

Chris asked, "What will happen to her when she goes home?"

Father Emilio replied, "It is unfortunate that there is so much poverty outside of these resorts. Her family was no doubt expecting that Polonia would return home with some money that the family needed to feed the other family members and pay the rent. So, Chris you can help Polonia save face with her family by giving her some money and sending her on her way."

Chris thought for a few moments and asked, "Father Emilio, what would happen if I went with Polonia to see her family? Would they allow me to stay with them and buy their groceries and pay their rent for the next week?"

Father Emilio spoke to Polonia again in Spanish. Chris could not understand anything that was being said but from Polonia's body language and the smile that came over her face it was evident that she agreed to whatever Father Emilio was telling Polonia. Finally, Father Emilio said to Chris, "It has now been arraigned. You will go with Polonia to her family. They live about an hour from here in Boca Chica which is closer to Santo Domingo. I will call them and let them know that you will be staying with them for a week and that you will help them with the money they need. If you give them $250 US dollars you will have been a great help to them and to Polonia."

Chris and the priest shook hands and Father Emilio made arraignments for the resorts driver to take Chris and Polonia to her family.

When Chris and Polonia arrived at her family's house Chris was again surprised by the poverty of the people and yet amazed by the friendly reception that he received. It seemed that there were throngs of children everywhere he looked. The house where Polonia's parents lived was a concrete block house with a flat roof and breadfruit trees in the yard. There were goats roaming the streets that seemed to know what they were doing even though it appeared that there was no one around to watch after them.

Polonia's mother appeared at the door of the small house and there was the smell of goat meat roasting on an open fire coming from somewhere nearby. Polonia's father appeared from around the corner of the house and a gaggle of children appeared out of no specific direction. Polonia's father held out his hand and then unexpectedly grabbed Chris and gave him a full embrace. Polonia's mother drew back into the house and Polonia followed her. Polonia's father, Raul, did not speak but took Chris's suitcase into the house and soon returned with a bottle of rum and two small glasses. Raul poured out two shots of rum and offered one to Chris.

Chris refused the drink, but Raul pushed the drink into Chris's hand so that he had no choice but to accept it. Raul tossed the drink down his throat and motioned for Chris to do the same. Chris had never drunk rum before and did not know what to expect. Chris mimicked Raul's action and tossed the rum down his throat and an explosion occurred. Chris started to cough uncontrollably and to wheeze as if his lungs were on fire. Raul looked at the spectacle and realized that Chris, even though he had been announced as a professional baseball player, was yet a boy in a man's body and that Raul would have to take into consideration all of what Chris was and was not capable of doing.

The two men sat on stools in the yard of the house that Polonia had grown up in. After sitting for what seemed to Chris an hour but was only about 15 minutes a man appeared and pulled up a stool to form a group of three men. Raul produced another glass and poured another round of rum. Raul and the new man tossed the rum in the same manner that Raul had tossed his drink before. Chris merely stared at the glass of rum in his hand and wondered who the new man sitting in the circle of stools might be. After a second round of rum was tossed by Raul and the other man, the other man spoke to Chris.

"My name is Pablo; I speak both English and Espanol and I'm Raul's cousin. You are Chris the baseball player from America, and you have brought Polonia home to her mother rather than disgracing her. You are to be thanked for what you have done for Polonia and her family is very grateful to you for bringing her home." the man now identified as Pablo said to Chris.

Chris listened to Pablo and somewhat wondered at what the man was driving when he said that he had not disgraced Polonia and Chris said, "What do you mean that Polonia has not been disgraced."

Pablo replied, "Polonia is only 15 years old. She was persuaded by her friend Henrietta to go with her for the week to stay at the resort at Punta Cana because she wanted to be alone with Manny. Henrietta needed Polonia to go to keep you company while they were being intimate.

"Those girls thought that you would go along with their scheme until you pulled the plug on what they had planned. Manny and Henrietta had been together before, and Henrietta's mother had forbidden Manny to be with Henrietta. The girls made up a story that each one was visiting the other so that Henrietta's mother would not know that Manny was back home and staying at the resort with her daughter." Pablo sadly told Chris.

Chris was getting the picture for the first time. Manny needed Chris to come with him to the Dominican Republic not because he wanted to show Chris around but because he needed Chris to complete the story that Henrietta and Polonia had worked out so that Manny and Henrietta and Manny could be together. Chris said, "I'm slowly getting the picture. I'm just not ready to be in a hotel room with somebody that I have never met before. Please tell Polonia that I'm sure that she is a wonderful person but I'm just not ready to have a relationship with anybody yet."

"You are wise for your age, and we are thankful for that. You are welcome to stay here with Polonia's family while you are in the Dominican. I'm sure that Raul and family would like to show you around our part of this island. Me and Raul are ex-baseball players, and we would like to take some batting practice with you." Pablo smiled as he said batting practice.

"I will be more than happy to hit some ball with you and Raul as soon as you are ready." Chris replied.

"First, Polonia and her mother, Juanita, have cooked a feast for us and we will eat roasted goat with all the food that we can hold," as Raul put another glass of rum into Pablo's hand.

Within a few minutes Polonia appeared at the door. It was apparent that she had been crying. Her face had been scrubbed clean of all the traces of makeup that she was wearing when she and Chris first met at the airport, and she was wearing a much more conservative outfit. Polonia told the three men to come inside because the dinner was ready to be eaten.

The feast was superb. Chris had never eaten roasted goat before and found that it had a strangely different taste from any other meat that he had ever eaten. Chris did not exactly make up his mind that he would be someone who would go out of his way to have goat a second time. On the other hand, the side dishes of black beans and rice and plantain were very tasty, and Chris had extra helpings of both. There was a chutney that went along with the black beans and rice that made the flavor of the dish exceptional.

After the dinner Pablo and Raul proceeded to finish off the bottle of rum that Raul had originally produced when Chris arrived earlier in the day. While Chris was offered more of the rum he politely refused, and the three men sat together in the yard while the women continued to talk among themselves in the house. Pablo was interested in knowing about Chris's experience in professional baseball and asked many questions concerning the Puerto Rican winter league and the major league players that Chris had played with that winter. Chris answered all of Pablo's questions and they generally discussed Chris's prospects for the next season. Chris said that he hoped to again play for Gastonia in the Western Carolinas League to start the season and that he hoped to advance to AA baseball after a short stay in A ball.

Finally, after several hours of talking to Pablo about Chris's prospects Polonia appeared at the door and told the men that it was time for the party to break up and for the men to get some sleep. Through Pablo's interpretation Polonia told Chris that she was going to take Chris to Santo Domingo and show him the sites of that city that had its roots from the time that Columbus discovered the new world.

Chris was shown to a room by himself and was made comfortable. The house had a functioning bathroom that allowed Chris to wash and prepare to go to bed and everyone stayed out of his view, so he did not know how much of a sacrifice Polonia's family was making so that Chris would feel welcome.

The next morning the sun was up, and Chris could hear the movement of people in and out of the small bathroom. Soon there was the smell of coffee and beacon frying in a skillet. Raul peeked his head into the room that Chris was occupying and retrieved a pair of pants that had been strung over a chair that sat in the corner of the bedroom. Raul hurriedly put the pants on and headed towards the kitchen from which the morning smells of breakfast emanated. Chris took all of this to be a sign that he needed to get his morning oblation in the bathroom completed quickly and join the family in the kitchen.

Raul motioned for Chris to sit down and poured a cup of coffee and put it in front of Chris. Soon Juanita placed a plate of fruit and small pieces of bacon on the table and the family looked at Chris to start the process of feeding themselves. Chris thought for a moment and decided that he would produce some cash from his wallet and place it on the table as a gesture of good faith and because it was evident that the family needed the cash. Chris placed $350 US dollars on the table and Juanita quickly took the money off the table and put it out of sight.

Polonia was also sitting at the table but was very quiet and hardly lifted her eyes up from the table. It was painfully obvious that the young girl had been scolded by her family and that made it somewhat awkward for everyone at the table to engage with each other. Finally, Raul motioned for Chris to follow him, and they together walked down the road until they came to a small shack that turned out to be the home of Pablo. Raul motioned for Chris to remain outside as Raul went in to find Pablo. Soon there was a rustling about and a blerrie eyed Pablo appeared at the entrance of the shack being propped up by Raul.

Pablo staggered over to a large bucket of rainwater and stuck his scruffy unshaved face and head into the water. Chris became concerned the Pablo had drowned himself because he kept his head underwater for what seemed like a full five minutes. After the long immersion in water, a gasping Pablo stood upright and tossed his hair back to reveal his wet face. Pablo looked around and saw Chris standing in the yard and said in Spanish, "¿Quién es este extranjero de pie delante de mí?" (Who is this foreigner standing before me?)

Chris, realizing that Pablo had been speaking to him looked intently at Pablo, and said, "Don't you remember me from last night?"

Pablo's memory started it kick in and he said, "You're the American baseball player who was trying to sleep with little Polonia, you ought to be ashamed of yourself."

"I don't know what happened between last night and now, but you have everything mixed up. I brought Polonia home to her mother and did not take advantage of her in any way." Chris replied to the obviously hungover man who stood before him.

Pablo stuck his head back into the bucket of water for another extended time and again came up gasping and slinging his wet hair back and forth. Pablo then recognized that Raul was also standing near and said, "You must be right because if you had tried anything with Polonia, Raul and you would not be here now. You, young man, would be dead and Raul would be in jail. So why are you here and what do you want?"

Chris pointed to Raul and said, "Ask him he brought me here."

Raul and Pablo spoke in Spanish and after a few minutes, Pablo nodded his head in agreement and again turned to Chris.

Pablo spoke and made an apology to Chris for forgetting that they had met the day before and had become acquainted over dinner with Raul and his family the night before. Pablo then said, "Mr. Baseball player, your friend has asked me to take you to Santo Domingo and show you around our city. Raul said that you have given his family some US dollars and I hope that you will bless me with some money also. We are a poor country; we depend on the kindness of American tourist like you for enough to get us by."

Chris dug into his pocket again and produced some Peso Oro, the national currency of the Dominican Republic and handed it to Pablo. Pablo looked at the Peso Oro's over and spit on it and threw it to the ground. Chris was somewhat surprised by Pablo's reaction to Chris's presentation of the Dominican money and reached down to the ground to pick the money up. Pablo growled, "It's worthless senior. We trade in American money; you can't get a rotten tomato with Dominican money around here."

Chris put the Peso Oro's back in his pocket and pulled out his billfold and handed Pablo a fifty-dollar bill that Pablo immediately put in his pocket. Pablo then put his rather smelly arm around Chris's neck, and they walked back to Raul's house.

Chris thought to himself, "Why are so many people intent on self-destruction?" Chris thought of Manny and Henrietta back at the resort in Punta Cana and how Manny's baseball career could be jeopardized by a wrong move on his part, not to mention Henrietta's if she were to get pregnant. Then he thought of Polonia and the risk she had taken when she tried to get Chris to stay with her at the resort. Chris thought about Pablo and his obvious drinking problem. Chris even thought about how he had been attacked by Ronnie Willis when he was still in high school. All of this caused Chris to realize that people are totally depraved and in need of a changed life. "What causes people to act the way they do and is it a universal condition of mankind that we humans seek to do ourselves harm as a condition of life?" Chris asked himself as he, Raul and Pablo walked back to Raul's house.

As they approached Raul's house Chris saw Manny standing in the yard and realized that something had taken place that was about to involve Chris in something for which he was not sure that he was ready.

Manny saw Chris and Raul walking toward him and immediately started to speak to Raul in Spanish in an excited tone, but it was obvious that Manny was being apologetic and seeking some sort of reconciliation with Raul. Manny then turned to Chris and said, "I have made a big mistake bringing you with me to the Dominican. I thought that I could trust you to go along with my plans to be with Henrietta and have some fun with her, but you could not keep yourself satisfied with having Polonia with you without involving her family and me in this affair."

Chris looked at Manny and then at Raul and did not know for a few minutes what had set Manny off the way it evidently did. Perhaps Chris was missing something that had been said or he had done something wrong. Chris was confused and hoped that this confrontation would soon pass. Chris said to Manny, "What have I done and what has happened that brings you out here to Boco Chica this morning?"

Manny looked disgusted and said, "Chris we are supposed to be friends. I brought you to the Dominican to get laid and to have some fun at the beach, but you had to go and ruin the whole thing by bringing Polonia back to her mother. Polonia's mother has called Henrietta's mother and now I'm in trouble and Henrietta is in trouble and it's all because of you!"

Chris thought about it and replied, "Manny, I did not mean to cause you any harm. However, you know that I am a follower of Jesus and that I will not compromise my faith in Christ to put a young girl like Polonia in a position that I would not want my sister to find herself in. As far as you and Henrietta I am in no position to judge what you two are doing is either right or wrong. That is between you Henrietta, Henrietta's mother and God. All that I can answer is for me and I made a choice that I feel was the right one. I don't know what you said to Raul, but I know that I could not have faced him if I had spent the night with his daughter and he found out about it.

"I think the best thing that we can do is for me to spend the day with Raul and family and find out how I can help them with the problems they are having and then be on my way back to Murfreesboro to see my family. You will need to figure out your next moves, Manny. I hope to see you back in the states when baseball season starts."

Manny looked at Chris and shook his head, "We could have had a really good time, and no one would have known the difference. Yeah, I'll see you in the West Carolinas League."

With that said Manny turned his back and walked to the bus line to wait on the next bus back to Punta Cana. Chris did as he said and stayed a little longer with Raul and family. With Pablo's translation help Chris was able to understand the needs of the family and the general needs of the Boco Chica community. Chris gave all the money he had on him to Raul just before he went down the concourse at the airport for his flight that eventually took him back to Nashville where he was met by Kay and Joe, Swamp Goddess was too busy at school to come.

Chapter 14
Chris Works Out With the College Baseball Team

Chris was very happy to be with his parents and to get to their house in Murfreesboro. Kay had made a pot of stuffed cabbages and the house was full of the aroma of Chris's favorite dish.

Swamp Goddess was busy talking on the phone from the bathroom where she spent most of her time. She did stick her head out to greet Chris but hastily retreated after a quick hello. Joe spoke the most as Kay was busy in the kitchen. Joe wanted to talk about Chris's time in Puerto Rico and his prospects for the upcoming season. Chris wanted to know when the MTSU baseball team started practice and if it would be appropriate for Chris to go over to the college and try to work out with the college players. Joe said that he could arrange for Chris to take batting practice with the baseball team because the baseball coach was a friend of his and Joe was sure that the college baseball players would enjoy taking swings with a professional.

The family had a happy time that evening. It was the first time they had all been together for many months. Chris needed the time to reconnect with the only people that he had ever known and who cared about him without trying to see how far he could be pushed.

It was late January and there were cold days in middle Tennessee, but not every day was a cold day. Joe drove Chris to the athletic office at MTSU and told Chris to find Jimmy Earl the baseball coach who was also the assistant basketball coach. Chris walked into the athletic office and was met by a group of students trying to talk to one of the kinesiology instructors about the upcoming exam schedules and each of the students was also seeking help with the subject matter. Evidently the study of kinesiology was a hot topic among the physical education majors at MTSU. Later, Chris determined that kinesiology was the make-or-break course for physical education majors that included most of the student athletes at MTSU.

Chris was able to find Jimmy Earl sitting with the head basketball coach, Ken Tricky, discussing the strategy for an upcoming basketball game. Chris interrupted the conversation and introduced himself, making it clear that he was related to Joe and that Joe had set up the meeting. Jimmy Earl stood up and extended his hand to Chris and said, "Your dad is very proud of you Chris, and we are more than happy to allow you free reign with the facilities, weight rooms, and anything you might need before you head to Florida for spring training. As far as working out with the baseball team you need to see Potts, my assistant and he will get you squared away."

Chris expressed his thanks to the basketball coaches and set off to find Potts. Potts had been a football manager and a baseball manager at MTSU for a long period of time. He was a guy that was having a hard time cramming a four-year degree in to six years of college. It was that old nemesis kinesiology that had kept Potts at MTSU and as far as Potts was concerned things were not all that bad. Potts enjoyed being around the baseball team and the team relied on Potts because Jimmy Earl was much more interested in basketball than in the players and practices of the baseball team.

Chris found Potts in the baseball dressing room under the visitors' side of the football stadium. Chris walked in and introduced himself and Potts had no idea who this new kid was and what he wanted. Chris finally said, "My father is a professor in the education department and asked Coach Earl if I could work out with the baseball team until I go back to spring training with the Pirates."

Potts looked at Chris and said, "Your father is a good man, and he has helped out many of the student athletes in our program. He also talks about you all the time and keeps us all up to date on your progress in the Pirates organization. You are welcome to workout with the baseball team and if you need anything all you have to do is ask."

Chris thanked Potts and asked when baseball practice would begin. Potts told Chris that the players usually got out of classes and headed to the locker room in just a few minutes from then, and just as Potts was saying so a group of about five guys strolled into the locker room and started to change into their workout clothes. Each of the players looked Chris over and wondered who this new kid might be until one of the guys said, "You played for West in Atlanta, I remember playing against you in high school."

Chris introduced himself and explained that he would be taking batting practice with the team for a few weeks until he had to report to the Pirates training camp in Bradenton in the middle of February. The players all nodded their approval and slowly one by one approached Chris to ask questions that every nonprofessional player wants to know. "What makes you different from the rest of us?"

Chris had never thought of that difference between himself and any other player, or whether there was a difference between a player that was paid to play baseball and these college players. In one sense of the word "professional", the college players were being paid to play baseball because they were on athletic scholarship that was a form of compensation for playing the game. On the other hand, each of the college players wanted to have the word "professional baseball player" associated with their name. A professional baseball player commanded an infinite amount more respect from baseball fans than a mere college baseball player.

To be a professional baseball player meant that you had a chance to play baseball at the highest possible level of the sport. Playing on a college team meant that a player could only achieve a status that was limited by the player's eligibility to play under the rules of the NCAA and those rules placed time limits on every player's time to play for a college.

A professional baseball player was not limited in the amount of time he/she had to develop as a student athlete, and a player could eventually play in the "Big Leagues" if he/she was good enough and the organization for which he/she played recognized the player's skill and promoted the player to the big leagues. Therefore, it was a big deal that Chris identified himself as a professional player and the MTSU players gave Chris a large amount of deference.

Eventually, Potts organized the practice session. It was a chilly winter day in middle Tennessee. There were low dark clouds that whizzed by on wind gusts that sent a chill on the exposed parts of each of the players' bodies. Everyone knew that batting practice was going to sting everyone's hand and that getting a warm shower after practice was something to be thought of as the wind blew and every now and then a spit of snow came across the baseball field.

In the late 1960's batting gloves were not in wide use and not used during batting practice that mid-January day when Chris worked out with the MTSU baseball team. For the first several minutes of the practice session the team engaged in calisthenics and stretching exercises. The players paired off and warmed up their arms by playing catch with one another. Batting practice followed with the expected position players hitting first. A group of 3 or 4 players stood around the batting cage that had been rolled into place. One of the younger underclass pitchers acted as the batting practice pitcher and one of the underclass catchers caught. Potts limited each batter to 10 swings so that the 30 odd players would each get a chance to take their turn in the batter's box. After the 5 players that were called up to take their swings, Potts randomly selected another group of 5 who were standing either on the infield or outfield shagging any ball that might be hit in their respective position.

After a few minutes of batting practice, the outfielders started playing a game among themselves that they referred to as "short hop." The object of the short hop game was to throw the ball from one outfielder to another so that the ball would land close to the other player's feet and bounce up and hit the other player in the family jewels. In order to guard against injury, the outfielder on the receiving end of the throw would have to play the throw on the short hop. The game of short hop made the players develop their skills of fielding a ball that took a short hop and developed a quick reflex and eye-hand coordination. The consequence of not cleanly fielding the short hop was obvious and potentially catastrophic.

After about an hour of Potts calling other players into the batting cage to take their swings, Potts finally called Chris to come in from the outfield and take his 10 swings. While batting practice was taking place Potts would call in other pitchers to throw to the hitters. When Potts called Chris to take his swings Potts decided to replace the underclass pitchers with the best pitcher that MTSU had. The pitcher, Craig Cunningham, threw the baseball almost underhanded in what is referred to as submarine style pitching. Cunningham could make the baseball break in ways an overhand or even a sidearm pitcher could not accomplish. Potts told Cunningham to see if he could strike Chris out.

Chris stepped into the batter's box to take his 10 swings and Cunningham came set to deliver his best submarine pitch. Chris had very little experience with hitting pitches thrown in the manner that Cunningham threw. Chris had closely watched as Cunningham warmed up and particularly noticed that the motion used by Cunningham caused the ball to be released at a very low trajectory so that the arch of the ball naturally dipped as it approached home plate. As the ball traveled from the pitcher's hand it naturally rose and then dipped. After Cunningham had completed his warmup tosses, Cunningham motioned to Chris that he was ready for Chris to take his swings.

The first pitch that Cunningham delivered was a foot outside and Chris did not swing. The second delivery started out low, rose as it traveled toward home plate and then dipped in a perfect parabola as it came into the strike zone. Chris swung and made solid contact as was his customary practice. Chris's hitting philosophy was to keep his eyes on the ball and swing the bat to the spot that the ball was likely to arrive in a fluid and compact manner. The sound of the bat on the ball was a small but distinctive "thwack" and the ball left the bat at a high velocity and on a line over the second baseman's head into the outfield grass.

Cunningham watched the ball as it hit the outfield grass and one of the outfielders gave chase. It was then that Cunningham decided to bare down and not let Chris get good wood on another pitch. On his third offering, Cunningham decided to throw a curve that broke from right to left and downward in the strike zone. It was a pitch that Cunningham had developed as his most potent strike out pitch and he had been successful in using that pitch to strike batters out since he was in junior high. The pitch was also thrown with a higher velocity so that the break on the pitch was sharp and acted more like a slider than a curve. Cunningham delivered the pitch, Chris swung, and the same result occurred as had occurred on the first swing. "Thwack" and the ball left Chris's bat at high velocity and caused the outfielders to chase the ball down.

The barrage of solid contact on pitches thrown by MTSU's top pitcher continued until Chris had completed his 10 swings. The players in the batting cage area all stood silently by and then slowly went back to talking about unrelated topics that had nothing to do with what they had just witnessed. Finally, one of the players, Mike Boyd from Dalton, Georgia who was also the field goal kicker on the MTSU football team and referred to as "Slink" by the other players said, "That Chris kid can hit." The other players nodded in agreement and looked at each other and wondered if it was possible that a professional baseball player was actually that much better than the college players standing around after Chris took his swings.

After everyone got their chance to take batting practice and the attention of Potts was directed to infield practice, the business of taking ground balls and practicing throws to first base and to home. The outfielders likewise practiced throwing to cutoff men and fielding ground balls. The practice ended with Potts yelling, "Take it to the house." All the players then sprinted to the locker room and all sorts of fun among the players started in earnest.

Bars of soap were thrown at players in the shower and a game of dodge the projectile allowed the quick and agile to avoid being hit by a solid bar of soap as they showered. Other such childish behavior also went on and everybody had a good time playing practical jokes on their teammates. Eventually, the players got dressed in their street clothes and headed in different directions. As he was getting ready to leave, Chris was confronted by Craig Cunningham and asked, "What did you think of the pitches that I threw to you during batting practice?"

Chris replied, "I have never seen anything like it. Very hard to make solid contact with stuff that good."

"But you seemed to hit every pitch as if you knew what I was going to throw, and you knew where every pitch was going to be located." Cunningham said with a cautious smile.

"Well, it did seem that you telegraphed what you were going to throw and where it was going to be located." Chris said also with a chuckle.

"How was I giving my pitches away?" the pitcher asked.

"When you place the ball in your glove you hold the ball in different positions. Your fast ball is held with your fingers plainly visible to a batter and your location can be seen from the placement of your feet on the rubber." Chris told the pitcher standing before him.

"You were able to get all that from just watching me pitch this one time?" Cunningham stated with a new respect for the professional baseball player he had just met.

"Well, you know, the organization pays us to hit baseballs and in order to do that it is much easier if you can see the pitch coming and know where it might be located." Chris was almost embarrassed to be telling Cunningham how he could read his pitches with so little effort, but Chris did not want to show up anybody unnecessarily.

After practice Chris went to the weight room to continue his strength training routine that he had neglected since he left Puerto Rico and ran into some of the MTSU players also working out with weights. One of the players started a conversation with Chris as they waited for others to finish their reps with the weight machines.

The general aspects of the conversation centered around the life of a minor league professional baseball player as he played during the season and how Chris was taking long bus rides from town to town in the Western Carolinas League. Chris was happy to answer any question that anybody asked and gave everyone the impression that Chris was a regular guy who just happened to be paid to play baseball. Chris also asked questions about college life and wanted to know how much emphasis was placed on getting good grades or whether grades were important at all. Finally, the conversation turned to a topic that every draft age male had on his mind; what would happen if the draft board called and wanted that person to report for an induction interview.

There were various opinions on the subject of being drafted into the army and being required to go to Vietnam and fight. One of the younger catchers was gung-ho for the proposition of going to Vietnam and killing Viet Cong soldiers. Because it was still early in the war in Vietnam, opposition to the war had not gotten to the point that it finally reached on college campuses after many American lives were lost after the escalation of the war occurred in 1968. It was still early 1967 and while there were about 500,000 American troops in Vietnam, antiwar sentiment had not reached the tipping point that it eventually reached in 1968 and 69.

Chris had not thought about what military service might require. Chris thought of himself as having been in the Navy until Joe retired and went back to college and was willing to let the war play itself out. While Chris was still in high school, he began a friendship with a classmate who was an antiwar activist. Lloyd and Chris would often have discussions about why America was fighting in Vietnam. Because Joe was a military man Chris was expected to favor the prowar sentiment of the Johnson administration that followed the Truman doctrine which held that all communist regimes were inherently anti-American and that if Vietnam was allowed to become a communist state that other countries would follow suit like the falling of dominoes. (The domino effect was the Eisenhour Doctrine that contended that Asian Countries would in turn become communist if the United States were to allow any one of the countries in southeast Asia to come under the influence of China or Russia.)

After his session in the weight room, Chris was hungry and went to Joe's office and waited for Joe to complete his duties. Chris and Joe were both ready to eat. Joe drove and they talked about baseball as they went.

Kay had prepared a meal of pork chops, mashed potatoes and gravy, together with applesauce. It was one of Chris's favorite dinners. They sat at the kitchen table and Chris and Joe quickly ate all that was put before them. Swamp Goddess turned up her nose at the meat and potatoes because she was a finnicky eater and often insisted that Kay fix a different meal just for her. As they were finishing supper, Kay informed Chris that he had received a letter from the Selective Services System. When Chris turned 16 and was still in high school, he was required to register for the draft and was subject to being called into active duty in the US Army unless he had a deferment, which allowed the potential draftee to remain undrafted as long as he was pursuing his education. At that time there was a deferment for college students, however there was no deferment for professional baseball players.

Kay and Joe were both anxious to see what the Selective Service wanted with Chris. They were not as anxious as Chris. Chris took the official-looking envelope and opened it so the whole family could see the contents. The letter asked that Chris report his status. It asked if Chris was attending college or if he had some other deferment from the draft and finally the letter asked Chris to report to his draft board in Nashville on Tuesday February 7, 1967, and be prepared to take a physical examination. February 7 was only a few days away and Chris and the family were all concerned about what might happen to Chris when he reported to the draft board.

Joe as a military veteran advised Chris that he had nothing to worry about and that military service was an honorable duty of which all true Americans should take advantage. Kay was skeptical and thought Chris should immediately apply to college in order to get a student deferment. Swamp Goddess retreated to her bathroom lair and stayed out of sight. Over the next few days debate among Chris's family raged about what Chris should do vis-a-vie the Selective Service.

Chris prayed. He was convinced that God had placed a calling on his life and that God had a special purpose for Chris, and it was up to Chris to be completely open to the leadership of the Holy Spirit. Chris believed that God would show the way that Chris was to follow and when God revealed the way that Chris was to travel then Chris had to fully embrace that revelation and act on it. After Chris prayed, there was no clear answer, so Chris prayed again this time more earnestly.

God hears the prayers of his children. Just as a good father of children born to him, a father will hear the cries of his children and not leave them to fend for themselves. Chris believed that God heard his prayer, and that God would answer Chris's prayer. God answered Chris's prayer, but it was not what Chris expected and the answer had a profound effect on Chris's life and the lives of many others.

The immediate answer was that Chris had to report to the Draft Board in Nashville on February 7 and that he would have to have a physical examination in preparation for an interview by the Selective Service. After that Chris would receive further direction not only from the draft board but also from God.

Chris's family wondered why Chris suddenly had no apprehension about his appointment at the draft board. They did not comprehend that there was a higher power leading Chris even though both Kay and Joe were believers. It did not occur to them that Chris would receive a direct word from God about what was about to happen in his life.

CHAPTER 15
BASEBALL AND THE DRAFT BOARD

Chris reported to the Selective Service office on Broad Street in downtown Nashville on February 7, 1967, which was at the height of America's involvement in the war in Vietnam. On the nightly news there were reports of the daily casualties suffered by the United States and reports of the number of Vietnamese soldiers killed by American forces. Reporters gave reports from the battlefield and showed American jets bombing the port of Hai Phong and the city of Hanoi in North Vietnam.

The average person in the United States in 1967 was unaware of the life and culture of the Vietnamese people or the history of the colonial aspirations of the French that led to the US involvement in a war so very far away from America. The American public had not yet come to see that the aspirations of other people in other cultures should be taken into consideration when foreign policy would lead to a conflict that would result in the death of so many Americans and Vietnamese.

In 1967 America was in the midst of its own cultural revolution. The civil rights movement, unrest in the streets, a sexual revolution, a growing awareness of gender equality all played into the changes in lives of the American people. Into that mix of cultural change was the war in Vietnam with nightly news from the battle fields and the political front that assured the American people that the United States was engaged in a war to protect freedom and democracy.

The US national government pitched the war as a means of protecting the rights of the South Vietnamese government from the communist regime in North Vietnam with its ties to Communist China and Russia. In reality, the South Vietnamese government was as corrupt as any government in the world including many African and South American dictatorships. The South Vietnamese president Ngo Dinh Diem had asserted dictatorial powers in South Vietnam until he was assassinated in 1963 by what many felt, at the time, to be a coup supported by the American CIA. Diem was replaced by Nguyen Cho Ky who in turn was replaced by Nguyen Van Thieu in November 1967. South Vietnam was eventually reunited with North Vietnam in 1975 after the United States withdrew from Vietnam and a peace accord was brokered in Paris between the North Vietnam and the United States in which South Vietnam was a reluctant participant.

Vietnam had been torn apart by war since before the Japanese invaded French Indochina (Vietnam) in September 1940. For centuries Vietnam had come under the influence of the Chinese and then the French. Catholic missionaries brought western religion to Vietnam and were perhaps responsible for political corruption in the area.

When the Japanese invaded French Indochina in 1940 it was to prevent oil supplies from reaching China from the port at Hai Phong. After World War II the French reasserted their presence in Vietnam. By then the Viet Minh, a military organization formed by Ho Chi Minh in the spring of 1941 was a part of the Indochinese communist party that expressed its purpose of achieving the independence of the Democratic Republic of Vietnam. The Viet Minh engaged in guerrilla war against the French and succeeded in driving the French out of Vietnam in 1954.

A treaty known as the Geneva Accords allowed for the temporary division of Vietnam into North and South Vietnam with elections to be held in 1956 to reunite the country. Ngo Dinh Diem became the leader of South Vietnam. Diem was a Catholic and anti-communist who consolidated his authority in the south and refused to allow the elections called for by the Geneva Accords.

A second Indochinese war broke out that pitted the North Vietnamese communist régime against the Diem led South Vietnamese military also referred to as the Arvin. It was around that time that the United States began to send military advisors to South Vietnam to assist the Arvin in its defense of South Vietnam from a group of insurgents referred to as the Viet Cong.

The Viet Cong was an armed communist revolutionary organization in South Vietnam, Laos and Cambodia that fought under the direction of the North Vietnamese against the South Vietnamese and their American allies. The Viet Cong was formed in 1960 under the leadership of Nguyen Van Hieu and remained active until American forces left Vietnam in 1975.

I have digressed. In February 1967 Chris had his physical at the Draft Board offices in Nashville. He was given an interview and was told that he would need to report to the Army induction center in Nashville on Wednesday March 15, 1967. The Ides of March were an ominous portent for the induction of a draftee into the US Army.

In the meantime, Chris contacted the Pirates organization to inform them of the events going on in his life. The Pirates told Chris that there was nothing they could do to keep Chris from being drafted and serving in the Army. The Pirates wanted Chris to keep in touch with the organization and to let them know when he had completed his service obligation. Chris even got a call from his manager at Gastonia to wish him well and God's speed in his service in the Army. Chris continued to work out with the MTSU baseball team and was told that when he got back from the Army that he would be welcomed to give hitting instructions to the college players.

On Wednesday March 15,1967 Kay and Joe insisted on driving Chris to the Army induction center in Nashville. Kay packed a lunch bag and Joe emptied his wallet and gave the money to Chris for his travels to Fort Lewis, Washington that was the Army boot camp for soldiers that were expected to be replacements for soldiers returning from their tour of duty in Vietnam.

Chris swore an oath to defend the constitution of the United States. Kay kissed Chris and gave him a tight squeeze. Joe shook Chris hand and had to be reminded by Kay to give Chris a hug. With that Chris got on the bus and started the next portion of his life, leaving his family and baseball behind was very traumatic and it was many miles before Chris could bring himself to speak.

CHAPTER 16
LIFE IN THE ARMY

In 1967 Army boot camp was an 8-week affair of changing a man from a civilian to a soldier capable of going into battle with a company of men and overcoming the enemy with fire team precision. Chris was on a long bus ride from Nashville to Fort Lewis near Tacoma, Washington, a bus ride that took 2 days and nights to accomplish. The bus ride was in the company of other drafted men each of whom had his own story of how he was going to be separated from the life that he knew and thrust into a life that would profoundly change how he perceived life and how he would choose to live his life.

On the third morning after Chris was sworn into the Army the bus arrived at the main gate of Fort Lewis and the men in the bus were lined up in front of a Drill Sargent and were told that within the next 24 hours that they would begin the process of becoming a soldier of the United States Army and would most likely be assigned to travel to Vietnam and engage in battle. There were men from all walks of life. There were young men from big cities, from small farming communities, from the deep south and the great Northwest, from California and from Tennessee. Each man was there because it was his legal obligation to submit to the draft. The draft was the law of the land because a decision had been made that American foreign policy demanded that the United States would fight in a war that had been started many years before, for a cause that was unclear, against people that were committed to riding their country of the colonial interest of Europeans and Americans.

Chris was put in a line that caused each man to give

up his individuality and conform to the group. Each man's head was shaved. Each man had to strip off his clothes and be inspected to make sure he did not carry lice of other disease carrying organisms. Each man was issued the uniform that he would wear and the boots that he would polish during his stay in boot camp. Each man was herded through the lines that led to physical and mental evaluations. All the while Chris submitted to the examinations and kept his mind on his relationship with Jesus and prayed that Jesus would see him through the stripping off of the old Chris and the coming of a new and different version of Chris.

The new draftees were taken to a barracks and assigned a bed and locker. The men were introduced to their drill sergeant and the lieutenant that was in charge of changing these men into a fighting unit that would serve the foreign policy of the United States in a war in Vietnam. The lieutenant like the men over which he had authority had also been drafted into the Army. His name was Albert Davis and was to be referred to as Sir by all the men under his control.

The drill sergeant's name was Bill Ottinger and was to be referred to as drill sergeant at all times by the men in his charge. Lieutenant Davis gave specific instructions as to how each man was to keep his bunk and locker in order and the lieutenants instructions were maliciously carried out and supervised by the drill sergeant. Any variation from the instructions of the lieutenant or the drill sergeant was met by immediate discipline and correction from the drill sergeant.

Compliance with the instructions of the lieutenant and the drill sergeant was demanded and if there was any rebellion in the ranks it was met by swift and cruel retaliation. The intent of the basic training was to transform ordinary citizens into a battle-ready group capable of being led into a war zone in order to meet the needs of those who set American foreign policy.

Chris accepted the training and commands of the drill sergeant and the lieutenant and did as they instructed. Chris had an enthusiastic attitude and was soon recognized for his potential leadership skills. Many of the men in Chris training class were older than Chris as they had stayed out of the draft by being deferred by being college students. Even the younger draftees that were near Chris's age had been to college but had failed out or dropped out because they realized that they were not college material.

One fellow draftee that Chris knew from high school was Ray Brammell who had gone to West End High School with Chris and had played football with Chris. Ray's football locker was next to Chris's locker, and they became friendly with each other. Ray's father had achieved success in the real estate sales business and Ray's family enjoyed a higher standard of living than the standard that Joe was able to provide while he finished his PhD at Vanderbilt.

Ray was somewhat lazy and one Friday night during their Junior year at West, Ray invited Chris to spend the night at Ray's house. Chris was interested in staying over at Ray's because Ray promised that his family always ate steak on Friday night and Chris would be well fed. Sometimes dinner was meager at Joe and Kay's because there was not that much money in the household budget for steak. Although Joe often said that the family enjoyed steak every meal. However, Joe referred to hotdogs as tube steak and also referred to pork-n-beans as bean steak.

After Chris got to Ray's house that was closer to the Green Hills section of Nashville and thus a more expensive neighborhood than the area close to Vanderbilt where Chris lived, Ray's motives became clear. Chris discovered that Ray wanted Chris to spend the night so that Chris would read out loud the novel <u>Catcher in the Rye</u> by J.D. Salinger to Ray. Evidently, the English class that Ray was in required that that novel be read by the next Monday and Ray did not want to spend his energy reading. Chris protested, but eventually he read the book out loud, and Ray laid on his bed and listened.

Ray graduated at the same time that Chris graduated from West. Ray in the fall of 1966 enrolled at the University of Tennessee with the pronounced intent of having a real good time. Ray had a great time in Knoxville that fall and attended all of the Tennessee football games and drank plenty of beer and whisky, but he also neglected to attend the classes that he had signed up to take that quarter. The result was predictable. Ray really had a great time and failed out of college and immediately became eligible to be drafted into the Army.

Chris and Ray sat together on the bus from Nashville to Fort Lewis and were put in the same training class with the same drill sergeant and lieutenant, but their experience was very different. While Chris was compliant and eager to follow the instruction of the drill sergeant, Ray was rebellious and questioned every word that came out of the drill sergeant's mouth. While Chris did not question the motive of his superiors, Ray reluctantly went through the physical training that was required in the first few days of boot camp.

The drill sergeant took notice of Ray's reluctance to follow instructions and also took notice of Chris's willingness to surpass the metrics that the Army prescribed for determining the fitness of the draftees. Ray came to the Army overweight and completely out of shape. Chris, because of his baseball playing and regular physical workouts, was trim and in very good physical condition. One of the first physical tests that each draftee had to complete was the hand over hand crossing of the monkey bars for a total of ten yards. It was no problem for Chris, but for Ray it was a terrible struggle. By the time that the training reached the point of running the mile Ray needed help and fortunately Chris was able to assist Ray in completing the mile run within the specified time.

With Chris's motivation and Ray's determination not to allow Chris to show him completely up, Ray made it through the physical competency portion of basic training and both Ray and Chris advanced to weapons training.

For two weeks the draftees had to run the five miles from their barracks to the firing range and become competent in the use of the M14 semi-automatic rifle that was the standard issue weapon of the United States Army infantry in 1967. The M14 was slowly being replaced by the M16, also a semi-automatic battle weapon that was also known as the AK15 by the non- military public. The M14 was heavier than the M16. The M16 at times was prone to jam until later modification to the design and the type of ammunition used by the Army corrected the problems. When Ray and Chris were in boot camp they had to qualify in the use and maintenance of the M14 but by the time they were deployed to Vietnam the M16 was the standard issue battle rifle of the US Army.

At first Chris was uncomfortable with his ability to use and maintain the M14 battle rifle that was issued to him. On the other hand, Ray was excited about the prospects of using a rifle that had the ability to do so much damage to any potential enemy that he might encounter in Vietnam. Chris was very careful in taking aim and squeezing the trigger of his rifle. Ray was apt to fire his rifle quickly and use all the ammunition issued to him rapidly. Chris took notice of whether the bullets he fired hit the target in the pattern that the drill sergeant recommended. Ray was not cautious in the way he aimed the M14 and blasted away in the general direction of the target on the firing range. Eventually, both Chris and Ray qualified to Army standards and completed their basic training.

They graduated from basic training and were sent for advanced individual training at Fort Polk, Louisiana. They were both sent to Light Weapons Infantry AIT. That training was another eight weeks of more training on the weapons that were available for use by infantrymen such as the 50-caliber machine gun, the mortar, the recoilless rifle, the 45-caliber pistol, hand grenades, anti-personal mines and various other weapons that the light infantry employed in battle and especially the weapons that would be used in Vietnam. The individual training also gave the men instruction in the use of communication devises and map reading.

After having spent 16 weeks of basic and advanced training Chris and Ray were assigned to an infantry unit that was to be shipped out to Vietnam because there was an acute need for light infantry to meet the combat needs of the war that was going on throughout South Vietnam. Chris was granted a weeklong furlough and made arraignments to travel to Murfreesboro to say his goodbyes to Joe, Kay and Swamp Goddess before deployment to Vietnam.

Chris arrived at the airport in Nashville and was greeted by Joe and Kay. Even Swamp Goddess was anxious to see Chris as he stepped from the airplane onto the tarmac. Chris looked very different in his olive drab dress uniform than he did when he left to go to basic training. Chris had gained muscle and he was very conscious of how he was received by everyone at the airport. Chris seemed to be withdrawn and very aware of the people in the concourse that led to the baggage claim.

While he was in basic training and even in advanced training Chris felt that God was always by his side and that God cared about everything that was going on in Chris's life. Chris felt the love of Christ and even when he was pushed to comply with the physical demands of the instructors Chris did so with a grace and self-assurance that the instructors had not encountered in any of the thousands of draftees that came through basic and advanced individual training in 1967. Chris was exceptional in his calmness, demeanor and confidence. Chris had what some might say was another world view of life. It was true, Chris believed that as a Christian that he was not to be conformed to this world but to take on the otherworld aspect of the life of Jesus Christ.

The second round of instructors believed that Chris would have been an exceptional officer had he been chosen to be sent to the officer's candidate school rather than to individual advanced training by his initial drill sergeant. Chris readily accepted his assignment because he believed that it was at God's direction that he was serving in the United States Army and that everything would go as God had planned from the start.

On the other hand, there was a war going on and the Army had quotas to meet and there was a manpower shortage that required the Army to train draftees for combat and send them to Vietnam to fight. In other words, Chris was a draftee that met the needs of the United States' policy makers to send American soldiers to Vietnam for the perceived purpose of protecting Southeast Asia from the menace of communism. That foreign policy was the declared purpose of the United States involvement in Vietnam even if the people of that region could have cared less about the form of government as long as it was not a government that was imposed on them by a colonial power.

The day finally arrived, and Chris was driven back to the airport in Nashville to begin his trip to Vietnam. There were kisses from Kay and Swamp Goddess and Joe even hugged his only son and they all said their goodbyes and promised that they would see each other again when Chris got back from the war. Chris told his family that God would comfort them, and that God would protect Chris from worry and fear. What God's ultimate purpose was for God to decide and as far as Chris was concerned that was sufficient and Chris would in fact see his family again either in this world or in the resurrection. Chris words were not as comforting as he intended them to be and both Kay and Swamp Goddess began to cry. Joe also was not comfortable with Chris's pronouncement and preferred to strike a more positive pronouncement and guaranteed that Chris would return to the family alive and well.

The boarding instructions were announced, and Chris disappeared down the jetway and he was gone.

Two days later Chris arrived in Vietnam. He arrived in a C-130, a four-engine turbo prop Army aircraft from Fort Bragg, North Carolina. Chris landed at the Bien Hao Air Base along with Ray. They were a part of the 199th Light Infantry Brigade stationed at Long Binh and assigned to protect the air base and the surrounding villages in this South-Central part of South Vietnam.

Chris and Ray arrived in Vietnam in September of 1967 about six months after they had been drafted. Long Binh was about 25 miles north of Saigon. The primary mission of the 199th Light Infantry Brigade was to enhance security and clear the region around Saigon of Viet Cong strongholds and resistance to the South Vietnamese government. The squad that Chris and Ray were assigned to regularly patrol territories assigned to their squad and went on long marches designed to announce the presence of the United States Army to the local population.

While on patrol the company size force to which Chris's squad was assigned were subject to being ambushed by Viet Cong guerrillas who would set traps and land mines in and around the areas that the squad patrolled. The Viet Cong often hid in elaborate tunnels that they had constructed in the region of the country.

The small villages that the company passed through hid the Viet Cong soldiers who were also operating in that part of South Vietnam.

The local civilians were caught between the daily patrols of the American Army and the terror they faced at night if the Viet Cong suspected the village of being too friendly to the Americans. Civilians mainly had to keep to themselves and comply with the demands of the Americans by day and the demands of the Viet Cong by night.

As Chris and Ray passed through the countryside, they witnessed both generosity and cruelty at the hands of both sides of the conflict.

Chris remembered the words of the famous civil war general who said, "War is hell." It was evident that the civilian population of that part of Vietnam just wanted to be left alone and not terrorized by either side of the conflict. The war was taking a terrible toll on the lives of the people. Chris was moved to tears because of the despair that he saw in the faces of the civilians in the villages that his squad and company passed through as they marched through South Vietnam.

On the other hand, soldiers often would help the civilian population by providing medical supplies and equipment. Soldiers would hand out their MRE's to the civilian population so that they could feed their children and themselves when the Viet Cong looted their supplies. Unfortunately, when the Viet Cong learned that the civilians were accepting supplies and food from the American's they would execute the people because they accused the civilian population of collaborating with the enemy.

When the company was not on patrol there was much down time that allowed the men to lay around until the officers found work for the enlisted men to perform. Much of the work was of no consequence but was ordered to keep the men busy and out of trouble. During his down time Chris often thought about baseball and missed playing. The other men in his outfit knew that Chris had played professional baseball and would try to get Chris to play catch.

Eventually, the Colonel in charge of the brigade heard that Chris was under his command and organized a company baseball team that would play against other company teams in a makeshift league. Chris was offered the responsibility of being the manager of his company's team. Chris was happy with the assignment and accepted the opportunity to get some playing time in while he was in the middle of a war zone.

The weather in South Vietnam was tropical and was suitable for playing baseball when it was not the rainy season that lasted from June to September. By the time Chris was asked to help form a baseball team for his company it was December and the warm climate made it perfect for playing baseball. Chris recruited players that had at least high school playing experience and found two pitchers that had been recruited to play college baseball before they failed out of college and were drafted.

The players that Chris persuaded to play for the company team were motivated to join the team because it got them out of the boredom and monotony of the downtime associated with being a soldier in a war zone waiting to go on patrols of waiting to be ambushed by an enemy that often blended in with the civilian population.

Chris was given free range as to when to schedule practice sessions and the games with other company teams that were scheduled on weekends. Chris organized practices in the same manner as the professional teams that he had played for, and everything was run in an organized manner. Chris carefully evaluated his players and was careful to place his players in positions that they could reasonably handle with the skill level that each player possessed.

By the end of January 1968, the team that Chris had assembled had won every game that they had played. The team relied on Chris as its rightfield power hitter and Chris made a reputation for himself as not only a great baseball player but also a dependable soldier that the officers of the 199th Light Infantry Brigade could rely on to accomplish the mission of their command.

From Chris's point of view, he was obliged to perform his duties as a soldier to the best of his ability. As a baseball player Chris believed that God had given him the ability to play baseball at an elite level and that he was obligated to use the talent that he possessed to the glory of God. Chris kept those thoughts in his mind and was not in the habit of sharing his feelings with anyone. Chris kept his motivation for service to God and the Army as a devotion to duty without calling attention to himself. Chris's nature was to keep to himself and not go to Saigon with Ray and the other soldiers in his squad to visit brothels and bars that catered to American soldiers. Chris was content to commit himself to the study of scripture and prayer for the people of Vietnam as they had to endure the hardships of living in a war zone and being terrorized by both the Americans and the Viet Cong.

CHAPTER 17
THE TET OFFENSIVE

On Tuesday, January 30, 1968, Chris had been in Vietnam for five months and had been put in charge of the company's baseball team and was given great deference by the officers and non-commissioned officers under which Chris preformed his duties. The baseball team that Chris played for and for which he was responsible was to play a game on the following Saturday at the baseball field at the Bien Hao Air Base that was about 20 miles from the base at which the 199th Light Infantry was stationed. Chris had called a practice of the team for that afternoon, and all seemed to be in place around the area where the soldiers were encamped.

After practice the sergeant called the men to a meeting because there had been sightings of enemy movements in the area and there was the possibility of enemy activity even though it was also the eve of the Tet holiday in Vietnam. The Tet holiday is the lunar new year celebration and is considered the most important holiday on the Vietnamese calendar. Because the Tet holiday was at hand the sergeant was not overly concerned about the activities of the Viet Cong but warned his men to be on the lookout for civilian intruders in the compound at which the platoon was camped.

No one expected that the local Viet Cong forces to be in the mood of starting anything because the American Army had reduced the ability of the local fighters to mobilize a sufficient force to threaten the American positions at Long Binh. What was not known was that the North Vietnamese Army had infiltrated the area around Saigon and was prepared to launch a surprise attack that later became known as the Tet Offensive.

At about 3:00 AM on January 31, 1968, Viet Cong and North Vietnamese forces began their attack on American and South Vietnamese positions with a barrage of rocket and mortar shells landing on the American positions. The rocket and mortar attacks were followed up by infantry attacks that caught the Americans asleep. American soldiers were killed and confused by the attack that took place at a time when they believed that a truce was in effect.

The American forces were able to respond and by the end of the day on January 31 the American forces were able to set up defensive positions to prevent their positions from being overrun by the attacking forces. Chris was ordered to become a part of a firing team that unleashed a withering amount of small arms fire against attacking Vietnamese soldiers. Many men were wounded by the exchange of bullets and exploding shells in and around the positions held by the company of men including Chris.

During the battle Ray made sure that he remained close to the place in the firing line where Chris was positioned. Ray instinctively knew that Chris would keep his wits about him and would not succumb to being overly excited by the events that were happening all around the battlefield that Wednesday. Chris kept his cool and responded to the orders of the officers and sergeants in a manner that promoted confidence in all the men around him.

As the battle raged, wave after wave of North Vietnamese soldiers tried to break the firing line that the Americans held but to no avail. The mortar rounds fired by the North Vietnamese in support of their troop's advances were ineffective and spiritic. In contrast round after round of artillery fire from distant location controller by the American Army were accurate and kept the Vietnamese advances at bey. Also, American jets dropped napalm on Vietnamese positions and helicopters provides close air support to the Americans.

The fighting lasted hour after hour and the Americans held their positions at Long Binh. At other parts of South Vietnam, the Viet Cong and North Vietnamese forces had more success. The American Embassy in Saigon was attacked and held by the Viet Cong for 8 hours until a company of Marines landed by helicopter on the roof of the building and fought their way down to secure the Embassy. The Tet Offensive tested the will of the Americans to remain in South Vietnam as the American public became more polarized over American involvement in the war.

Chris remained in combat in the aftermath of the attack on the 199th base at Long Binh and continued to take his place in the ranks of soldiers that served faithfully. Chris was a model soldier. He respected the officers and went out of his way to help his comrades in arms as they went on patrols and dealt with ambushes. In particular, Chris saw to it that Ray stayed out of trouble with the sergeant and the lieutenant from whom the squad took their orders.

The Tet Offensive continued until the rainy season in Vietnam brought it to a conclusion. The squad that Chris and Ray belonged to continued to go on patrol, but the baseball games came to an end when the Tet Offensive started.

The squad and the company marched through III Corps Tactical Zone the area surrounding Saigon pursuing the Viet Cong and increased activity from North Vietnamese Army units. When the 199th Light Infantry received intelligence that there were sightings of Viet Cong or North Vietnamese at any particular location in Dong Nai Province the company responded. Eventually, the 199th was sent to Cho Lon to engage in house-to-house combat.

Chris fought as directed by the sergeant and officers but hated to do anything that would cause unnecessary hurt or even death to those against whom he was ordered to fight. One afternoon Chris's squad was ordered to go house-to-house down a long seemingly deserted street in Cho Lon when the squad was ambushed by a group of North Vietnamese troops.

Chris and Ray dove for cover behind a low stone wall as bullets whizzed by their heads. Others in the squad were not as quick as Chris and were caught in a cross-fire from which they could not easily find cover or even return fire because they had to lie in a small ditch while bullets slammed into the pavement all around them.

From the low wall behind which Chris and Ray were protecting themselves they could see the situation in which the remainder of the squad had gotten themselves. Chris realized that quick action was necessary to protect the lives of the other squad members.

Chris told Ray to stay under cover and to fire his M16 in the direction from which the firing at the pinned down members of the squad was coming. As soon as he told Ray what to do, Ray began to question Chris's authority to give him an order. Ray did not like to do anything that Chris told him to do because Ray believed that he was better off, and his family was higher class than Chris's family. Of course, that made absolutely no sense in a war zone and especially in the middle of a fire fight in which the lives of the other members of the squad were at stake.

Ray shouted at Chris, "You stay here and use your M16 to return fire. I'm getting out of here and going for help."

"We need to work as a team. I am going to flank the Viet Cong that are firing at the squad that is in the ditch and draw their fire away from the ditch." Chris replied.

Chris had no time to have a discussion with Ray as he got to his feet and headed to the other end of the wall behind which he and Ray were located. When Chris changed his position, he could more clearly see where the Viet Cong were firing from. Chris quickly took off to a position at the corner of a house about 20 yards away from where the enemy fire was coming. Chris took a hand grenade from his belt and threw it like he was throwing it from right field and placed it within 2 feet of the position of the ambushing soldiers. The grenade exploded and several of the Viet Cong went down and the firing from that position stopped. There was another group of Viet Cong firing at the Americans pinned down in the ditch about 30 yards further to the left of the place where the first group of Viet Cong had been positioned that Chris attacked.

In the meantime, Ray had vacated the place where he and Chris had originally been when Chris told Ray to stay and fire at the enemy. Ray, true to his word, abandoned his spot behind the low wall and ran in the opposite direction from where the Viet Cong were firing at the men sheltering in the ditch.

Ray did not get 10 yards from the low wall when a third group of Viet Cong opened up on Ray and he went down. Chris could see all of what had happened to Ray, and immediately deep sorrow filled Chris's heart. Chris thought about all the time that he and Ray had spent together and realized that Ray was a lost sinner, and his life was gone, and Ray was lost forever.

While Ray had made a bad decision to not do as Chris had told him to do, it did reveal the presence of other enemy soldiers that would need to be dealt with if the squad and Chris were to survive the ambush. Chris had no time to do anything but to react to the present situation.

Chris made an assessment of the situation and quickly changed his position so that he could direct his fire directly at the location from which the second group of Viet Cong continued to reign bullets on the remainder of the squad. Chris took aim and immediately one of the enemy soldiers was hit and fell. That caused the second group of Viet Cong to direct their fire at Chris. When the Viet Cong started shooting at Chris the men in the ditch were able to change position and run to the low wall where Chris and Ray had been.

From that point the sergeant ordered the men to open up on the position from which the second group of Viet Cong were located as they crouched behind the low wall. A withering amount of M16 automatic weapons fire was directed to the location from which the group of Viet Cong soldiers were firing. When that happened Chris was able to throw another grenade accurately at the Viet Cong position with similar results and soon the firing between the two groups of soldiers quieted. The Americans began to stand up from behind the low wall and to survey the area in which the fire fight had taken place. They did the wrong thing.

Chris shouted at the sergeant to stay low behind the wall because there was another group of Viet Cong in the nearby vicinity. Chris yelled, "Stay down and don't expose yourselves."

As Chris's words came from his mouth the third group of Viet Cong soldiers who were behind the Americans started firing and several of the Americans were hit. Chris quickly changed his position so that he was hidden from the direction from which the bullets were flying. Chris was somewhat out of position and could not leave where he was without exposing himself.

Chris decided that he had to get to a better location from which he could more accurately engage the Viet Cong that were keeping the squad pinned down. Chris ran across a street and into an open door just as a hail of bullets exploded on the pavement and on the wall of the house he had just ducked into.

Chris reloaded his M16 by ejecting the spent magazine from his rifle and inserting another clip into his weapon. At that time there were problems with the M16 jamming during fire fights in Vietnam. Up to that point the M16's used by the squad operated well and there were no problems with the rifle's performance, however that situation was about to change and cause problems.

After the third group of Viet Cong started firing at the squad located behind the low wall, the sergeant ordered that his men move to the other side of the wall. The squad succeeded in crossing over the wall and pulled the wounded men with them. Chris was on their right flank and slightly behind the wall and he could maneuver in any direction he thought would enhance the squad's chances.

Chris signaled to the sergeant and tried to get a sense of what the sergeant wanted him to do. The sergeant had been hit in the leg and was not in a position to make any decisions. Chris was not aware of the sergeant's condition but became aware that something was not quite right when the corporal signaled to Chris that he needed to try to get help from any other squad that might be in the area.

Evidently the walkie talkie was either damaged or was out of commission and was not available to contact the lieutenant. Chris looked the situation over and decided that the best thing he could do was to find the location of the third group of Viet Cong that had killed Ray and who were now pinning the squad down. Chris started to work his way from house entrance to house entrance along the street that the squad had been patrolling. Chris finally came to an open lot and was able to cross an open space between two houses and to get one street over from the street that he and the squad had been on. From that point Chris sprinted down the street to a point where he believed that he was behind the position of the Viet Cong soldiers that he had observed when they opened fire on Ray and the squad.

Chris found another space between houses and slowly emerged on the street from which he and the squad had been located. Chris could make out the backs of the Viet Cong soldiers and realized that he had not been seen in making his dash to get behind the enemy. Chris was about 30 yards behind the Vietnam soldiers, so he crept slowly and quietly back up the street until he was near enough to see all the soldiers and have them under his gun.

Chris yelled at the soldiers and fired a few rounds from his M16 when it suddenly jammed. Chris did not know whether the Vietnamese soldiers recognized the problem that Chris was having with his weapon and if the Vietnamese soldiers were aware of the situation if they would bring their guns to bare on Chris. So, Chris, in the middle of the situation in which he found himself prayed. Chris asked God to intervene in the situation and God did.

God is in the business of answering prayers and protecting his children. Chris was a child of God and God had promised that those who are called, unconditionally elected, will experience the goodness of God. The bible promise is that all things will work together for good to them that love the Lord and are called according to his purposes. At that moment God's purpose was fulfilled. Chris was protected. The Viet Cong soldiers were disarmed and safe. The men in Chris's squad were spared any further jeopardy and for the moment peace was restored.

Jesus promised that if those who believe in him will continue to abide in him and live by his words, a believer can ask whatever they wish, and it will be done for them. Chris lived by that promise and when he asked God to protect him Chris was doing exactly as Jesus had said for Chris to do. Chris had to also admit that the promise of God did not apply to non-believers and that the prayer he had prayed would not have been answered had he not put his full trust in Jesus and lived by his commands. Chris asked himself if the exclusion of non-believers was fair from God's perspective when so much death and misery was all around him.

"Why is the belief in Jesus Christ so necessary for inclusion in the elect group whose prayers will be answered?" Chris asked himself as he made his way to the place where Ray's body had fallen only a few moments before.

Chris saw that Ray had been hit multiple times and his body was badly torn by the bullets that had hit him. Chris remembered the time that they had spent in high school playing football and the training that they had taken at Army boot camp and at individual training. Chris felt ashamed that he had not taken the time to ask Ray to believe in Jesus Christ because Chris believed that it would have made a difference in how Ray would have faced death and Ray would have had the opportunity to seek salvation.

Chris wondered if Ray would have accepted Jesus Christ as his personal savior if Chris had reached out to Ray with the Gospel message that Chris embraced when he was 10 years old. Chris had felt the presence of God when God answered Chris's prayers and believed that answered prayer was a part of the grace of God to God's children. Chris had just experienced God's grace when the Vietnam soldiers did not recognize that Chris's M16 had jammed. On the other hand, God could have made it so that Chris's rifle would not have jammed as easily as causing the Viet Cong soldiers to surrender, but that would have caused more blood to have been spilled.

And perhaps even the death of more men on both sides of the fight. Eventually, Chris had to come to the belief that he could not understand all the province of God and had to accept the fact that he only had to believe that "all things work together for good to those who love the Lord and are called according to His purpose."

The day that Ray died Chris vowed that he would reach out to every man in the entire brigade and provide every man with an opportunity to accept Jesus Christ as his personal savior. How Chris would bring about that goal required prayer and faith that God's will would be accomplished.

The squad mourned Ray's death because everyone in the squad had become close to each other after having been in Vietnam for the last six months. Chris had reached the midpoint of his duty in Vietnam and those who had reached that point all exclaimed that their time was on the downslope. Chris felt that he had a mandate from God to share the Gospel of Jesus with anyone that would give him the opportunity to discuss his faith, but he found that there was a great deal of resistance to Chris's efforts to share his belief in Jesus.

Chris would approach a member of the squad and after he had said a few words and explained that he wanted to make sure that the other squad members were saved and would receive the protection of Christ, Chris was treated with very different reactions from his fellow squad members.

Some of the men listened to Chris's urgent plea for a few minutes and then told Chris that they already were Christians and did not need to make any further profession of faith. Chris would ask if their prayers were being answered and generally, they would say, "well not lately."

Others told Chris that they were not interested in knowing about Jesus and all they wanted was to get out of Vietnam as quickly as the Army would let them. Still others were openly hostile to Chris and would curse at Chris and tell him to go fuck himself.

To some however, what Chris was saying struck an urgent chord and they wanted to have the same luck that Chris had had when his rifle jammed the day that Ray was killed. Chris tried to explain that a belief in Jesus was not like having a good luck charm but most of those that allowed Chris to talk to them merely regarded a belief in God as a talisman that would keep them on the right side of good luck.

Chris tried to reconcile his own faith with the rejection of the soldiers that he went into combat with but could only come to the understanding that his job was not to determine who would accept the Gospel of Jesus, it was merely to be a witness of the saving grace of God. It was at that time that Chris realized that God determined who he had called and that no matter what Chris said or did that if God had not first entered into a person's spirit it was impossible to direct them to God's irresistible atonement. Chris had to accept the reality that not everyone would accept the invitation to become a Christian even if God would have all mankind to become saved.

Chris thought about the last minutes of his friendship with Ray. They had known each other for several years but they really did not know the true meaning of each other's lives. As far as Chris knew, Ray was a decent person. Ray did not go out of his way to hurt anyone or cause anyone to suffer but on the other hand Ray did not go out of his way to be of help or comfort to anyone either. By contrast Chris loved to help people. Chris thought of his time in the Dominican Republic and his dealings with Polonia and her family and how he had tried to be of help. Chris thought of the Viet Cong soldiers that he could have killed when he chose to capture them instead and what the difference was

between his mind set and the others that refused to accept Jesus.

CHAPTER 18
THE IRON TRIANGLE

After the fire fight in the streets of Cho Lon Chris's squad was part of the 199th Light Infantry that was sent to the area surrounding Saigon to pursue the Viet Cong into an area known as the Iron Triangle. The Iron Triangle consisted of deep forest and jungle. It was a staging area for the Viet Cong and to North Vietnamese soldiers that had moved south to bolster the ranks of the Viet Cong guerrilla fighters. The Viet Cong, despite being outnumbered and without artillery managed to carry on fighting not only against the South Vietnamese Army but also the Americans sent to South Vietnam to prevent the Communist North Vietnamese from controlling the entire country.

Chris was sad that not many of his comrades were interested in his urgent plea for them to accept Jesus as their savior because he knew that the squad was entering a time in their tour of duty in Vietnam that they were most vulnerable. After a man has dealt with the routine of being in the Army for almost 18 months, they tend to let down their guard and become careless even when the situation calls for concentration and a complete awareness of dangers that being in a war zone portend.

The men of Chris's squad had been dealing with marches into the jungle of the Iron Triangle for several weeks and the Viet Cong and North Vietnamese had avoided contact with the Americans. They always seemed to vanish when the Americans and South Vietnamese were on patrol. It was the belief of the men in Chris's squad that the Viet Cong were too weak and too outnumbered and out gunned to get into a battle with the American Army. After weeks of the routine of marching on patrol the men let down their guard and it was at that exact moment that the Viet Cong were present and had gotten so close to Chris's squad that Chris could see the white of their eyes.

General Westmoreland and the American Army decided that the way to clear the Viet Cong from the Iron Triangle was to engage in what they called a hammer and anvil operation that they named Operation Cedar Falls. The general parameters of the operation were to remove all the civilian population from the Iron Triangle including the city of Ben Suc which was the largest population center in the area. Once the civilian population was relocated by the South Vietnamese Army and government the whole area would be defoliated to give the Americans a free fire zone. After accomplishing those two objectives three divisions totaling about 30,000 men would be deployed. One division would take up position along the Saigon River that formed the southwestern edge of the Iron Triangle. A second division would be deployed along the Than Dien Forest to the north and the Thí Tinh River that formed the eastern and northern boundaries of the triangle. The third division would enter the triangle from the east and drive the Viet Cong towards the other two divisions.

Chris's squad was a part of the third division, and they were tasked with driving the Viet Cong from their underground bases of operation. Chris watched as the South Vietnamese Army brutally gathered up the civilian population and herded them to settlements that were hastily constructed to house the deported civilians. If there was any resistance to the relocation of the civilians it was met by brutal force.

Once the civilians were removed from Ben Suc the Army bulldozers moved in to remove structures that had been burned out. After the bulldozers came a heavy bombardment to cave in the tunnels that formed the network of structures that housed the headquarters of the Viet Cong military and governmental operations. Lastly the forest and jungle were defoliated by the spreading of deadly chemicals that acted to destroy the vegetation, pollute the water, and poison the food supply of the enemy soldiers and civilian population. The chemicals were also referred to as Agent Orange.

After all the preliminary actions were taken, Chris's squad as part of the hammer division moved into the Iron Triangle to engage the Viet Cong. However, by the time all the preliminaries were accomplished the majority of the Viet Cong had fled the area and went into Loas and Cambodia.

When Chris's squad started marching into the Iron Triangle, they were met by the smell of smoke from burned out buildings and homes, the stench of dead livestock and the foul odor of Agent Orange that had been used to defoliate, poison and pollute the once lush country. Some of the men began to suffer from respiratory difficulties and coughing spells. Chris even felt nauseous because of the agent orange that had been sprayed throughout the area surrounding Ben Suc and the whole Binh Durang Provence. The company was being led into the Iron Triangle by a seasoned Captain who had progressed up the ranks.

Captain Hank Berthelot had enlisted in the Army as soon as he could after graduating from high school. After basic training at Fort Gordon, Georgia, Hank was sent to Vietnam in 1962 as an advisor to the South Vietnamese Army. Very soon Hank was promoted to sergeant and was recognized for his leadership qualities and certainly because of his love of the Army way of life. The Army liked Hank so much that he was sent to West Point to further his education and to hone his leadership skills. On graduation from West Point, Hank was again sent to Vietnam and after a second tour of duty in Vietnam Hank was again promoted this time to Captain. Hank was given command of a company of 200 men consisting of four platoons as they marched into the Iron Triangle.

The Viet Cong fighters had mainly escaped from the Iron Triangle and fled to neighboring Loas, Cambodia and hid among the Mung Mountain people. There was, however, still a Viet Cong regiment hidden in the underground bunkers that the Americans thought they had eliminated by the arial bombardment of the Iron Triangle. The Viet Cong had their sights on ambushing the company of men that Hank Berthelot led into the Iron Triangle on January 8, 1968.

The company of Americans were vigilant and prepared for enemy activity as they marched into an area that was only partially defoliated. The company of men that Hank commanded were given an area that was supposed to be devoid of the enemy and was not in contact with the other part of the division that marched into the Iron Triangle that fateful day. Hank deployed the platoons under his command in columns into the jungle with point men several yards ahead of the formations.

Suddenly, one of the point men tripped a wire that set off an explosion that in turn started an intense fire fight. Chris's squad that was a part of the company led that day by Captain Berthelot was towards the rear of the column and was soon engaged by the Viet Cong from all sides. Bullets were coming at the squad from all directions. Men in Chris's squad were hit, and some were immediately killed. Chris jumped into a low gully and managed to crawl to a natural depression that protected him from the bullets that were flying at him. The American soldiers began to return fire at the Viet Cong, but they were well hidden in the jungle. The Viet Cong also had committed more men to this ambush than the Americans had anticipated would still remain in that part of the operation.

Men on the American side of the fight for one of the few times in the Vietnam War were outnumbered and out gunned. Hank was wounded and took a bullet in his leg that put him on the ground, but he was protected by a squad that was able to keep fighting despite the losses they were taking. Hank surveyed his situation and realized that his position would soon be overrun by the Viet Cong. Hank had very little choice to make, and he called an artillery and rocket strike on the location from which he was making the call. Artillery shells exploded all around him and shrapnel hit Hank on his neck and chest. Two of his fingers were blown off and yet he continued to direct the artillery to keep firing.

Chris was still in the depression that he had crawled into when the battle had started, and he stayed covered by dirt and debris as the men in his squad were all cut down by enemy bullets. From his vantage point Chris could hear Captain Berthelot give the orders that brought a rain of explosions to his exact location. While he could hear what was going on and he could feel the percussion of the rocket hits and shells all he could do was to stay where he was and hold on to the life that God had given him.

The Viet Cong were surprised by Captain Berthelot's action and many of them also lost their lives in that ambush attack.

After the smoke cleared the only two men from the company that Captain Berthelot led into the Iron Triangle that day was Chris and the Captain. Captain Berthelot was severely wounded and was unable to speak because of the wounds to his neck and throat but he managed to hold on to his life. Chris ran to where Hank lay and began to administer as much help as he could. Chris placed his hands on Hank and prayed out loud so that Hank knew that Chris was calling on God to keep Hank alive. Chris knew that Jesus had promised that he would protect those who believed in him and rested in the fact that Chris was safe and protected even as the battle had raged around him.

The sun was hot even on the January day that Chris and his squad marched into the Iron Triangle. All around Chris lay dead men who mere minutes before had been alive and trying to kill other men. Chris sat in the dirt and cried. Death had come close to Chris and yet he was alive without a mark or even a scratch. The bodies of men who were the sons of their mothers and fathers both American and Vietnamese, brothers of sisters, husbands or wives and the fathers of children were scattered and broken. Chris wondered why these dead men had taken up the fight that brought them to their deaths. Surely, men of reason, men who act rationally do not have to blow each other apart in order to achieve their objectives.

Chris wondered, was it worth keeping the communist out of South Vietnam that caused the United States to send men and a great amount of wealth to southeast Asia to engage in war? Was America just another colonial power trying to gain a foothold in Indochina to exploit the resources and population of that region for the sake of business? Were the Viet Cong fighting to free their country of imperialist or were their other unknown motives that led these dead men to try to annihilate each other? Did God have a hand in these men's wills that caused them to throw their lives onto the trash heap of history and bring misery to their mothers, fathers, sisters, wives and children?

Chris asked God to give him an answer to the questions that ran through his mind and in his spirit that hot January day in the Iron Triangle of Vietnam. Chris had prayed for answers before and eventually God had answered his prayers. In some cases, it took a long time before Chris received an answer, but in some cases, Chris had an answer to his prayer almost before he stopped praying. On that day the answer was not immediate, and Chris knew that it might take the rest of his life to understand why what had happened that day happened, but he did know that God was true to his word and that God would answer.

CHAPTER 19
BACK TO BASEBALL

Chris had been in Vietnam for over 12 months and his required tour of duty had ended. The tour of duty seemed to be longer than the 12 months required by the Army for drafted soldiers as Chris's life during that time had changed. Chris was definitely a changed man. While he was in Vietnam, Chris met an Army Chaplin, Lieutenant James Ritchie as they were both leaving Vietnam and got into a long and complicated discussions with the Chaplin regarding the meaning of life and the part that God plays in a man's life on their flight back to the United States.

Chaplin Ritchie graduated from the University of Alabama and volunteered to join the Army as a Chaplin. Ritchie was a Christian Scientist, and his beliefs were very strange to Chris. Ritchie was no stranger to combat. Ritchie often volunteered to go on patrol missions with Army regulars especially in the area of South Vietnam that was close to the DMZ.

The DMZ or Vietnamese demilitarized zone was established as a dividing line between North and South Vietnam in 1954 as part of the Geneva accords that were to temporarily separate North and South Vietnam until general elections could be held to reunify the north and south. The DMZ stretched from the Vietnamese coast along the Ben Hai River to the Laotian border.

By 1964 several fire bases were established by American forces approximately 5 miles south of the DMZ from which patrols were launched. The patrols were for the purpose of keeping track of North Vietnamese infiltration to the south along what became known as the Ho Chi Minh trail. North Vietnam brought men and supplies to the Viet Cong fighters through Loas on this route. American forces established a fire base at Khe Sanh from which to launch patrols.

Ritchie was sent to Khe Sanh to act as Chaplin to the Marines and Army Special Forces units based there. While performing his duties as Chaplin, Ritchie often went on patrol with the soldiers in order to meet the spiritual needs of the soldiers while they were in the field. Jim Ritchie saw plenty of combat while he was stationed at Khe Sanh. While on patrol there were ambushes that resulted in men being wounded and killed. Ritchie ministered to the soldiers and his life was profoundly changed by what he experienced. Ritchie left Alabama as a gung-ho Army volunteer and was profoundly changed by his experience in Vietnam as were many others including Chris.

Chris and Ritchie met after both men had experienced combat in South Vietnam and while they were leaving the country and headed back to the United States. They met at Bien Hao airbase just outside of Saigon in October of 1968. Ritchie was headed back to the University of Alabama Law School to pursue a law degree because he no longer wanted to be a Chaplin. Chris was headed back to Murfreesboro and then to the Pirates training facility in Bradenton, Florida to hopefully resume his career as a professional baseball player.

Chris saw Ritchie while they were waiting for the commercial flight on which they were both scheduled to take from Vietnam to Honolulu, Hawaii and then to Seattle to Fort Lewis where they would receive further orders. Ritchie had been in the Army for almost 6 years and had spent two tours of duty in Vietnam while Chris as a drafted soldier was nearing the end his two-year enlistment. Ritchie noticed that Chris was looking at the Chaplin's insignia on his uniform and surmised that Chris was interested in talking to him.

Ritchie came near to where Chris was sitting and immediately Chris stood and gave the hand salute that was required of enlisted men when an officer came into his presence. Ritchie returned the salute and said, "Soldier are you in need of an ear to listen to you."

Chris responded, "Sir, I would like to talk to someone that can help me make since of the year that I have spent in the war zone here in Vietnam."

Ritchie said, "Maybe we can both come to some understanding of what has happened to us while we have been here and resolve some things before, we get home. I would like to have this conversation but first tell me who you are and what has happened to you while you have been here."

With that said the two men started to tell each other who they were and what had happened to them. When they had recited to each other their personal information, Ritchie said, "It seems that we will be able to get to know each other during this long flight home. I suggest that we disregard the formalities of rank and speak to each other as men of equal rank and with a common desire to answer the question of what did all of this mean and how can we come to a conclusion of this part of our lives."

Chris said, "Yes Captain Ritchie, it would seem that we have had a common experience of living through war. I have asked God to give me answers to my question of why all of this happened to me and the men that were killed. My friend died. I watched men that I knew be blown apart. I saw many Vietnamese killed and many homes and villages destroyed. I saw the jungle poisoned, rivers polluted, crops destroyed, and people displaced. I asked God why this happened?"

"Chris, call me Jim. I have been trained to listen to questions like you have posed. My belief system is different than your I suspect, but we can talk about this all day and all night and maybe I can help you come to a conclusion about the questions that you have asked of God." Captain Ritchie replied.

With that said, Chris got to the heart of the issue and said, "What is in the hearts of men that they want to go to war? Can't those in charge realize the amount of suffering they are causing when they order men to wage war on other men? It not only causes suffering on the enemy but on the soldiers of their own army when men start shooting at each other."

Ritchie looked intently at Chris and replied, "Those questions are beyond our comprehension. Nations go to war because of greed, jealousy, fear, and avarice. Those feelings are matters of human imagination and are not the reality of the physical world, if such a reality even exists. You see Chris, none of what you see really exists. The mind of man is full of thoughts, but the reality does not exist outside of the minds of men. You ask about suffering; suffering does not really happen. Your mind only sees what you are predisposed to believe about to nature of man. If you see men at war with each other it is because you are at war within your mind. War is not reality."

Chris did not understand anything Ritchie had said. Chris had never been exposed to the beliefs and teachings of Mary Baker Eddy or the Christian Science religion. So, Chris asked, "What do you mean? Are you telling me that everything that the both of us just went through is just a figment of our imagination and it really did not happen?"

"Reality as we perceive it in our consciousness is not subject to physical reality, and there may not be a physical reality at all." Ritchie said with an assurance that disturbed Chris.

"Jim, I cannot believe that you are a Chaplin in the United States Army and that your personal belief is so out of touch with what you have told me happened while you were in the field and faced death at the hands of Viet Cong soldiers." Chris replied.

"I am not here to convert you to my beliefs, Chris, but my beliefs are my beliefs, and you should never question anybody's belief system. You will never convince me that your belief in Jesus Christ will replace my belief in Christian Science." Ritchie asserted.

Chris thought for a moment and slowly began to say, "Jim do you not believe that there is good and evil in the world and especially in the hearts of men?"

"Good and evil are within the mind of men but what is to say that my concept of good is the same as your belief. My good thought may be what you would describe as evil. All the thoughts that come to you may or may not be anything more than your conception that fills your mind at any given time." Ritchie argued as he continued to assert his belief in Christian Science.

"But Jim, you and I have just had similar experiences in the war. We have both seen men killed, blown apart by other men. We have both come through the battles being fought between men and even children, is there not something to be said about why this has happened? Why did I need to come to Vietnam? I was perfectly happy playing baseball in the United States. I have nothing against the North Vietnamese, and communism is just a political philosophy that does not affect me." Chris replied as the two men sat next to each other on a commercial jet liner while the aircraft flew over the Pacific Ocean.

Ritchie thought that he had a response based on his belief in Christian Science, but he held that explanation back and instead took another tact, and said, "When I graduated from college, I decided that I would join the Army and apply to become a Chaplin. I was sent to a school in Fort Jackson, South Carolina and underwent training on how to conduct religious services for every religious belief that could be found among the troops to which I would be assigned. That training has allowed me to become familiar with the beliefs of every religion and every sect of every religion that is recognized by the Army. Therefore Chris, I understand the prospective that you have as an evangelical Christian. I do not condemn you for your beliefs. Actually, I admire you for being committed to your belief, but what you believe is not what I believe so don't try to convert me."

"Jim, I am not trying to convert you, as if I could, all I want to do is try to understand why I had to witness the depravity of mankind played out in the jungle in Vietnam and to seek an understanding of how I am to respond when people ask me what I did while I was a soldier in the United States Army." Chris thoughtfully answered.

Ritchie had to let that question sink into his mind for a few minutes, but finally said, "You do not have to say anything. It is actually no one's business to ask you to explain the war in Vietnam to them. Everybody will have an opinion about the war, and you will not be able to answer anybody in a way that will convince them that the war was justified or that we should have killed every enemy soldier we came in contact with. "

Chris replied, "You may be right about what other people might say or think, but it is for me to answer my own questions that I am more concerned about. I believe that all things are directed by God for the good of those who are believers and are called according to his purposes. In my way of thinking there is some good reason that I was sent to Vietnam, but to find the good in it will take perhaps a long time to understand. Maybe, I will never understand and will need to rely on God's promise that it was for my good that I was sent to Vietnam to witness the depravity of humans. On the other hand, I believe that I have been under the protection of

God and his Holy Spirit during the time that I spent in Vietnam and also for my entire life. How can I explain how my rifle jammed and yet the Viet Cong did not realize that they were free to shoot me? How do you explain that when Captain Berthlo calls the strike down on us that I survived without a scratch?"

"Maybe it was all a figment of your mind, nothing but an illusion, maybe you and me sitting on this jet airliner is not real. Perhaps the whole world as we imagine it is nothing more than our minds playing tricks." Ritchie offered in response to Chris's continuing questions.

"If that is the case, why don't we get up, open the door and walk out on the wing of this airplane?" Chris shot back in a rather annoyed manner.

"Now Chris, don't get belligerent on me. We are just having a friendly conversation among fellow soldiers on their way home." Ritchie said, trying to diffuse the tension that he heard in Chris's voice.

"You are right, I have been thinking about this too long and I am tired. I am going to take a nap. How soon before we get to Hawaii?" Chris asked.

Ritchie looked at his watch and said, "A nap will be good for the both of us. We have another 3 hours before we reach Hawaii."

With that said both men let their seats back and closed their eyes and were sound asleep just like that.

A stewardess nudged Chris and Ritchie awake and told them to put their seat backs into the upright position because the airplane was on its final approach to the airport at Honolulu International Airport. The pilot announced on the intercom that the flight would be on the runway for an estimated 2 hours while the flight was refueled and re-supplied. The passengers would be allowed to leave the airplane while it was being refueled but the passengers should not leave the airport facilities. The scheduled departure for the Seattle-Tacoma International Airport was at 12:30 AM with arrival at 9:00 AM on the west coast.

Both Chris and Ritchie decided to stretch their legs a bit and walk around in the Honolulu airport while they were in Hawaii. Chris got off the airplane first and headed for the first place he could find that was outside. Ritchie made for the first restaurant he could find that was serving food in order to have a cup of coffee and a snack to chew on.

When it was time to get back on the airplane Chris had decided that he had had enough of Ritchie's company and looked for an excuse to find another seat on the airplane. Chris saw another Army Captain that was also on the same flight and asked him if he would feel more comfortable sitting next to a fellow officer than sitting by an enlisted man. The captain agreed to change seats and when the flight was ready to take off again Chris found himself sitting next to a fellow draftee who had been wounded and was returning home to Derby, New York, a town slightly east of Buffalo. Chris never saw Captain James Ritchie again and that was soon enough for Chris.

The soldier now sitting next to Chris was much less talkative than Ritchie and that left Chris alone with his thoughts as the flight progressed from west to east through the night. Soon Chris was back asleep. While in Vietnam Chris had learned to fall asleep quickly and stay asleep until he had to respond to an officer, his sergeant, or the noise of the enemy firing in his direction. Falling asleep in a coach chair leaning back as the jetliner crossed the Pacific Ocean was no problem. Chris only dreamed of playing baseball again when he got back to the United States of America.

Chapter 20
Home Again

Great expectation was aroused in Chris as his final leg of his flight from Vietnam to Nashville neared its conclusion. Chris very much wanted to see his mother, father and even Swamp Goddess. Finally, after four full days of travel that included a full day at Fort Lawton processing center that was in the vicinity of Seattle, where Chris received his orders to report to the Army Reserve Center in Nashville, Tennessee on December 10, 1968, to serve 2 years in the Army National Guard. That obligation was a part of the requirement to complete his obligation as a drafted enlisted man.

The American Airline flight from Chicago to Nashville arrived at the Nashville Airport on time and the jet taxied to a stop on the tarmac near the main gate. There was no band playing, no welcome signs, no speeches by politicians recounting the bravery of the soldiers on the flight even though there were 20 or 30 soldiers in uniform on the flight. Many of the soldiers had served in Vietnam though only a few had actually been in combat.

Kay spotted Chris as he departed the airplane and walked down the stairs from the door of the jet to the tarmac. Kay squealed with delight as she saw her first born descend from the American Boeing 707 320B. Kay alerted Joe and he beamed with pride seeing Chris in his dress uniform walking towards him ready to embrace his family after having been away for 24 months and having gone through close fighting and artillery shelling while he was gone. Swamp Goddess even ran to Chris and put her arms around him.

It had only been a few days since Chris was in a war zone and only days since he was close enough to the fighting to experience death tugging at his sleeve. While he was happy to see his family and feel the hugs and kisses of his mother, he was different from when he last saw his family. He was different because no one can go through being in a battle in which your life may be required by some unknown person pulling a firing string and sending an artillery shell in your direction. The uncertainty of life in a war zone in a far country would have caused a profound change in anybody that had to endure the constant question of whether the next shell would be the last shell that you hear.

Joe and Kay did not recognize the difference in Chris right away. It took a few days for the changes in Chris to become evident. Kay noticed that Chris was very quiet while the family had meals together. Chris responded to questions in short abrupt answers as opposed to the usual happy and open way that had characterized his responses to family discussions before he went to Vietnam. Chris was not angry or sad, he was very noticeably silent and withdrawn. Finally, Joe asked Chris if he would like to go to the movies. The spaghetti western <u>The Good, the Bad and the Ugly</u> was playing at the movie theater in Murfreesboro that week and Joe, being a fan of westerns, wanted to go. Chris wanted to be with Joe, and they went to the theater.

Clint Eastwood, Lee Van Clief, and Aldo Rea played the respective parts of the protagonist who during the Civil War were trying to outdo each other in order to recover bags of gold hidden by a Confederate Soldier in a cemetery. While on their way to retrieve the gold each man had to fight with and overcome each of the other protagonist. Near the end of the movie there was a scene in which the Union Army was in an artillery battle with the Confederates. That proved to be too much for Chris to take and he got up and walked out to the theater lobby and waited for the movie to end. Joe finished watching the movie and found Chris sitting on a bench in the lobby when the film was over.

Joe asked, "Why did you leave the movie? It was just getting to the end. There were only a few minutes more."

"I had to go to the bathroom, and I didn't want to disturb the audience by coming back into the movie at that stage of the film." was all that Chris could say in reply.

"I believe you. But if you want to talk about anything with me, I will be happy to hear what you need to say." Joe replied.

"I know." Chris said in a hushed voice that led Joe to believe that his only son and a person after his own heart could not say what it was that was bothering him. Joe was wise enough to let Chris come to his own feelings. Joe decided to let the issue rest at least for the moment.

When Chris and Joe got back to their house, Chris told Joe and Kay that he was tired and that he was going to lay down until he was called for dinner. Joe took Kay into the den so that they could not be heard and said, "Chris could not finish watching the movie. He is bothered by something the happened to him while he was in Vietnam. We need to give him some time for him to get over the shock of being in a war and suddenly coming back to America."

Kay was completely in agreement with what her husband said and added, "He has been through things that we can only guess about. When he is ready, I am sure that he will open up and let us know what happened while he was away."

At supper that evening Swamp Goddess, being a direct and outspoken person said, "Chris, tell us what happened to you over there in Vietnam. You haven't told us any of your stories and I for one want to hear what the American occupation of South Vietnam is like. Did you fight any battles, did you kill anybody, did you see anybody get blown away?"

Before Chris could answer, Kay said, "This is not the proper place to talk about that. Ali, let your brother enjoy his dinner and let him decide when he wants to tell us what is on his mind."

Chris spoke in a very low tone and said, "The war in Vietnam is terrible. I saw much suffering at the hands of the Americans that was needless. Yes, I had to kill Viet Cong soldiers that seemed to be children, but it was kill or be killed. I hated the situation that our government put me in. I am glad that I am no longer in Vietnam, but I grieve for those that are still killing each other every day."

Chris's words surprised everyone at the table that evening. No one spoke for what seemed like an eternity, but finally Swamp Goddess said, "We are all so happy that you are safe and at home. We all prayed every day while you were gone that you would come home safely."

"I am glad that you remembered me in your prayers. I have never stopped praying for each of you even when I was in the jungle and facing uncertainty, I hung on to the belief that the protection that Jesus promised to those called to believe on Him would be granted to me while I was fighting to stay alive and return to America. I believe that the only reason that I am here today is because of the protection of the Holy Spirit. I believe that when I feel that I am weak and alone that I am still anointed by God and that I will reign with Jesus in His kingdom." Chris said as his affirmation of faith in the power of the Holy Spirit to protect and accomplish the will of God in His chosen.

No one at the table had anything further to say until the dinner was finished. When the table was cleared Chris helped his mother with drying the dishes as Kay washed the dishes by hand that evening. On several occasions during the process Kay would reach out to Chris and pull him close to her and say, "I am so happy that you are home." then Kay would weep silently but it was tears of joy at having her son next to her safe from the war in Vietnam.

Chris had arrived in Murfreesboro in mid-October 1968 only a few weeks before the Presidential election and Chris was very interested in getting caught up on all that had happened in America while he was in Vietnam. Chris had heard that President Johnson had announced that he would not run for president again in 1968 and that had led to some very disturbing events.

President Lyndon Johnson was from Texas. After the assassination of President John Kennedy, Johnson became president and ran a successful campaign for re-election in 1964. During his administration the 1964 Civil Rights act was passed and signed into law in July 1964. At that time the former Confederate States that had been solidly in the hand of the Democratic party began to shift into Republican control as a reaction to the Civil Rights act of 1964. Much of the south including Texas was reacting to what they considered the liberal norths final battle of the Civil War to give black people equality with the "good ole boy" political coalition that had controlled the southern states since reconstruction.

Added into that mixture of anti-civil rights backlash in the old south was a new breed of Republican candidates that sprang from the radical far right wing of the GOP. In the 1964 presidential election Johnson ran against Berry Goldwater of Arizona. Goldwater captured the Republican nomination with the slogan that, "I would remind that extremism in the defense of liberty is no vice! And moderation in the pursuit of justice is no virtue!" Even though Johnson won the presidency in a landslide victory in 1964 a divide in the America

political psyche was developing that would have profound influence in America ever since that election. The
Republican party became more radicalized. There were
more contentious elections in the future of the country.
Civility between competing political factions became
non-existent and the radicalization of the Republican
party became the norm.

By the time of the 1968 presidential campaign, with
the political climate rapidly changing in the south, the
war in Vietnam growing more and more unpopular,
Johnson saw the handwriting on the wall and decided
that it was time for him to step aside and hand the government over to another generation of political leaders.
Bobby Kennedy the younger brother of the very popular assassinated president announced his candidacy for
president, and he campaigned throughout the country
to enthusiastic and growing crowds of supporters.

On April 4, 1968, Martin Luther King, Jr. was shot
and killed as he stepped out of his room onto the landing of the Lorrain Hotel in Memphis, Tennessee at about
6:01 PM. Dr. King's assassination set off riots throughout the urban centers in the United States. Nashville
was not spared the anger of the black population. A riot
centered in the black colleges campuses in Nashville
ended in confrontation between college students, many
of whom had recently returned from active duty as soldiers in Vietnam, with the Metro Police force who likewise had many returning members who had served in
Vietnam. The Metro Police force at that time was nearly
all white while the student population of Fisk and Tennessee State were all black.

The rioting in the major cities of America lasted several days. Many were killed, wounded and arrested
during the riots following Martin Luther King Jr's assassination. Tension between southern whites and blacks
spilled over to all areas of the United States shifting political aspirations of those who saw the racial tension as

a political opportunity to gain political power with those who did not champion racial equality.

Richard Nixon sensing the growing divide between those who believed that white supremacy could be couched in terms of law and order resurrected his political fortunes from the trash heap of his failure in the 1960 presidential election and his defeat in his campaign for governor of California in November of 1962. At his news conference following his defeat in the California Governor's election Nixon had famously said, "Now you will not have Nixon to kick around anymore." However, Nixon's political aspirations resurfaced after the passage of the 1964 Civil Rights Act and the backlash of the south that allowed a path to victory for a politician as skillful as Nixon who saw an opportunity to win in the south and garner enough electoral votes to win the presidency. Nixon set his strategy with the only caveat being the rising popularity of Bobby Kennedy as a populist candidate who was running on an anti-war platform and was considered to be a unifier rather than a divider like Nixon.

On June 5, 1968, Bobby Kennedy was assassinated in Los Angles by Sirhan Bishara Sirhan shortly after declaring victory in the Democratic Presidential Primary. Kennedy's assassination threw the Democratic Party's nominating process for the office of president into confusion. Eventually, the Democrats held their party's convention in Chicago on August 25 through the 29. By then there was much political and social unrest throughout the United States. Groups of protesters descended on Chicago to voice their opposition to the war in Vietnam and to call for even more civil rights legislation.

A group called the Youth International Party (YIPPIES) was led by Jerry Rubin, Abbie Hoffman and Tom Haden in protest during the Democrat Convention in Chicago. Bobby Seal, the leader of the Black Panther

Party also showed up at the Chicago convention and riots ensued. It seemed as if 1968 was the year of the riot and the phrase "Burn baby burn" could be heard in many streets throughout America. It was a time when many ROTC buildings on college campuses were torched by students opposed to the war in Vietnam.

Into this mixture of racial, social and political unrest in the United States, Chris had returned from being shot at and bombed in Vietnam. It was no wonder that Chris kept to himself. He had gone from a foreign combat zone to a situation of domestic violence and unrest and a situation in which soldiers returning from Vietnam were treated with suspicion. The younger population of the United Stated in 1968 came to believe that the war in Vietnam was being prosecuted by leaders who could be accused of war crimes because of the way the war was being conducted against the people of Vietnam. It was often heard on the streets of America the chant by protesters of, "Hay, hay LBJ how many kids you kill today." The suspicions of the American population led to a shunning of those returning from service in Vietnam. Chris was not immune to that treatment. In turn Chris could only rely on his belief that God had not sent him to Vietnam without knowing exactly what He was doing and that at some point Chris would understand that his time in Vietnam was for his own good because he was a believer and felt the call of Jesus on his life.

It was also the first time that Chris could vote in the presidential election. Kay and Joe were set to vote for Richard Nixon because Joe did not like liberal Democrats and because he did not believe black people needed affirmative action. On the other hand, Chris thought back to the time he had been on choir tour in Meridian, Mississippi and had seen racial discrimination up close and personal. Chris decided that he was a Democrat and that he would vote for Hubert Humphrey as the first presidential candidate to come close to his beliefs.

Chris also supported Albert Gore for senator from Tennessee because he seemed to have a sensible approach to the war.

When the votes were counted both Humphrey and Gore were beaten. Nixon was elected as president and Bill Brock a conservative Republican from Chattanooga and an heir to the Brock Candy Company fortune was elected to replace Al Gore. Throughout the old Confederate South, Nixon and his Republicans received more than enough votes to turn the liberal coalition of norther and mid-western Democrats out of office.

Chris could see before his very eyes that politics in America had taken a sharp turn to the right and that America was facing a generational change.

Party politics was only part of what Chris observed. There was a distinct intervention in politics by religious groups that espoused a right-wing agenda that led to an intolerance of those that did not believe as they believed. The so-called moral majority claimed to be speaking for most Americans who believed in God and that the liberal courts had gone too far in protecting the rights of criminals and racial minorities. Their beliefs were bolstered by movies such as <u>Bullitt</u>, a crime drama starring Steve McQueen that depicted a hard-working police officer whose efforts to bring criminal elements in San Francisco under control were being hampered by a District Attorney who was trying to make sure that the criminal's rights were protected.

Chris noted that there was a backlash in the people that he encountered in Tennessee, who felt that the Supreme Court of the United States had gone too far in protecting the rights of blacks and criminals in the country. The moral majority's unofficial spokesman was the pastor of the Liberty Baptist Church in Lynchburg, Virginia. Pastor Jerry Falwell became an outspoken critic of what he described as the decay in the morals of

America. As it turned out the moral majority was very supportive of the Republican Party and Richard Nixon in the 1968 presidential elections. Some news reporters suggested that it was the moral majority that put Nixon over the top in many of the southern states that he carried in that election.

There were decisions by the Supreme Court of the United States in such cases as <u>Griswold v. Connecticut</u>, in1965 that dealt with the right of married couples to use birth control contraceptives in the privacy of their home without government intervention. In that case Justice William O. Douglas, a Franklin Roosevelt appointee in 1939 wrote in his majority opinion that the United States Constitution had a penumbra or rights within the first ten amendments to the Constitution that guaranteed the right of privacy to American citizens. That decision and the introduction of "the pill" an oral birth control contraceptive ushered in a sexual freedom for women in the country that had not been previously experienced.

There seemed to be contradictions within the whole society that caused a social revolution in America. On one end of the spectrum was the moral majority and its preaching of the moral decay in the United States, an assertion of giving the police more powers to combat crime, and a feeling that the courts and congresses legislative acts had gone too far in recognizing the right of minorities and especially black people. On the other hand, there was an openness to sexual freedom and the expectation of greater personal freedoms of civil rights in the general population. Imposed on those societal issues was the war in Vietnam that had no end in sight.

Into this landscape of American society Chris had returned from being shot at and bombed in a faraway country when he was still a very young man with his life before him.

Chapter 21
Chris is Spoken to by Jesus and Chris Seeks Wisdom

After being at home with Joe, Kay and Swamp Goddess for a few weeks Chris decided that he needed to get back in touch with his manager at the Gastonia Pirates in the Western Carolinas League. Chris tracked Pop down on a Monday morning in December 1968. The conversation started innocently enough when Pop answered his phone and Pop said, "Hello."

Chris identified himself and then said, "I am back from serving in the Army and I am ready to play baseball again. Can I report back to the Pirates training facility in Bradenton in February."

Bob Clear who told Chris to call him "Pop" when they first met after Chris was sent from the Instructional League to Class A baseball in Gastonia, North Carolina of the Western Carolinas League replied, "Who did you say you were again? I am having a hard time hearing you. You have caught me while I am at work here at Parkdale Mills and they are running the spinning machines and it makes it hard to hear."

Chris could hear the noise of the machinery of the plant over the phone, so he mustered his loudest voice and repeated who he was. Pop heard him this time but was still having a hard time knowing why Chris was calling and what it had to do with him. It was obvious to Chris that Bob Clear was having a hard time remembering that Chris had been a player on the team that Bob Clear managed during the baseball season just the previous season. With that bit of information Chris determined that he needed to call the Pirates headquarters in Pittsburg for further discussion of his return to playing professional baseball.

After a few failed attempts to get someone on the telephone to discuss the reason for Chris's call Chris finally talked to the General Manager of the organization and spoke with Joe E. Brown. The GM recognized Chris's name from several reports that had come to his attention from the time Chris had entered the Pirates organization until the time that Chris was drafted into the Army. "Young man what can I help you with today?" the GM asked as if he were the proprietor of a retail sales store.

"Mr. Brown, I have returned from serving in Vietnam and I would like to resume my place in the Pirates organization. I would really like to resume playing for Gastonia and show the organization that I still have what it takes to play professional baseball." Chris said as directly as he could.

"Chris, as I recall you were making real progress before you were drafted and were sent to Vietnam, but the organization has changed since you left. Bob Clear is no longer the manager of the Gastonia Pirates. We now have Frank Ocean in that position. Frank was the third base coach under Danny Murtaugh and when Murtaugh left we put Ocean into our minor league system." Joe E. Brown told Chris.

"Well Mr. Brown, I understand that Pop Clear is not the manager, but what I am really asking is, can I get my job back and play baseball this year for the Pirates organization?" Chris asked with some annoyance because he believed that the General Manager was purposely avoiding the reason that Chris was calling in the first place.

"Young man, we make decisions everyday about who will play in our organization. I understand that you were a good player when you were with us before you left the organization and joined the Army, but you left us and now we have moved on and somebody else has taken your place. Sorry kid, we have released you and you are free to do or go wherever you want." With that last exchange the GM for the Pirates hung up the phone leaving Chris to wonder what he should do next.

It looked as if being drafted into the Army was going to be more costly than Chris had anticipated when he received the notice from the selective service to show up for an interview. Chris decided that he needed to pray about what was to come next in his life. That is exactly what Chris did. Chris went to his room, shut the door and talked to God.

God honors the prayers of the righteous. In the case of Chris, he always prayed that God's will would be done in his life. Chris was willing to accept whatever assignment that God had for him. Chris believed that if he aligned his personal will with that of God's will that all aspects of his life would come under the direct control of God and that the outcome would be perfect just as God is perfect. A belief that God is perfect is an important first step in becoming a righteous person. Once Chris had decided that God was perfect it was not hard to believe that whatever God required of Chris would also be perfect. It would not only be perfect it would be good, and Chris knew that he would see the goodness of God's will worked out in Chris's life. It was a matter of being submissive and mindful of the purposes of a godly life.

As Chris prayed, he began to think of the ways that he could be of service to God. It came to Chris's mind that he could continue his education, or he could try out for another baseball team if he could get noticed by another organization. At first nothing specific came to Chris's mind but he was willing to be patient. Many times, a Christian needs to be patient and wait on God to move the believer in the right direction. Chris decided that he would wait on the Lord.

For the next week Chris stayed around the house in Murfreesboro and to Kay's complete joy went everywhere and did everything that Kay was doing. Chris went to the women's church meetings that Kay attended on a weekly schedule. Kay would beam as she introduced Chris to the other ladies in her group. The other ladies were more than pleased that Chris accompanied his mother to the group meetings. The group would discuss current books that the group was reading, and Chris even enjoyed hearing about the different stories that the women described. Generally, the books described the efforts of missionaries sent by various church denominations to foreign countries for the purpose of building hospitals or schools to bring the Gospel message to the tribes of Africa or the countries of southeast Asia. When the ladies began to talk about the missionary efforts in Vietnam Chris had to excuse himself because it was still too recent in his memory to listen to those stories. Chris had seen the actions of the evangelical church in Vietnam and was not very happy with the results of how they responded to the needs of the people.

One afternoon Chris was at home when Joe came home from his teaching duties at Middle Tennessee State. Joe supervised student teachers in the Middle Tennessee area and often traveled to high schools in the area to check in on the progress of students who were seeking teaching certificates from the state. Joe had been to Shelbyville Central High that day to check in on a student teacher who was also playing on the MTSU baseball team. Chris had told Joe about Chris's conversation with the Pirates General Manager and told Chris that he was being treated unfairly and that Chris needed to get back into baseball shape by again working out with the college baseball team.

Joe even suggested that Chris enroll in college and take some courses until he could determine what his baseball future was going to be. Chris had been a slightly above average student in high school, but he also had an IQ that was more than two standard deviations above average, meaning that Chris would have no problem with getting through college if he chose to go that route.

Again, it was time to turn to God for answers. Chris prayed. Chris's prayers were earnest and direct. Chris prayed that God would lead him to do what God had set out for Chris as God's plan. Chris told God that he was open to do what God wanted him to do. Chris would go where God wanted him to go. If God wanted Chris to go to college, he would go to college and study hard any subject that God set before him. If God wanted Chris to use his natural talent to play baseball Chris would play baseball and play as if he were playing for God's enjoyment. If God had any other plans in mind Chris would be receptive to any direction that God wanted him to take.

Hebrews 11 verse 8 tells of the calling of Abraham by God to go to a place that he did not know. To his credit Abraham did as God instructed and left family and his former life. Abraham set out for an unknown land because he heard God's call and acted on it. Chris was facing the same call. Chris might have to leave everything that he knew behind and go to a place that he did not know, but by faith Chris was ready and willing to do whatever he was called to do. All that Chris did know was that God would be with him no matter where God sent him.

It is often unclear to a believer to know what God has in mind for His followers in situations like Chris was experiencing. Sometimes it is best to wait on God to reveal His desires for a believer's life. Fortunately, Chris had time to wait for the leadership of the Holy Spirit to direct Chris in the right path. On the other hand, a young man like Chris is often tempted to take matters into his own hands and rely on his own feelings in the pursuit of his next moves. Chris was anxious to get moving. He had been sent to war in Vietnam. Being drafted was not something that he would have chosen for himself. Chris was not sure how being in Vietnam was going to work for good in his future even though he believed that God was very much in control of his life.

While Chris was thinking about all these seemingly incongruous events that had taken place in his life, he decided that he needed further spiritual guidance. Chris picked up his Bible and began to read the Gospels. The first four books of the New Testament of the Bible tell the story of Jesus form the announcement of his birth to his crucifixion and to his resurrection and finally to his ascension back into heaven. When Chris was called to be a follower of Christ, he decided that the best thing he could do for himself was to try his best to read and understand the life and teachings of Jesus.

Chris read the first four chapters of Matthew and stopped. He did not know why he stopped but he felt that something really important had to happen to him before he continued his reading and studying of the scriptures. In the first four chapters of Matthew the lineage of Jesus's paternal ancestry is listed, the story of the announcement of the birth of Jesus's cousin, John the Baptist is recounted, the announcement of the birth of Jesus to Joseph, the visit of Mary to her cousin Elizabeth, the visit of the Magi, the descent of the Holy Spirit on to Jesus and the pronouncement of God that Jesus was His beloved son during Jesus's baptism, Jesus's wilderness experience and his confrontation by Satan, and Jesus's choosing of his disciples. Chris took all of the scripture to heart, and he loved Jesus. Chris went to bed.

What came next was very dramatic for Chris. Chris began to dream. Chris heard the voice of Jesus. When Chris heard Jesus speak to him in his dream he knew at once that the Lord had heard his prayers and that the

Lord was responding to the help that Chris was seeking. Chris wanted to know why he had been sent to Vietnam and what good would come of that time away from his family and baseball.

Jesus did not speak to Chris in audible words but more in deep thought, but Chris knew non-the-less that it was Jesus speaking to his mind in the same way that Chris prayed. Slowly, Chris realized that Jesus had a plan and calling on his life and that the next three chapters of the book of Matthew would be very important for Chris to study and try to understand. Matthew 5,6, and 7 are referred to as the Sermon on the Mount. Those chapters of Matthew are the direct teachings of Jesus and the foundation of the Christian life. The Sermon on the Mount may not be the entire teachings of Jesus or even the actual sequence of the teachings, but these words of Christ form the basis of what Christ expects of his followers. Jesus was telling Chris that in order to receive an understanding of how Chris was to view his experience in Vietnam, Chris would need to understand how Jesus thought men should view their life in relation to God and to other men.

Chris began to formulate an understanding that Jesus wanted Chris to carefully incorporate the core teachings of Jesus into his life and to live according to those commandments found in Jesus words in the Sermon on the Mount. When Chris awoke, he could not wait to start his study of the scripture found in chapters 5, 6, and 7 of Matthew.

The 5th chapter of Matthew starts with the Beatitudes. The Beatitudes are 8 pronouncements of qualities of life that lead to a blessing from God. Those that would obtain blessings from God show these characteristics in their lives. The first characteristic that Jesus enumerated is being poor in spirit. Jesus says according to Matthew 5: 3 that, "Blessed are the poor in spirit, for theirs is the kingdom of heaven."

Chris read that verse and stopped and wondered what these words meant and how these words were to be incorporated into his life as a part of his persona. Chris asked himself how do I become poor in spirit so that I will have a place in the kingdom of heaven? What is being poor in spirit? Chris thought that being poor was not something that he wanted. Chris wanted a life in which he played professional baseball and got paid big league money for hitting home runs.

Jesus had come to him in a dream and told Chris that he had to understand and live by the words of Jesus recorded in the Bible and especially in Matthew 5. Chris had just started his study and already he was running into a problem about what Jesus said for Chris to do. Chris needed to regroup and find someone to help him understand.

Chris decided that he needed to talk to someone that had studied the scriptures for a longer time and who could help Chris understand what Jesus meant. Chris asked Joe to help him find someone who could explain how he could become poor in spirit. Joe asked Chris why he was interested in studying the Sermon on the Mount. At first Chris was reluctant to tell Joe that Jesus had come to him in a dream and told Chris that it was of utmost importance that Chris live by Jesus's instructions in the Sermon on the Mount but when Chris told Joe about his dream, he did not think that Joe would act the way he did.

When the family lived in Nashville, they attended the First Baptist Church in downtown Nashville that was very close to the Southern Baptist Sunday School Board's Headquarters. The First Baptist Church was attended by many employees of the Sunday School Board. Those employees were tasked with preparing literature and publications used by Southern Baptist churches for teaching Sunday school lessons, commentaries on books of the Bible and other publications for church use.

Joe had been involved in a Sunday school class at the First Baptist Church in Nashville taught by Herschel Hobbs a well-recognized Bible scholar. Hobbs had written a commentary on the whole Bible and Joe suggested that Chris go to Nashville and seek an audience with Herschel Hobbs to explain what being "Poor in Spirit" meant. Joe did not offer to go with Chris, nor did he offer his own understanding of what the meaning of Matthew 5: 3 might be. Joe simply said go to Nashville and seek your answer from Herschel Hobbs. Chris called the Southern Baptist Sunday School Board and was able to track Herschel Hobbs down and got his telephone number.

Chris called Herschel Hobbs and to his amazement Chris was able to get a meeting with Hobbs on the next day. Chris borrowed the family car and drove to Nashville and went to the address that he had been given by the Bible scholar.

Hobbs lived in the Greenbriar section of Nashville on a street that was lined with oak and popular trees. Hobbs's house was a modest two-story house with a detached garage and a lawn that was well kept but not extravert with ornamental plants and bushes. The front yard was surrounded by a white picket fence and the driveway was not paved but strewn with gravel that looked as if it had been there for many years. Chris parked the car behind a car already parked in the driveway and walked up a walkway of pavers to the steps leading to the front door.

Chris knocked and a lady who appeared at the door asked who was knocking and what he wanted. Chris replied, "My name is Chris and I have an appointment to see Mr. Hobbs today."

"Dr. Hobbs is in his study. Please come in and wait in the living room and I will let him know that you are here." was the older ladies' reply.

Chris sat on a sofa for what seemed like only a minute or two and he was greeted by a man who introduced himself as Herschel Hobbs and he held out his hand to Chris for Chris to shake.

"Dr. Hobbs I want to thank you for seeing me today. I have some important matters to ask you about." Chris shook Herschel Hobbs' hand as he spoke.

"Chris, I have a feeling that we will have an interesting conversation this afternoon. Please follow me to my study. Would you like anything to drink? I am going to have a cup of coffee while we talk." Hobbs said as he led Chris to a room full of books where Hobbs sat behind a desk that was well organized.

Chris found a chair in front of the desk and sat down. Before Chris could say anything, Hobbs started to speak. "You have been spoken to in a dream by our Lord and Savior Jesus Christ. I have also been spoken to in a similar manner and I was expecting your call. In all the years that I have had a personal relationship with Jesus he has spoken to me many times, but he has never spoken to me in a dream as he did just recently."

Chris was amazed to hear the words that the Bible scholar had just spoken to him. Chris looked into Hobbs' eyes and saw a genuine glow that came from the old man who obviously had spent a lifetime seeking the will and presence of Jesus. "Dr. Hobbs, then you already know why I am here to speak to you today?" Chris asked.

"I am not fully aware of what you have to say. Let's start by getting acquainted. Tell me about yourself. Please call me Herschel and I will call you Chris." The old Bible scholar replied.

Chris told Hobbs the major parts of his life story and reminded Herschel that Joe had been in his Sunday school class when the family lived in Nashville while Joe was getting his PhD at Vanderbilt. Chris related that he had been drafted to play baseball for the Pirates and that he had been drafted into the Army and had recently returned from Vietnam. Chris told Dr. Hobbs of his being called to become a follower of Jesus when he was a 10-years-old and the family was living in Hopkinsville, Kentucky. Hobbs listened with a quiet but intense interest.

Chris then told Hobbs of his discussion with Jim Ritchie on the flight back to the US when he left Vietnam. Hobbs was not interested in hearing what Ritchie had to say and said, "You didn't fall for that did you Chris?"

To which Chris replied, "No sir."

Hobbs then asked Chris to describe in detail his dream and the words that he heard Jesus say.

"Jesus spoke with an intensity in his voice that I have never heard before. The words penetrated my mind. There was no question that what Jesus had to say was to be obeyed and that my very being depended on following exactly His directions." Chris began.

Hobbs nodded his head, "The commands of Jesus are not to be taken lightly. There is power not only in the words but in the direction that the words will take His followers."

Chris continued, "When I was 10, I knew that I had been called to follow Jesus. I did not know where it would lead me, and I had no idea that I would hear his voice again with explicit instructions to study and understand the recorded words of Jesus in the Sermon on the Mount. I have prayed for Jesus to lead me almost every day of my life. I prayed when I played baseball and was injured. I prayed when I was in Vietnam and when my time in Vietnam was over that I would reach an understanding of what the purpose of my time in Vietnam was for. Now Jesus has spoken to me, and I am here with you to seek your help in understanding what it means to be poor in spirit so that I can see the kingdom of God."

Herschel Hobbs listened to Chris's plea for help intently. He slowly unfolded his hands and said, "I have studied the Bible all my life. I have written a commentary with the help of others that I hope brings clarity and understanding to the Holy Scriptures. I must admit however, that each individual who seeks to understand the words of God must receive assistance from the Holy Spirit to hear and understand the message that God is willing for each of us to have as our own. Have you prayed that God would give you a clear message as to what being poor in spirit is to mean in your own life? I can tell you what I believe the words of Jesus mean to me and if that helps you understand for yourself then I will have accomplished what I am supposed to help you with today."

Chris replied, "I must admit that I am having a very hard time calling you Herschel. To me it would be more appropriate to call you Dr. Hobbs. Can you allow that."

"Sure." That was all that Dr. Hobbs replied.

Chris continued, "Dr. Hobbs, I cannot remember when I have not prayed for understanding of what God would have me to do or to become. This, however, is different. I have never had Jesus so clearly tell me to study the Sermon on the Mount as an answer to my prayer concerning what God wants me to think and believe."

"When you say, 'Jesus told you to study the Sermon on the Mount' then I would take that to mean that the words of Jesus should have a message for you regarding a direction that Jesus would have you to take immediately." Dr. Hobbs said with an assurance in his voice that came from years of prayer and walking closely with

God.

With that said Dr. Hobbs turned his back to Chris and reached for a book that was on the bookshelf behind his desk. After looking for only a moment Dr. Hobbs came up with a book and handed it to Chris. The book was a compilation of sermons given by Charles Haddon Spurgeon in London from the late 1850s to the mid-1880s Dr. Hobbs handed the book to Chris and said, "Over the years I have received inspiration from reading the sermons of Charles Spurgeon and I think that you will also receive a blessing from reading the thoughts of Pastor Spurgeon. Do you know anything about Spurgeon?"

Chris acknowledged that he was unfamiliar with Charles Spurgeon but readily accepted the tender of the book of sermons and said that he would make sure that he returned the book as soon as he finished reading it.

"Dr. Hobbs, we have talked around the question that I came here to ask you. I still would like to know what you believe is meant by Jesus's words concerning being 'poor in spirit'. I think that based on our conversation up to this point that you have been thinking about how to respond to me and also to deal with the dream that you said you had that told you that we would meet to-day." Chris insisted.

Dr. Hobbs thought carefully before responding to Chris. He was silent for several minutes and then spoke slowly and softly. "The starting point of a relationship with God is to understand the nature of we humans and the nature of God. We humans are born in sin. We are sinners from the time of our conception, and we remain sinners until we are saved by the unmerited grace of God. If you read the eight Beatitudes, you may come to the conclusion that they are a progression of thought. In verse 3 Jesus is telling us that we must acknowledge who we are in relation to God. We as humans from a spiritual point of view are not only poor, but we are also totally bankrupt, not able to escape from our condition of poverty in relation to God.

"It is only when we acknowledge that there is nothing that we can do to escape our condition of nothingness that we have the possibility of a relationship with God. Secondly, in verse 4 Jesus says, 'Blessed are those who mourn, for they shall be comforted.' which suggests that in order to come to God we must not only acknowledge who God is, but we must be exceedingly sorry for our total depravity.

"Now I have given you my understanding of what the first two Beatitudes mean to me, but I was not spoken to by Jesus in your dream. Jesus asked you to study the Sermon on the Mount and that is exactly what you should do. You should ask the Holy Spirit that is in you to open your mind to the words of our Lord and Savior so that you will know what Jesus wants you to know and to do about His instructions to you."

Chris heard every word that Dr. Hobbs said and thought that he understood that Dr. Hobbs had given him an idea of how to approach the study of the Sermon on the Mount. Chris wanted to get going on his study and begin reading the sermons of Charles Spurgeon. Chris thanked Dr. Hobbs and held out his hand. Dr. Hobbs took Chris's hand and pulled him to an embrace. "Chris, it has been a long time since I have felt a closeness with a young man like you. It gives me great hope that the Holy Spirit is at work in the younger generation. One word of caution, do not become conceited. Study the scriptures with a sense of humility. Do not rely on your own intellect. Rely totally on the Holy Spirit to lead you in the right direction." With those words of caution Chris and Dr. Hobbs embraced once again, and Chris walked to the family car and started the hour-long drive back to Murfreesboro.

Chris had time to think about his meeting with Herschel Hobbs and the advice that he received. When he drove to the house in Murfreesboro, he thought about playing baseball and what his future as a professional athlete might mean in relation to what Jesus was asking him to do. Chris wondered if playing baseball would be in his past or whether playing would be in accordance with the direction that the Holy Spirit would lead. When Chris got off I-24 and turned toward home he decided to pull over and have a snack at a fast-food restaurant. Chris found a McDonalds and ordered a Big Mac at the drive through speaker and received his hamburger through the drive through window. The process made him think of prayer and answered prayer. Chris spoke to an unseen person who took his request and then he trusted that his request would be filed by an unknown source. In a sense that was how prayer worked.

When Chris prayed, he made his request known to God without seeing God. Chris knew that God had heard his prayer and would respond to his prayer when he got to the place of receiving. How wonderful it was that God heard and responded to prayer. At that moment, while he was eating a snack at McDonalds on Highway 41 in Murfreesboro, Tennessee it was time for Chris to receive an answer to his prayers. God spoke to Chris.

All true followers of Christ are given spiritual gifts. There is a wide verity of spiritual gifts that God gives to believer to accomplish God's purposes. To some is given the gift of preaching, to others the gift of teaching, some receive the gift of exhortation, the gift of hospitality is among the gifts God bestows. One of the gifts that scripture recognizes is that of diligence. Chris felt that he had been given the gift of diligence when he played baseball. Chris took playing baseball seriously. He practiced hitting a baseball as often as the weather allowed.

Chris worked out with weights to strengthen his

arms and legs. Chris fielded fly balls until he knew exactly where to go to catch a fly ball from the sound that the bat and ball made when the ball made contact with the bat no matter if the contact was solid or weak. Chris ran the stairs in the gym and in the stadium to build up his stamina and speed so that he could steal bases and easily go from first to third on a sharply hit single. Chris did all this because he wanted to be the best baseball player that he could be. Chris wanted everyone to say that Chris was the best player there ever was.

Then that day after meeting Herschel Hobbs in Nashville and thinking about the dream that he had in which Jesus admonished him to study the Sermon on the Mount, Chris realized that he had a higher calling from God. That higher calling was starting to take shape in his mind and in his spirit. Jesus was calling Chris to follow Jesus more closely. In every aspect of his life Chris was to devote his talents and abilities to Christ. Jesus was demanding that Chris take up the life of Jesus. The study of the Sermon on the Mount was of utmost importance to a correct alignment of Chris's spirit with the Holy Spirit so that Chris would be able to realize the calling that Jesus had placed on his life when he was first bidden to walk the isle and make a public profession of faith when he was a boy in Hopkinsville, Kentucky. Whatever and wherever the Holy Spirit was to lead Chris, he was to do it as if he were doing it specifically and totally for Jesus and that included playing baseball.

After getting home Chris went to his room and read a sermon by Charles Spurgeon entitled "The Secret of Health", based on Psalms 42:11 of the King James version of the Bible. That verse provides, "Why art thou cast down, O my soul? And why art thou disquieted within me? hope thou in God: for I shall yet praise him, who is the health of my countenance, and my God." Chris read the sermon with undivided attention.

In that sermon Spurgeon states that we are born spiritually dead and that we all suffer a need for spiritual health because our natural state is sin. Spurgeon says that if we could cast out our sinful nature, we would be spiritually healthy. In that regard Spurgeon says that pride is a deadly sin. However, when we flee from iniquity and live a godly life, God will restore our health. Spiritual health is measured by the closeness of our relationship with God. God is a God of infinite mercy, and infinite atonement. If God begins to heal a believer, he will not stop the healing process until it is complete. The work of the Holy Spirit is intimately involved with the work of Jesus. When the Holy Spirit descends on man it is to glorify the ascension of Christ to the right hand of God where Jesus reigns in glory.

The words of Spurgeon were new to Chris, and he had to think about the meaning of what he had read. Chris took Dr. Hobbs's advice and asked for understanding from the Holy Spirit. Chris prayed for wisdom because he believed that God always positively answers a request for wisdom to lead to an understanding of God's will in every believer's life. Chris would soon receive the wisdom that he needed to serve Jesus in a way that would bring joy and fulfillment to Chris.

CHAPTER 22
BASEBALL TAKES ON A SPIRITUAL DIMENSION

Kay called the family to dinner and within a few minutes, Joe, Kay, Chris and Swamp Goddess were sitting in the kitchen eating meatloaf, green beans, and mashed potatoes. A dish that Kay had mastered and that everyone in the family enjoyed except Swamp Goddess because she turned up her nose at just about everything that Kay did during that part of Swamp Goddess's life. Joe quickly finishing his plate of food, because he had learned during the time spent in the Navy that he was always on call and to eat quickly just in case the ship he was on demanded his attention. Joe asked "Chris, how did your meeting with Herschel Hobbs go? Did you get answers to the question that you have been asking?"

"Yes, my meeting with Dr. Hobbs was very helpful. He loaned me a book of sermons by Charles Spurgeon that I have begun to read, and I think that it will be most helpful to me in figuring out my next moves." Chris announced to the family.

Swamp Goddess asked, "Do you think that reading a bunch of religious garbage will help you be a better baseball player? Isn't all that religious stuff just a bunch of mumbo jumbo and people speaking out of the wrong side of their mouth?"

Kay was quick to respond, "No our beliefs are not mumbo jumbo. There is a real reason that your brother is studying the Bible. He will learn what to do and how to do it. Besides it can't hurt him and it's good to read the Bible stories. I am sure that you to would get something good out of reading the Bible yourself."

"Oh mother, you are always taking Chris's side of everything, and that is not even the question that I asked him. What does religion have to do with playing sports? Shouldn't you be out chasing fly balls or doing something like that if you want to be a baseball player?" Swamp Goddess asked with an exasperated tone in her voice.

At first Chris did not want to get involved in that conversation. He was content to keep his mouth shut and ignore Swamp Goddess when she got into one of her moods when she thought that everything that went on in the family was stupid and a waste of time.

Joe also kept quiet in response to Swamp Goddess. However, Joe did say to Swamp Goddess that he was willing to take the family to the Dipper Dan ice cream parlor and treat everybody to ice cream. Kay said, "Joe we just finished dinner and you want to eat again?"

Joe said, "Sometimes it is good to have dessert and we could all use some Dipper Dan ice cream tonight while we think about how we are going to get Chris back on the baseball field next summer."

Chris declined the ice cream treat and said that he needed to spend his time seeking an answer to a question that he had been asking himself and he said, "I need some time alone tonight. My conversation with Dr. Hobbs has led me to believe that there is a spiritual aspect of every activity in which Christians engage. I am seeking the spiritual essence of being a baseball player."

To that announcement Swamp Goddess burst out laughing because she thought that all that religious stuff was nothing but a waste of time. "I am ready for ice cream, and I am heading to the car."

Kay said that she did not want ice cream and declined Joe's invitation. Joe headed for the car because he wanted to eat ice cream and he wanted to get Swamp Goddess out of the house before any further confrontation developed.

After Joe and Swamp Goddess left, Kay looked at Chris and sighed, "That girl is headed in the wrong direction and one of these days she is going to regret it."

Chris did not respond to Kay's lament but did reach out and grab Kay's hand and said, "Mom, I have learned that prayer is the best solution to all problems, but if a person is not wanting to listen to God speaking, there is not much anyone can do to cause them to understand what God has in mind for that person."

"I am so afraid that Swamp Goddess will never believe that she is a child of God and that she will reject Christianity." Kay said in a plaintive voice.

"Mom, it is not up to us to force anyone to believe as we do. If a person is called by Jesus that person must still accept that calling and respond by accepting the grace and mercy that is offered in that calling." Chris said as he tried to console Kay from her fears that her daughter was headed in a direction that was not in line with what Kay had been taught from her childhood.

Chris knew very well that Kay anguished over Swamp Goddess's rejection of even a belief in God. To Chris it was further evidence that unless Jesus calls anybody to believe that it is impossible to accept Christ as your Savior. Chris would often think about his own calling and how he had felt the direction of Jesus. Chris had seen clear evidence that the Holy Spirit was at work in his own life and in the lives of others. He was also able to discern that in some there was an absolute rejection of God. Chris did not come to this understanding all at once. Chris's understanding of the direction of the Holy Spirit and his love of God and of Jesus took time to register in his own spirit.

As indicated at the start of this story there was an extremely close relationship between Chris and Kay because Joe had spent many years away from the family while he was in the Navy. Swamp Goddess's rejection of her spirituality was perplexing to Kay because she never doubted that God was real and a vital part of everyone's life. Chris sensed Kay's angst and did his best to comfort his mother's fear that her daughter would never be saved.

"Mom, there is still time. We have both seen that changes in a person's life can and will happen even when we least expect that change will occur. We will continue to pray for Swamp Goddess and leave the results to God." Chris lovingly said to Kay as he continued to hold her hand and comfort her. Actually, Chris was more concerned that Joe would encourage Swamp Goddess to rely on her own judgment and not be open to a call from Jesus that would be life changing.

Chris knew that he needed to turn his full attention to what had prompted him to seek an audience with Herschel Hobbs earlier that day. Chris knew that he needed to study the scriptures and especially the Sermon on the Mount that Jesus had told him was necessary if he was going to have a complete understanding of the spiritual essence of baseball. After comforting his mother as best as he could Chris returned to his bedroom and pulled out his Bible and found Matthew 5 and read the Beatitudes again. He read, "Blessed are the poor in spirit, for theirs is the Kingdom of heaven." Again, Chris had to ask himself what is the meaning of these words so he prayed. and then it came to him. a person who is poor in spirit is totally dependent on God and when a person is totally dependent on God, he finds himself in God's presence.

Then Chris read, "Blessed are those who mourn, for they shall be comforted." The Holy Spirit then led him to understand that these words could be interpreted so that a person would be extremely happy if he realized the responsibility of his sinful actions and repents. In that way he will be forgiven. Once a person is forgiven then he can have a personal relationship with God.

Next Chris read, "Blessed are the meek, for they shall inherit the earth." the Holy Spirit led Chris to believe that the meaning of this Beatitude was that a person would be extremely happy who will allow himself to follow God's commandments, because he will reap the benefits that God gives.

The 4th Beatitude states, "Blessed are those who hunger and thirst for righteousness, for they shall be satisfied." the Holy Spirit interpreted this to Chris to mean that a person will be extremely happy who desires to follow godliness as if it were his only choice, because that person will take on the very nature of God.

"Blessed are the merciful, for they shall obtain mercy." is the next Beatitude. Chris realized that a person would be extremely happy if he was as forgiving as God is forgiving because he will be forgiven with the same measure of forgiveness that he gives.

The next Beatitude reads, "Blessed are the pure in heart, for they shall see God." A person will be extremely happy when his motives are in tune with God's will in their life because that person will see God's purpose fulfilled.

"Blessed are the peacemakers, for they shall be called the sons of God." Chris realized that a person who brings about peace when all around there is no peace, will be happy because that person will be acting as God's child.

Chris then read what he considered to be a troubling beatitude that says, "Blessed are those who are persecuted for righteousness sake, for theirs is the Kingdom of heaven." Chris realized that being rejected and persecuted by the ungodly was exactly what happened to Jesus and therefore he felt secure that if Chris was acting in such a way that he was going to be persecuted that he would be on the right path to the Kingdom of heaven.

The last Beatitude states, "Blessed are you when men revile you and persecute you and utter all kinds of evil against you falsely on my account. Rejoice and be glad for the reward is great in heaven for so men persecuted the prophets who were before you." Again, Chris realized that Jesus had gone through the same tribulation. Chris came to understand that in his life he would be insulted, persecuted, falsely accused, and people would commit all kinds of evil against him because of his beliefs in Jesus. When that happened, he was to be extremely happy because he would be greatly rewarded in heaven just like those who were persecuted before him.

Chris was beginning to see a pattern in the structure of the Beatitudes. In order to become as God envisioned his creation, man would have to acknowledge that he was in need of God. Mankind would then need to understand that they were totally depraved and had to be sorry for their sinful nature. Men would have to seek to follow God's commands in order to relieve themselves of their depravity. Once a man had come to the conclusion of his own unworthiness then he could begin to take on those attributes of God that God wanted to impart to his creation. A person who takes on the attributes of God as if it were his only choice would start to become a forgiving person who is able to overlook another person shortcomings just as God overlooks our shortcomings. When the person aligns his personal desires with those of God, he will begin to see God's purpose fulfilled and he will bring about peace where there is no peace because he will be acting in a God like manner.

When a person has achieved the blessings of life that God has to offer, he will begin to be treated just as Jesus was treated when he was here on earth. A godly person will be ridiculed, argued against and even persecuted for his beliefs when they are in tune with God. This is going to occur on earth until the time that Jesus returns because we are all to take up the same cross that Jesus took up and we are to follow his lead.

After Chris had thought of these things and had prayed that he would be able to live in such a manner as Jesus had instructed, he became exhausted and began to fall asleep. In the middle of the night Chris awoke and he prayed again. He prayed that the Holy Spirit would fill his life with a love for Jesus that went beyond all other love that he could muster for anyone or anything. He told Jesus over and over that he loved Jesus and he wanted to be completely dedicated to Jesus's service as he pursued his career as a professional baseball player.

When he awoke the next morning, he again picked up his Bible and continued to read Matthew chapter 5 where Jesus says, "You are the salt of the earth; But if salt has lost its taste, how shall its saltiness be restored? It is no longer good for anything except to be thrown out and trodden under foot by men." While he was still in the spirit, Chris realized that Jesus was telling him to remember that Christians are to be influential in all their dealings in this world. As an influencer people would always be looking at a Christian ballplayer to see if there was any difference between him and all the other ballplayers that were talented enough to play professionally. The thoughts began to form in Chris's mind that he had in fact been called not only to be a good ballplayer but to be the best ballplayer that he could be and to play the game in such a way that it would bring honor and glory to God.

With that assurance and the leading of the Holy Spirit Chris got up, went to breakfast with his family and then got on the telephone to find an agent that would get him in touch with the next professional baseball team for which he was going to play.

Chapter 23
A New Team and a New Start

Agents who could be enlisted to represent Chris as he sought a new baseball team to play for was not an easy task. Chris had the presence of mind to call his friend and former teammate, Richie Hebner, from when he was playing for the Gastonia Pirates, to ask about a potential agent that would represent him in finding a new team. Eventually, Chris found a sports agency in St. Louis that was willing to take him on as a client. Hebner advised Chris to seek out the National Sports Agency which he said was a well-respected group that undertook the representation of a great many baseball players.

Chris called the National Sports Agency number that he got from directory assistance and was put through to a man that specialized in representing young baseball players in the minor league organizations of Major League Baseball Teams. Chris spoke to Bob Bird who told him that he would call back after looking Chris up in the data system that his agency kept on every potential professional baseball player in the United States.

Chris waited patiently for a return call from Bob Bird and after about two hours the phone rang at Joe and Kay's house in Murfreesboro with the sports agency on the other end of the line.

"Hello Chris, Bob Bird here, I have looked you up in our files and I believe that we can adequately represent you and find you a new team within the next few days if you're inclined to hire us to represent you." Bob Bird said with an assurance that was both disarming and exciting to Chris.

"Mr. Bird, I'm very happy to hear that you're willing to represent me and help me to find a new team to play for in this coming season. Can you tell me what a contract of representation between your company and me would entail." Chris replied also with enthusiasm.

Bob Bird took this time to explain to Chris the details of a representation contract between a baseball player and his company. It generally broke down to a contract of representation in which the agency would undertake to negotiate on behalf of Chris a contract to play professional sports. Chris had the right to either accept or reject the contract negotiated on his behalf by the sports agency. The sports agency would be paid a contingency fee of 10% of the negotiated salary on behalf of Chris. There was also a disclosure that the sports agency would not engage in side deals with the professional team in order to increase their compensation. After discussing these points, Chris agreed that he would retain the sports agency and Bob Bird to represent him in finding a new team. Bob Bird got Chris's address and said he would send a contract to Chris right away.

Chris also asked why the sports agency was willing to represent him. In reply Bob Bird was able to say, "Chris, when I looked you up in our files, I saw that you had quite a season before you were drafted into the army. Your batting average, for a prospect of your age is exceptional, the exit velocity of the balls that you made contact with is also in the above average range. Your fielding ability and your speed on the base pads put you in the 95th percentile. So it is with great pleasure that we will undertake your representation and find you a professional team in very quick order."

Chris listened to what Bob Bird had to say to him and was truly impressed with the statistical account that the sport agency kept even on a minor league player like Chris. Chris thought over the conversation that he had with Bob Bird and believed that it was providential that he was able to find that representation. Later that evening Chris sat down with his father and discussed the conversations that he had had with the sports agency and his prospects for playing baseball for the oncoming season.

Joe asked, "Do you really think that the sports agency that you talked to will be able to find you a new team to play with? You have been out of baseball now for almost two years don't you think that any team will be skeptical without at least seeing you in the batting cage and fielding flies?"

"Dad all I know is what I have been told. The agent that I talked to, Bob Bird, seemed genuine enough and he was able to spout out my batting average and other statistics as if he had tattooed them to his hand. I have a very good feeling about what Mr. Bird and the sports agency will be able to do for me." Chris replied.

Joe said, "I hear what you have had to say, but it seems more reasonable to me that you would try to find a team that would give you a tryout before entering into any agreement with a sports agency. You need to be very cautious in dealing with professional organizations. You don't have any experience in these matters, and I think it best for you to slow down and give it more thought before you enter into any contracts."

Chris was somewhat hurt by what his father had told him, and said, "Dad sometimes you just need to rely on the Providence of God. When I had talked to Mr. Brown in the Pirate's organization I felt as if my days of playing professional baseball were over. Today when I spoke to Mr. Bird it appeared that my ability to play baseball and to find a team is still before me. I believe that I am in this in order to serve God, and that God will watch over me."

The conversation between Chris and his father ended abruptly. When Chris said that he believed that God was going to watch over him, Joe got up from his seat in the living room and went into his bedroom where Kay was waiting to talk to him. Chris retired to his room and again picked up his Bible in order to study another portion of the Sermon on the Mount.

Chris read, "You are the light of the world. A city set on a hill cannot be hidden. Nor do men light a lamp and put it under a bushel, but on a stand, and it gives light to all in the house. Let your light so shine before men, that they may see your good works and give glory to your father who is in heaven."

Chris took this to mean that he was to always remember that because he was a follower of Jesus that he has the light of the words of Jesus in him. Because God has sent light into the world in the presence of Jesus and that light came to shed light into a dark and sinful place Chris felt that he had no choice in this matter. Chris was not to hide the light that is in him nor to let his light be extinguished but to make that light visible so that all will see that Jesus had called him. Chris felt as if he were a lighthouse guiding ships at sea to a safe harbor and thus showing the good works that would come out of his life.

The words of Matthew chapter 5, verses 14, 15, and 16 continued to resonate in Chris's mind. He went to sleep that night contemplating what the next few days would hold for a promising young professional baseball player.

Chris had spoken to the sports agent, Bob Bird, on Wednesday December 18, 1968, and Chris received another call from the sports agent on Friday December 20. In that call the sports agent said that he had good news for Chris.

"Hello Chris, Bob Bird here, I have been in a meeting with some of my colleagues to discuss your future in baseball and we have come up with a strategy that I think you're going to like." Bob Bird announced.

Chris replied, "Mr. Bird that was a very interesting thing that you just said to me. What do you mean by your colleagues and what do you mean by a strategy?"

"Chris you will be getting a call in the next few days from the manager of the Shreveport Braves, whose name is Lou Fitzgerald. Coach Fitzgerald has been with the Braves for a few years and the Braves organization wants you to report to their facility in Boca Raton, Florida on January 21. When you get there, you will be told what you will need to do. The Braves have a big operation in Boca Raton. Not only do they have their minor league facilities there but also their Major League spring training personnel are there. You'll be given an opportunity to mingle with the Major League players and you may even get into a grapefruit league game or two while you are in camp. Right now, it is anticipated that you will break camp around the 1st of April, and you will be assigned to the Shreveport Braves which is their AA affiliate. I'm going to send over to you a copy of the contract. When you receive the contract call me and we will go over the details. Chris, I think this is extremely good news for you and I hope you are pleased with our representation." Bob Bird gave Chris this information in an almost rapid-fire presentation.

Chris thought for just a moment and then replied, "Mr. Bird you have made my day. I am very grateful for your representation, and I look forward to receiving the contract. As soon as I get it, I will call you."

The excitement of the family at the news that Chris shared with his parents and Swamp Goddess that evening was felt by everyone in the family. Joe was happy. Kay was happy. Swamp Goddess said that she would be happy when Chris left for Florida because she would have the bathroom all to herself again. Chris thought about what had taken place and he started to think about the place of faith in his life. He remembered a sermon by Charles Spurgeon that he had read in the book of sermons that Dr. Hobbs had loaned him.

The sermon was based on John 4: 46-53. That scripture provides, "And there was a certain royal official whose son lay sick at Capernaum. When the man heard that Jesus had arrived in Galilee from Judea, he went to him and begged him to come and to heal his son, who was close to death. 'Unless you people see signs and wonders,' Jesus told him, 'You will never believe.' The royal official said, 'Sir, come down before my child dies.' 'Go,' Jesus replied, 'Your son will live.' The man took Jesus at his word and departed. While he was on his way, his servants met him with the news that his boy was living. When he inquired as to the time when the son got better, they said to him, 'Yesterday at 1:00 in the afternoon, the fever left him.' Then the father realized that this was the exact time at which Jesus had said to him, 'Your son will live.' So, he and his whole household believed."

The thought came to Chris that the royal official in the story told by the apostle John had similarities to his own situation. The royal official's son lay dying in bed. Chris's baseball career seemed to have come to an end. At a moment of desperation, the royal official probably thought he was above seeking Jesus for any other purpose, decided to travel the 15 to 20 miles from his home to where Jesus was so that he could beg Jesus to heal his son. Chris needed to make the trip to Nashville to see Herschel Hobbs and to seek his help in understanding the dream in which Jesus told Chris to study the Sermon on the Mount. When the royal official confronted Jesus, Jesus rebuked him at first and said, "Unless you people see signs and wonders you will not believe." Chris needed a confirmation that his encounter with Jesus was genuine. The royal official would not take no for an answer and continued to beg Jesus to come down to heal his son. At that point the royal official's faith was starting to form in a way that he continued to beg (pray) that Jesus would intervene in the health of his child. Chris continued to pray that God would answer his question concerning his professional baseball career. In response to the royal official, Jesus told him that his prayer had been answered and that his son would live. Chris believed that God in fact would answer his prayer and put him in the right place in order to pursue his career in baseball. With the assurance from Jesus that his son would be healed the royal official evidently did not feel it necessary to rush home. We get the picture of the official's servants coming to meet royal official as he is making his way back towards his home. Chris was able to reach out to a sports agent with the faith that he would receive positive news concerning his playing professional baseball in the next baseball season. Eventually, the royal official made it home and was able to see that the faith that he had in the ability of Jesus to heal his child was an actual event. Chris received word from his agent that he in fact would play professional baseball again.

John's account also has a very interesting ending. The royal official's family, because of the faith of the royal official, also believed and were saved. Chris continued to pray that there would be salvation throughout his family including his sister. Interestingly in the picture painted by John in his account in the 4th chapter of his gospel, faith comes from a fervent desire that Jesus would intervene. Faith springs from necessity. Faith then requires a change in heart. After Jesus confronted the royal official and told him that all he wanted was a sign, the officials attitude changed, and he prayed even more fervently for Jesus' intervention in the health of his child. The royal official was then comforted when Jesus told him that his son would in fact live. Faith had gone from desperation to fervent prayer to an assurance by Jesus. But this official's quest for faith did not stop there. When he finally met his servants on his way home his inquiry concerning the time in which his son was healed was met with the confirmation that when Jesus had told him that his son was healed that his son was healed. Lastly, the royal official made it home. I can see his child running to him and jumping up into his arms and the royal official examining his child with a gladness of heart that his faith had been rewarded. Not only that, the faith that he had exhibited was also imparted to his family. Chris prayed for the same result in his family.

Chris received the contract from Bob Bird by special delivery to his parents' house. He read over the contract and as instructed called his agent to discuss the particulars addressed by the contract. It was a rather standard players contract that for the most part gave the Braves organization complete control over the manner and method that Chris would be subject to while he played for the Braves.

The agent, Bob Bird, told Chris that the contract was basically a one-sided deal in which the organization dictated the terms and conditions of the deal between the two sides. Bird told Chris that it would not be until Chris had a longer track record with the organization before any significant changes in the contractual relationship between team and player might change.

Chris understood and told his agent that he would sign the contract as delivered to him and return it to his representative by special delivery that afternoon. To Chris it was the culmination of his faith. He believed that God had set a course for his career and that he could rely on God's protection and direction in his life including his life as a professional baseball player.

It turned out that there was a significant spiritual undertaking in the life of a Christian baseball player. The development of a God-given talent required a spiritual commitment to keeping his body strong and in shape. The mental aspect of playing baseball on a daily basis required concentration and a spiritual willingness to devote his time and effort to every aspect of the game itself. Lastly, there was a reliance on the providence of God to put Chris in the right place at the right time to become the salt and light that he was destined to become when he accepted Jesus Christ into his heart, mind and body.

Chapter 24
Extra Innings

A baseball player is not an ordinary individual. A baseball player must separate himself from ordinary pursuits and set himself apart from the world. A baseball player must develop a distinctive set of skills that require not only coordination and physical strength but also a dedication to the game of baseball. When we started out speaking about the fundamentals of baseball, we discussed how a batter stands alone in the batter's box waiting on the pitcher to initiate the action on the field. There is a certainty that the pitcher will throw the ball towards the plate because there is an umpire that will insist that the action starts within a very reasonable period of time. Certainly, almost everybody must join the game at some point or be declared to be disabled to perform.

While the batter waits for an opportunity to make solid contact with the baseball, the batter knows that a ball will be thrown. The batter in his/her own right must make up his/her mind whether he/she will swing away or take the pitch. Taking a pitch requires no effort. The batter suffers the consequence of a strike being called if the pitch is within the strike zone. If the batter does not swing, he/she has no hope of making solid contact and there is no possibility of a positive result. On the other hand, if the pitcher throws the baseball within the strike zone and the batter makes contact with the baseball, all sorts of activity occur.

When the batter swings and makes contact with the baseball and the ball is put in play, the batter must immediately leave the batter's box and make his/her way towards first base with all deliberate haste. That activity causes the defensive players to move from their stationary positions in order to attempt to field the ball and end the "at bat" by causing the batter to make an out. Putting the ball in play is only possible when a batter swings and makes contact. A passive batter who never swings at a pitch can never reach first base unless the pitcher cannot get the ball within the strike zone on four separate occasions during the "at bat" and the batter walks casually to first base. A walk is the result of the pitcher's mistake and not the batter's intent to make solid contact.

To my way of thinking there is a lesson to be learned from observing the actions of the batter as he/she attempts to make solid contact with a pitch. If a batter is too passive, he/she can only rely on the mistakes of the pitcher in order to reach first base. If a batter is overly aggressive and swings at anything that is thrown by the pitcher, he/she will strike out and the ball will never be put into play. It is the batter whose eyes are on the ball and who is able to guide his/her bat to the precise location and angle necessary to make solid contact with the ball that has the possibility of succeeding in the game of baseball.

The natural ability to hit a baseball and make solid contact cannot be casually dismissed, but in order to be a good baseball player a batter must continuously hone his/her skills to the point that he/ she can see the ball clearly, discern whether it is a strike or a ball, allow his/ her body to appropriately move, allow his/ her hands and arms to move to the appropriate location and pull the bat through in such a way that contact is solid and the ball is put in play.

Can we not learn lessons from this activity? Being too passive in life allows others to direct our actions. Being too aggressive in life causes too many mistakes and too many lost opportunities. It is the person who has the desire to make solid contact, make the right decisions and implement those decisions by taking appropriate action that succeeds in his/ her pursuits.

I have discussed at some length how the protagonist of this book, Chris, in all his ways continued to seek prayerfully God's will in his life. Chris was able to overcome the fact that he was always an outsider, suffered from rejection even if it were subtle, overcame injury and lack of instruction to become a professional baseball player. Then his life was turned upside down by being drafted into the army and sent to Vietnam and into a hostel war zone. Chris did his best to live by the commandments of Jesus and he was rewarded by the protection and wisdom that Jesus offers those that are willing to commit their lives to his service.

Chris's life was lived in contrast to others with whom he came in contact. Chris's encounter with Ronnie when he was in high school indicates that there was a presence of evil even when Chris tried to do everything he could to overcome the physical abuse that playing football in high school caused. The relationship between Chris and his friend Ray suggests that the protection that Jesus offers to believers is a reality that cannot be ignored. Chris's relationship with others in his family show that Chris had a deep commitment to understanding the commandments and instructions of Jesus and was willing to live by those instructions and commandments even if it meant leaving his family behind.

We are all on a pilgrimage set in motion by God's spirit. We are called upon to follow the leadership of the Holy Spirit to guide us in the direction that God intends us to take. We may be called upon to leave family, friends and everything else that we possess behind. If we desire to make solid contact and put our lives in play for the service of God and our neighbors, we must be willing to use our bodies, our intellect, and the spirit that God has endowed us with and put our lives in play for God's glory.

The end.

Acknowledgements

The writing of this book has been a work of great interest to many of the people that I love and who have assisted me in the writing and editing of this book. When I started writing these pages I was living in Dallas, Texas and was working as General Counsel at American Hail Company. The owners of the company allowed me the use my spare time to do most of the research and writing in the office the company provided to me and therefore I would like to thank Lou Sarabi and Hunter Rock the owners of the company for giving me space and time to conduct the necessary research and writing of the book.

While I was writing I passed drafts of the writing that I had finished to my son Nicholas who gave me critical feedback and suggestions as I continued the writing process. Additionally, Nadya Bean also read some of the drafts that I had completed and gave me encouragement to continue with the writing. I will also mention my friend Archer who also encouraged me to continue writing and who also gave me feedback on other important matters that were going on in my life while I sojourned in Dallas.

I left Dallas on December 21, 2022, and drove to Meldrim, Georgia to be with my sister and her husband Chris for the holidays. It was in Meldrim that I was able to finish the writing. My sister Cathy listened to me as I read her passages from the story to which she had firsthand knowledge and she offered approval and encouragement as well. I finished writing the bulk of the book on New Year's Eve while at Cathy and Chris's tree house. I thank Cathy and Chris for their hospitality and help to bring these pages to a completion.

I met Nguyen, Nha Vy while I was still in Dallas. She also likes to be called Samantha and that is her American name. I insisted that she give me a Vietnamese name so that we could both have American and Vietnamese names to call each other, and she did just that. Samantha's help and encouragement in the writing of this novel was steadfast and most appreciated.

A large portion of the story is based on events that took place in my life. My parents loved me and always encouraged me in every way possible. Without their support, love and steadfast desire that I succeed in life I would never have accomplished much of anything that is contained in these stories. I am truly grateful to them for helping me along this path that I have chosen.

By way of explanation. I have never played professional baseball. I played college baseball at Middle Tennessee State. I did not serve in the Army, and I have never been to Vietnam. However, when I was in law school, I had the great honor of sitting next to Hank Berthelot, who was awarded the Congressional Medal of Honor regarding the events that I have discussed as my main character was caught in an ambush while serving in Vietnam. I express my thanks to Hank for sharing his story with me.

I believe in the saving grace of Jesus Christ. As I have grown, I realize more and more that Jesus has always been close to me. I believe in the overwhelming love of God and the guidance of the Holy Spirit. The Holy Spirit directed my writing of this book; without the presence of the Holy Spirit this book would have never even gotten off the ground. I give all glory and honor to God for allowing me to complete this book.

Jeffrey L. Sakas

January 6, 2023

www.ingramcontent.com/pod-product-compliance
Lightning Source LLC
Chambersburg PA
CBHW070936010826
48976CB00028B/2185